M:

'I'll have to take you back to shore.'

'Not to Kororareka!' she said quickly, a desperate note in her voice. 'I cannot go back there!'

'Then...' Kit's voice trailed off as he realised what he had done. A woman alone with sixteen men on a sea voyage that would take many weeks. Sudden helpless rage surged up inside him. 'I should damned well throw you overboard, then! If I'd known...'

He stood up abruptly to leave before he lashed out at something or someone, and Jara caught his arm, dismayed at the abrupt change in him.

'Please! I will not be any trouble, I promise! Only please do not take me back to shore! I will do anything——'

'Will you?' he interrupted her harshly, and as she looked into his eyes she was shocked by what she saw there. Before she had a chance to move back his hands came up to her bare shoulders and he pulled her towards him, his fingers hurting her. 'Will you?'

Victoria Aldridge is a fifth-generation New Zealander and quite addicted to the country of her birth. She married young and very happily and spent some years travelling widely before settling down to have three children. Victoria Aldridge's husband has a design and build company in Wellington and due to his unfailing support she has been able, over the past few years, to involve herself deeply in her children's Montessori education, complete her BA and to write.

Previous Title

MELISSA'S CLAIM

DEEP WATERS

Victoria Aldridge

Masquerade is a trademark published by Mills & Boon Limited, Eton House, 18–24 Paradise Road, Richmond, Surrey, TW9 1SR.

First published in Great Britain 1990 by Mills & Boon Limited

© Victoria Aldridge 1990

Australian copyright 1990

ISBN 0 263 12629 3

Set in Times Roman 10 on 11¼ pt.
08-9008-80320 C

Made and printed in Great Britain

CHAPTER ONE

THE stranger came ashore at dawn, and Jara knew at once that he was different.

He did not look the same as the other whalers—he might wear the uniform moleskin trousers and heavy jacket but they were worn with a bearing, a dignity, that was strangely at odds with the shabby clothes. And dignity was something that Jara had thought she would likely never see again.

As he walked across the pebbled beach to where she stood stirring the pot of fish stew over the fire she quickly ducked her head, the better to peer at him from under her shawl without him being able to return her scrutiny.

It was unusual to see a man cleanshaven here—soap was much too valuable a commodity at Kororareka for men to waste on such vanities—but she had seen some of the officers from the Naval vessels which occasionally called into the whaling station who kept themselves immaculate even through the four month sea-voyage to New Zealand. Scarcely daring to hope by now, she quickly scanned again the dozen ships bobbing gently at anchor in the mirror-smooth waters of the harbour and checked for any vessels that were flying Naval flags.

There had been none the previous day and there were none now. The tide of ill fortune which had destroyed her little world so cruelly was still showing no sign of turning—an American or British Naval officer would have been too much to hope for.

She lowered her head and kept her eyes firmly fixed on her work as the man approached her. She might have only been at the whaling station for a week, but she knew better than to draw attention to herself; male attention in particular.

She heard his boots over the fine shingle and then saw them out of the corner of her eye as he stopped beside her fire. Still she kept her head down.

The stranger cleared his throat.

'Good morning.'

She gave no sign of having heard him; with any luck he would soon give up trying to communicate with her and would walk further up the beach to try the others in the settlement, who were still emerging sleepily from their huts.

'*God dag,*' he tried again after a moment. '*Ist du* . . . er . . .'

'I speak English,' she said abruptly, more from a desire to be rid of him than to help him in his obvious ignorance of Swedish. 'Everyone does here. What do you want?' She heard him expel his breath quickly in relief.

'I need . . . I need to speak to someone here. About getting men for a crew. Can you tell me who can help me, please?'

'Bjorn. Up there.' She pointed up the beach, still keeping her head averted. 'That big man there, with the red hair. He is just coming out of the *whare* closest to us.'

'*Whare*? What's that?'

'Hut,' she said impatiently, and without thinking she raised her head to look at him as she spoke. As soon as she did so she realised that that had been his intention.

She brought her head down again quickly, but not before she had caught a glimpse of warily observant brown eyes under thick fair brows. There was an almost tangible sense of tension emanating from him and this struck Jara as very interesting indeed; men who came

ashore here were—in her limited experience at least—
anything but uneasy.

Kororareka was set at the northernmost tip of New
Zealand; a tiny Swedish colony that existed purely to
process the carcasses of the great whales harpooned in
the waters of the Pacific Ocean, and to service the needs
of the men who killed them. Men came ashore here after
many long monotonous months at sea avid for a change
of diet, for the acrid home-brewed alcohol and for the
women who served them.

Jara's mother had been one of those women—if indeed
a fourteen-year-old girl could have been considered a
woman. It had no doubt been her extreme youth that
had worked against her when she had gone into pre-
mature labour with Jara seventeen years before. The
women of the settlement had brought her up the hill to
Jacques Perrault's trading post to be cared for by
Madame Perrault before hurrying back to their *whares*;
another ship was coming into the bay and that meant
more customers to tend to—there was no time to spare
for a sickly girl struggling desperately to give birth to a
baby that would no doubt be born dead anyway.

In the event, it was Jara who had lived and her young
mother who had died within hours of the birth. With
the baby's mother dead, a father who could have been
any one of a dozen of unknown men, and a distinctly
uninterested settlement to return the child to, the exasperated but kind-hearted Marie Perrault had no option
but to raise the small but perfectly healthy infant herself.
She gave the baby to a local Maori woman who had
recently lost her own baby to nurse and, as soon as she
was old enough to be weaned, the infant took her place
in the Perrault household.

Madame Perrault gave the child her mother's name—
Jara—but nothing else of her mother's background was
allowed to taint her young life. Jara's world was busy

and fulfilling with work, study and prayer. Of her mother's people, she saw nothing—the whaling settlement was barely a quarter of a mile away, and yet the inhabitants might as well have been on another planet for all the contact they had with the Perrault trading post up in the bush-clad hills overlooking the bay.

Marie had come to love the small, beautiful child and, having no children of her own, raised her just as she had always wanted to raise the many children she had longed for when she had been twenty years younger. Jara was taught geography, history and mathematics by Monsieur Perrault. A Franciscan priest who stayed with the devout Perraults for a year gave her lessons in Latin and perfected her handwriting. Books in French and English were procured at great expense to satisfy the child's growing curiosity about the world that lay beyond the blue seas of New Zealand.

For Madame Perrault was determined that the child— *her* child—was not going to stay on these godforsaken shores one single day longer than she had to. The licentiousness and brutality of the whaling settlement on the beach were far too close for Marie's peace of mind. From time to time a trading ship would visit with a man of the church on board, or sometimes Naval vessels from many countries with civilised men on board would call into the harbour for provisioning. From them she heard of the great wars that were taking place between the nations of Europe and a man in France named Bonaparte...

She would wait, she thought, until Europe was at peace again before she sent Jara to France, to be entered as a novice in the high-walled, ivy-covered nunnery in Marie's own town of birth. But as the years passed Jara seemed to grow ever more dear to her, and the thought of entrusting her to anyone else for the long and dangerous voyage to France became ever more daunting.

So Jara grew into young womanhood, raised sternly but with infinite care and love in the protected world the Perraults created for her. She was free to run and climb in the great forest trees growing close around the trading post, free to spend long, happy hours lost in her books as she daydreamed about the huge world that lay outside Kororareka harbour. But the beach at Kororareka, and the people who lived there, were strictly forbidden to her.

Sometimes the confinement became almost unbearable for a child who was by nature both inquisitive and sociable, but Jara always knew that the restraints were, in some way she was not allowed to ever fully understand, for her own good. Only once, when she was ten, had she ever deliberately defied Marie. She had wandered well past the limits of Marie's large, fenced vegetable garden down the hill towards the shore. It was a hot midsummer day, and the shimmering sea she could glimpse between the trees looked so cool and inviting...

Drawn by voices and the sound of laughter, she had come lower, until she was almost on the beach but still hidden by the trees. Although the bay where the whales were brought ashore was a little further up the coast, the smell of rendered whale blubber was quite overwhelming here, and Jara had brought up the hem of her skirt to cover her nose as she cautiously made her way through the bush.

There were a group of people sitting on the beach, eating and drinking together, but mostly drinking. Some appeared to be asleep but others were talking and laughing uproariously. They all seemed to be enjoying themselves hugely. Jara leaned forward to look more closely at this curious sight just as one of the men turned around to reach for the bottle pushed in the sand behind him. She froze in fright as he saw her, and a slow smile spread over his broad face.

He nudged the man next to him who turned to look at her searchingly before slowly getting to his feet. He came towards her somewhat unsteadily with his hand outstretched.

He said something to her in a language that she did not understand and she shrank back, ready to run away. But then he called her by her name and she stopped, puzzled by how he could possibly know who she was. He had reached out and pulled her towards the group, not ungently, and she heard her name being repeated by others in the group in a tone that was clearly one of surprise. She was pushed down to sit with them and she stayed there like some small terrified animal, her heart thumping wildly in her chest as she saw them all more closely. They were filthy, with clothes so stiff that they could have stood up by themselves—Marie would never have allowed such people anywhere near the store!—and she was sure she could see things crawling in the beard of the man who was sitting next to her. There did not seem to be any other children on the beach.

The man with the active beard smiled at her toothlessly.

'Jara,' he said again. She nodded and he nodded. 'Jara,' he repeated, and rested his hand on her arm as if in friendship. But despite her tender years Jara knew it was not a friendly hand and shrugged it off. The man laughed then, and brought a bottle up to her lips. She pushed it away and put her hand down to the ground to get up. The sand under her fingers felt soft and squishy, and when she looked down she saw that the gritty red sand was covered with fat white maggots, wriggling incessantly in the bits of whale meat that were strewn over the beach.

She had leaped to her feet and run for the safety of the bush, only to collide with Marie who had come down to search for her. Jara had received the only beating of her life that day; Marie had beaten her until neither of them could move any more. Then, with tears pouring down her face, Marie had sat beside the sobbing child and told her for the first time whose child she was, and why she must have nothing to do with the people who had so callously turned their backs on Jara and the girl who had given birth to her years before.

'It was your mother's name they were calling you by,' she said softly, stroking the child's hair soothingly. 'And you do look something like her, poor little thing that she was. It was she who named you, not me. Jara—such a heathen name, but it was what your mother wanted, child. But I'm your mother now, and I don't want you to end up as she did. That's why you must never, ever go anywhere near any of those people. Do you understand?'

If Jara had been strictly honest she would have admitted that she did not but, child though she was, she understood well enough that her mother was even more upset by what had occurred than she was herself. So she simply nodded obediently and the matter was never directly referred to by either of them again. In any case, nothing would have induced Jara to repeat her horrifying visit to the beach and it was with relief that she returned to the peaceful, predictable refuge of her books and her beloved forest.

But seven years later, when Jara was helping to serve in the store and found the young American Naval officers she was serving to be rather too persistent in their offers to improve her English, Marie decided that the time had definitely come when her precious daughter would have to leave for France. She could no longer pretend to herself that Jara was still a child, and her maturity could bring nothing but problems. Marie's strict views had tolerated no mirrors in the house, no frills or other frivolities in their clothing, no drinking or reading of novels—and she viewed her daughter's flowering with dismay. She had taken such pains to prepare Jara for her future life in the nunnery, and if she were to stay in Kororareka, it would only be a matter of time before the worst would happen and some woman-starved sailor would manage to take her by force or persuasion. Besides, Marie could not help but think, in her more pessimistic moments, that Jara had her mother's blood in her, and the blood of whoever it had been who had so thoughtlessly sired her; and who knew what kind of proclivities that might have given her...? The girl was quiet enough in a dreamy sort of way but there was a stubbornness there, an inner world that she sensed Jara often retreated to even while outwardly complying with the rules and restrictions of her parents. It was a duality that Marie believed was duplicity, and she was confident that only a life of discipline and prayer would ensure that Jara's lower nature did not emerge.

There was a French captain, Monsieur Ferrier, who called into Kororareka once every eighteen months. Marie and Jacques trusted him as a friend, and he had agreed to escort Jara in safety to the nunnery in France when the time came. He was due any month now, Marie told her daughter with rather more composure than she felt, and Jara was to prepare whatever she wanted to take with her. Jara, for her part, was almost delirious with delight at the thought of the great adventure that awaited her beyond the harbour! Marie was a little hurt by her eagerness to leave, but would not have shown it for the world.

Life, in the meantime, continued in its quiet pattern, marred only by a terrible argument that occurred one day between Jacques Perrault and a group of Maoris in his store over the price of a rifle Jacques had for sale. He was a peaceable and God-fearing man, widely respected by Maori and Pakeha alike for his fairness, but these men were drunk on liquor from the whaling station and aggressive with it. Jacques had been quite shaken by the event, and had had to sit quietly for a time after in the shady garden behind the house while he calmed down.

Very late that night, Jara had woken to the smell of burning wood and the sound of a woman screaming somewhere outside. She lay in stunned confusion for a moment before scrambling out of bed and sweeping together the dress and boots she had worn the previous day. She had no sooner climbed out of her window and run over the garden to the protection of the forest when she heard her bedroom door crashing open. In the light of the flames now beginning to take hold of the front of the house she saw the shapes of men moving around in her room, kicking over the bed she had been lying on a minute before, rifling quickly through the chest that held her belongings before running out again. There was no mistaking that they were the Maoris with whom Jacques had had the argument the previous day.

Marie had started to scream again, and Jara saw her in her white nightgown, her grey hair coming untied from her nightcap. Her pride and joy had been her beautiful flower garden—the first in Kororareka—and she knelt there now among the roses, holding Jacques's inert body in her arms as she pleaded and prayed for his life, for Jara's life, for her own.

As the men began clubbing them about the head with their heavy wooden cudgels, Jara hid her face, desperately shoving her hands into her mouth so that her screams would not give her away. But she could not cover her ears to the sounds that her parents made as they died, and the sounds went on forever.

She was found the next morning by some of the men from the whaling station who had heard the screams and seen the flames of the night, and who had come at daybreak to see what remained of the trading post. Jara didn't remember them coming, and she didn't remember them carrying her past the ruins of the house on the way to the whaling station, although they must have done so. All that was now mercifully a blank, a missing piece of her memory that she made no effort to retrieve.

Barely a week had passed since the nightmare, and somehow—Jara never knew quite how—she had managed to keep her sanity. She had been neither welcomed nor rejected by her mother's people; merely put to work on the multitude of tasks that needed to be done to keep the settlement alive. She accepted the hard work philosophically enough—she was used to scaling fish and collecting firewood. Even the foul job of helping to render down the flesh and blubber of the great whales meant that she did not have time to remember how she came to be in this place; did not even have time to raise her eyes to the hills behind the bay where the charred remains of what had once been her home now lay scattered and bleached under the hot summer sun.

It was the other sort of work that she was expected to do—that of helping to serve the needs of the many hundreds of whalers and traders who called in a steady stream at Kororareka harbour—that she knew she could never accept. On only her second day at the settlement, when she was still stumbling about numb with grief and shock, one of the women had thrust a pitcher of ale into her hands and ordered her to take it to a group of already drunken whalers at one of the makeshift tables set up on the beach outside the *whares*. She had gone to the table quickly and left the pitcher there, spilling some of it in her haste to be gone. Avoiding the hands outstretched to grab hold of her, she had fled back up the beach, collecting a bad-tempered cuff from Bjorn as she passed him.

Another more willing woman went to serve them and Jara took steps to ensure that she was not put in that position again. It was relatively easy to always be at the far end of the beach from the visiting men, and to stay anonymously behind the cooking pot and the endless piles of wood and seaweed she collected for the fires. It was not so easy to change her appearance so that no man could possibly take an interest in her. But it seemed that she had succeeded—the slight, immediately masked look of distaste she had seen on the stranger's face when he had looked at her told her that.

The problem was that not all the men here were as fastidious as this man obviously was. Nor could she reasonably expect to remain unnoticed here for very much longer. Sooner or later a man—or men—too drunk or too long without female company would force from her what all the other women at the settlement were more than happy to sell. It was imperative that she escape from this place, but she could not do that alone—and the man standing beside her now just might be the man to help her. If only she could be sure that he *was* different, and not like all the others...

He was walking away now, up the beach to where Bjorn the self-appointed leader of the settlement was yawning and sleepily scratching his great stomach in the early morning sun. So it was a crew he was looking for, was it? she thought grimly to herself. He'd have little joy from Bjorn there—Bjorn never did anything for anyone unless he could see an immediate profit in it for himself. Besides, there were no men to spare here or in any of the other tiny pockets of European settlement she had heard about that had sprung up further down the coast in very recent years. There were the Maoris, of course, but everyone knew that to take too many of *them* on board a ship was tantamount to suicide. Even one would be too many if he had been hand-picked by Bjorn.

The stranger was talking to Bjorn now, and Jara watched him for a moment as the two men squatted down by the fire outside the *whare* to talk. He was not a small man—Bjorn's height perhaps—but compactly built. She guessed that he was in his early twenties, but it was hard for her to tell a man's age when he had no beard; he might have been a little older. But with his short-cropped fair hair and open face he looked worryingly young to be here dealing with Bjorn. She was filling a bowl with fish stew for the leader's breakfast and, on an impulse, filled a second bowl and carried it over to them.

'And at present I've only sixteen men in my crew,' the stranger was saying. 'I need at least that number again...even twice as many if they're available.'

Bjorn grunted and took the bowl Jara proffered. With a look of surprise the stranger hesitantly took the other bowl. He had the far-seeing, crinkled eyes that sailors always had, but dark brown where one might have expected sky-blue. They were warm eyes, she thought suddenly. Perhaps even kind.

'Thank you very much.' It was a small thing, but it was the first time she had heard those words spoken here. She moved behind Bjorn and sat silently on the ground where the big Swede could not see her.

After filling his mouth with a spoonful of stew Bjorn said slowly, 'Your ship—what you come here for?'

'For the reason I told you. I need a crew.' Jara looked at him closely, wondering what reason he had for being so evasive. Bjorn shook his head reprovingly.

'You not a whaler, I see that.' He looked across the harbour to the great three-masted barque riding easily at anchor on the still water of the harbour. 'And you not trader either.'

'Why do you say that?'

Bjorn shrugged. 'Traders don't have ships like that. Too big, too fast. And I see that once you bore many cannons, like Navy ship. British Navy, I think.'

Watching him as closely as she was Jara saw the stranger's eyes flicker just for a split second before he said easily, 'She could well be. We salvaged her up the coast a few months ago—found her run aground on a spit and unmanned. I've no idea who had her before then. We're all from another ship—a trading vessel— that went down in the same storm. We've remasted and repaired her, so I suppose that makes her ours now.'

Bjorn snorted and spooned up the last of the stew. 'You tell the British Navy that when they want her back! But it is your business where you come from. Deserters, convicts...they all come here. So you want men, eh? How you going to pay them?'

'I can pay them.'

'*Ja*? Well then...' Bjorn pretended to think, idly wiping his spoon against his rough beard. 'I get you men if you can pay. Good men. Thirty men?'

Behind his back Jara sat up straight and caught the stranger's eyes. She shook her head slightly in warning.

'Can you get thirty men?' the stranger asked neutrally, even while his eyes narrowed to ask her *why*.

'I get you thirty men—you pay me twenty pounds each man. Then you pay them what you want. All right?' He cut through the stranger's explosive protest at the exorbitance of this amount with an airy wave of his hand. 'No, no need to thank me. I know men hard to get but I want to help you. You pay me now and then I get men for you. All right? That settled?'

'Not yet. I want to see the men first before I hand over six hundred pounds to you.'

Bjorn looked deeply offended. 'You suspicious man. I am doing you a favour, and you don't trust me?'

'Not at all, I'm afraid. I will have to see the men first,'
the stranger said firmly, and Bjorn's eyebrows knotted
together as he realised that bluff was not going to work
in this situation, no matter how desperate the stranger
was for a crew. The prospect of losing money in his
hand—and perhaps even more—visibly agitated him.

'But they good men!' he blustered. 'Good sailors!
They...' He broke off, warned by some instinct, to suddenly look over his shoulder. Jara, who had been shaking
her head emphatically, lowered her face just in time to
look down at the seaweed she was twisting nervously in
her hands. Thankfully the stranger himself had had the
sense not to give her away, but she was sure that Bjorn
would take the first opportunity he could later to beat
her anyway, just in case she was the reason the stranger
was being so obdurate. 'Get away from here, woman!'
he growled.

She got to her feet wordlessly and bent to collect
Bjorn's empty bowl. When she reached for the stranger's
scarcely touched bowl he tried to catch her eye but she
turned away quickly. She had done what she could for
him, and if Bjorn ever found out how she had tried to
sabotage his plans she would be in water so deep that
this brown-eyed stranger would not be able to help her.
Even if by some remote chance he should be inclined to
do so...

She had almost reached the cooking fire at the other
end of the beach when Helga met her.

'Stupid slut! I saw you!' She fetched Jara a solid blow
to the nose before she could duck and with a muffled
shriek Jara doubled over with pain, her hands over her
face. 'What you shaking your head at him for, eh? You
telling him not to pay Bjorn for Maori crew? Eh? What
business is it of yours? If he fool enough to pay for Maori
crew, what matter if they kill him before he leaves the

harbour? Eh? You keep away from Bjorn's business, you hear?'

Still bent over and gasping for breath, Jara barely managed a nod and the other woman moved off, obviously satisfied for the moment. But Helga was Bjorn's woman and it was only a matter of time before she told him of what she had seen. Jara knew that a broken nose was slight punishment compared with what Bjorn would deal out to her!

She made her way into the bush that lined the beach, stumbling over the rocks and undergrowth, blinded by her streaming eyes. By the river from which the settlement drew its fresh water she vainly tried to wash the blood from her face, finally giving up to throw her head back and hold her nose firmly between her fingers until the gushing stopped. By some miracle Helga had not broken it, and it felt merely swollen and very sore. Bjorn would no doubt take pleasure in finishing the job when he got his hands on her. Cautiously she leaned forward and regarded her reflection in the still water. A wavering stranger looked back, and rancidly lank strands of her hair escaped from her shawl to dangle in the water. A shiver of disgust ran through her and she thrust her fist into the reflection in impotent rage at what she had become. Seven days, it had been, since everything in her world had fallen apart. Seven days ago she had been happy, loved, poised on the brink of life. And now...

No! She clenched her fists, and willed herself not to remember, comfortingly vivid as some of her memories still were. She could take no more of this place and she had to think of her immediate future now, not dwell on the past.

It was cool there in the bush, and the soil beneath her knees smelt clean and damp and new. Sunlight streamed silver and green down through the delicate fronds of the *ponga* trees and danced on the glittering water. Overhead the forest birds fluttered and sang, just as they had every day of her childhood and just as they would when she had gone from here. *This* she would miss, she told herself fiercely, but nothing else in this place! She suddenly remembered the stranger and hurried back to where she had a view of the beach again. If he had gone already...!

He had gone and Bjorn was still sitting where she had left him, already well into the first of the many bottles of liquor he would drink that day. From something he had said to her once she was sure that he had fathered her mother, but even if he was her grandfather it had brought her no favours from him. He was a brutal man, with huge fists that he had used on Jara before now for all that she had only been in the settlement for a few days. She had very good reason indeed to fear him and his violent rages.

As she watched he got heavily to his feet, and from the way he hurled his mug to the ground Jara knew that the stranger had turned down Bjorn's offer of a crew. Perhaps he would have done that anyway, she thought— the stranger had seemed like nobody's fool after all, despite his youth and absurd good manners. Perhaps there had been no need for her to have warned him as she had. Perhaps Bjorn would never know what she had done after all. But as he turned to go back into the *whare* she saw Helga's squat little form hurry up to talk to him, and Jara knew exactly what she would be telling him.

Helga had never liked her. It had been Helga who had thrust her at the drunken whalers that day and who had berated her later for her foreign ways. 'You living here now,' she had told Jara fiercely. 'And you never going to leave! You remember that and try to do something about it. You got soft hands and fussy ways, and you don't even speak Swedish, and you a lazy slut too! You work and maybe you be of some use to Kororareka. But I don't think so. You useless slut! Useless!'

Useless and as good as dead if Bjorn found her now. She had seen him thrash a man close to death a few days ago, in a dispute over a game of cards, and a man was of much more value to the settlement than a woman not raised in the ways of the whalers.

She backed away from the beach noiselessly, taking care not to disturb the leaves as she passed and so draw attention to herself. She would stay in the bush until she worked out what to do. She would be safe enough there. The people of the settlement, due perhaps to some primitive fear of the unknown, rarely ventured into the dense bush; but Jara had played freely among the trees of the lush forests as a child, had always felt quite at ease there—at least until the Maori massacre of her family.

If she hadn't helped the stranger this morning she could have continued on as she had for a little longer, waiting for the time when the Perraults' friend Captain Ferrier came back to Kororareka. But now... now she was trapped here, perhaps while the stranger and his ship sailed on up the coast in search of another crew! She could still see the great barque on the harbour, and there appeared to be no sign of departure as yet, but that meant nothing.

Wearily she curled up in a hollow and rested her throbbing head on the bracken-covered ground. She closed her eyes, trying to clear her mind for some constructive planning, but found she could not stop thinking about the stranger. Bjorn had believed him to be lying, although the story about how he came by his ship had been possible if not probable and many ships were known to have met their end in the mighty gales which ripped across the northern seas of New Zealand. But for once Jara thought Bjorn was right, and the stranger was not a trader. Everything about him—his speech, his bearing, his appearance—denoted a Naval officer, and yet he had been quick to deny that, even while he must have known that a man like Bjorn would not like to be off-side with an officer of the British Navy. She had heard of deserters before, of course, who left their ships out of curiosity or for the local Maori women and who soon disappeared. In a country devoid of flesh-bearing animals, cannibalism was very common among the unconverted Maori tribes. But she had never heard of an officer deserting, or 'running' as the Navy called it. No, he was a very puzzling man altogether...

She lay all day hidden in the bush. From time to time she heard her name being called from the settlement, but she knew much better than to give in to her emptily grumbling stomach and go back to the beach and Bjorn.

As darkness fell she plucked up the courage to venture closer to the beach. With the day's work done the men were settling down at the outside tables for some steady drinking and more longboats had arrived from the ships in the harbour. One of them, she noticed, was coming across laden with men from the big barque. Making herself comfortable behind some large rocks on the edge of the beach, Jara settled down to watch what was going on. It was no different from any other night she had seen here—men eating and drinking, laughing and cursing each other. From time to time a man would get up and stagger to the water's edge to relieve himself, and as the night progressed someone was occasionally thrown into the sea to everyone's great mirth. She found herself looking for one particular man, but in the fading light it was hard to be sure that he wasn't there.

She finally fell asleep, to be woken some time later by the sound of loud voices far too close to her. She instinctively cringed back, before realising that she was not the object of their attention.

'I tell you—not so many!'

'Aw, come on, Helga! What does it matter how many if you're paid for it? Be a sport, lass!'

There was a chorus of rough male laughter and then the sound of Helga grumbling as she lowered herself to the sand just feet away from where Jara lay paralysed with fright.

'All right then. But don't you think I not counting!'

Jara came fully to her senses and regained use enough of her limbs to be able to slither away on her stomach from the ugly scene, unheard in the ensuing uproar, not caring where she went as long as she simply got away. She hid herself deep in the bush this time, blocking her ears to deaden the sounds of what was happening on the beach. She found herself praying that the stranger was not among the men with Helga, but common sense told her that it was much more than likely.

And if he *was* there, and she should find herself to be wrong about him, then her last hope of getting away from Kororareka had just been shattered.

CHAPTER TWO

CAPTAIN Christopher Montgomery, of His Majesty's Navy, aimed a vicious kick at the inert body sprawled at his feet on the beach.

'Get up, damn you! Get up!'

There was no answer except for a low groan and Kit clenched his fists in frustration. Blast them! If only he'd been able to think of a good enough excuse to keep his crew on board the *Courageous* last night they could have upped anchor and been off at first light, away from that wily bastard Bjorn and whatever he had planned for them. But it had been many months since any of them had so much as set eyes on a woman and even when he had commanded a crew of His Majesty's finest sailors Kit had always been tolerant of what his men did in port; most captains and commanders turned a blind eye, accepting that men driven hard at sea for months on end needed some form of physical release on land. Besides, the men still did not constitute a *crew* in any sense of the word as he understood it and until he had complete control of them he could not risk taking the *Courageous* out to sea. Very few of the men had any experience of sailing before, and it did not help that he had had to downplay his own knowledge of these seas, and of this ship in particular...

Suddenly despairing of ever getting away from this accursed country, he gave one last half-hearted kick at the uncaring body of Moody and slumped down beside him. He could have saved his breath and his temper and come with them in the longboat last night. What the hell did it matter anyway if Bjorn and his Maoris ransacked the boat while he drank and whored himself into oblivion along with everyone else in Kororareka? He'd hidden the purser's supply of gold coins under the floorboards in the great cabin, and there was precious little else that could be taken that hadn't already been picked over. As it was he had spent a long and uncomfortable night patrolling the decks alone, convinced that Bjorn would find the temptation of a ship guarded by only one man far too much to resist.

One of the first lessons that had been drummed into him as a midshipman was the old rule of never anchoring further than a pistol-shot from an unknown coast when a longboat was ashore. Expect the worst and you can only be pleasantly surprised... His caution had paid off when, some time around midnight, he had heard the soft splashing sound of deliberately muffled oars approaching from the shore. Taking careful aim he had fired a single shot into the sea in the direction of the disturbance, and had been rewarded by a muffled oath of surprise. He had heard nothing more after that, but the incident forced him into a decision he had not wanted to make. Faced with a choice between continuing to spend precious time in recruiting a crew here or pressing on with the men he had, he had finally decided on the latter course of action. The risks of taking out a severely undermanned ship still had to be better than taking on a Kororareka crew he did not know.

He had come ashore at first light to retrieve his men before a bolder attempt was made to take over the ship, but had found half of them in Moody's unconscious state, littered over the beach. The others, he assumed, were still in the *whares* with the overly obliging local women, and he was not particularly eager to recover them from there.

God damn them all! Why hadn't he killed them all weeks before, when he had first realised the impossibility of his situation? Or even earlier than that, when he had been so crazed with the need for vengeance that he would joyfully have given his last breath to be able to squeeze the life out of each and every one of them? But even that, he thought savagely, would have been a kinder end than any of them deserved; certainly a kinder end than they had allowed George and all the others... The discipline born of fifteen years of rigid Naval training had been all that had saved him then, and he knew now that while he lived—as futile as it might be— he had to keep trying. It was not only his duty, but the only chance he had of one day returning to England.

He tried to cheer himself up with the thought that it could have been worse; if it hadn't been for that foul-smelling crone sitting behind Bjorn yesterday he might have been tempted to overcome his instinctive distrust of the Swede and have agreed to let some of his men on his ship. As it was, the woman had probably saved his life—for the time being at least.

It was not, after all, such a cheerful thought, and he was relapsing into gloom again when a mis-aimed pebble hit him squarely on the back.

'Christ!' He leaped to his feet and looked back at the bush from where he gauged the pebble had come. He could see nothing but a grimy hand gesticulating wildly to him to approach. It seemed unlikely that Bjorn or one of his men would be skulking about in the bushes throwing pebbles at him, but still he hesitated. 'Who's there?'

'It is me!'

That didn't tell him a great deal except that the speaker was a woman. Then a face cautiously thrust forward through the undergrowth and looked quickly up and down the deserted beach, and he recognised the crone from yesterday. Good God, he thought in disgust—she looked even worse today. Now there was something wrong with her nose, and even under the mud it looked swollen and bruised. Long, unkempt, unbelievably greasy hair was escaping from the shawl pulled over her head and was hanging in strands over her shoulders, and her clothes looked as if she had not taken them off for several years at least.

'Please—come here!'

He was inclined to refuse, but he read unmistakable fear on the woman's face and, very much against his better judgement, he moved forward.

'Closer! They must not see me!'

Holding his breath Kit bent over and followed the woman as she wove a way through the thick under-growth, hoping to blazes that she had a good reason for putting him through all this and that he wasn't walking straight into a trap. She came to a stop at last and knelt down, motioning that he do the same. Taking care to sit some distance from her, he slowly did so.

'Listen madam,' he began courteously enough, 'I'm grateful for your help yesterday, but——'

'Ssssh!' she hissed, and they sat in silence for a moment while she appeared to listen intently to the sounds of the bush around them. He was surprised to see that she was not nearly as old as he had at first thought—perhaps even still in her teens. The hand she held to her lips was incongruously slim and well-formed and he found his eyes automatically following the curve of her arm under the stained grey smock she wore, to dwell on the unmistakable curves below...

Stop it! he ordered himself, and shook his head slightly in an effort to clear it. He was dangerously tired, and his senses were too blurred for him to think with complete rationality. And he had been nine months away from civilisation now—what other reasons could he have

for finding one of these whaling station women desirable
for even one moment? Surely he wasn't as desperate as
all that? Besides, she smelt abominable—almost as bad
as the slaughtering beach they had passed on their way
into the harbour. His stomach began to churn at the
very memory of it, and he moved back fractionally from
this unpleasant woman.

Apparently satisfied that their entry into the bush had
not been noticed, the woman let out a great sigh of relief.

'Good. I think everyone is still asleep. We are safe.'
By this time it had dawned on Kit that she spoke with
not a Swedish but a distinctly French accent, and he felt
a completely irrational wave of anger surge through him.
Her nationality provided yet another reason to heartily
dislike this disgusting woman. And here he was, sitting
in the bushes with her! Was she even sane? he wondered. She didn't look sane to him.

'Safe?' he said testily. 'I'm sorry, but... Look, just
what is it that you want from me?'

'I must get away from here at once. You have to take
me with you on your ship. Today!' She spoke low and
urgently, and with such apparent conviction that he
would comply that Kit found difficulty in voicing the
flat rejection that sprang to his lips. While he hesitated,
trying to find a gentler way of saying no and wondering
why on earth he felt he had to bother, the woman leaned
forward. 'Please understand that it is because of you
that I have to leave. If I had not helped you yesterday,
Bjorn would not have tried to kill me. So you see, you
have to take me away from here.'

'He'd kill you?' Kit looked at her sceptically. 'That
would be a little extreme, wouldn't it? And while we're
on the subject, may I ask why you *did* try to help me
yesterday?'

'Because if I had not you would have accepted Bjorn's
offer of a crew,' she said in surprise.

'Not at twenty pounds a head, I wouldn't have. I couldn't have. I haven't got that sort of money, and there's very little of any value on the ship.'

'But he would have come down in price, you see,' she explained impatiently. 'And once his men were on board they would have taken everything you have and murdered you and your crew if you had objected! It was because of me that he lost your ship, and if he should find me...'

'So he hasn't tried to kill you yet?'

'No, not yet,' she admitted. 'But I know he will, and I can not hide here in the bush forever. And if you are short of men I can cook, and clean, and I am sure I could be of help. Oh...*please*, you *must* help me to get away!'

He looked at her dubiously. 'Why me? Surely someone else——'

'No one else. You are the only one who owes me such a debt,' she said with such sublime assurance that Kit sat bolt upright with indignation.

'Listen, madam, I am in no way responsible for you——'

'But you are. Absolutely!' The woman threw her head back to stare at him with what he realised with astonishment was actually defiance. She looked so ridiculous with her dirty, misshapen nose, like a scruffy little mongrel trying in vain to look more important than it was, that he almost laughed. He resisted the temptation, however, as it began to dawn on him that her proposal might not be quite as outrageous as it had at first seemed.

Whether or not she was right about him being in debt to her was unimportant—he was in no position to afford a tender conscience, and if it were more expedient to leave her here to Bjorn's retribution, then he would most certainly do so. On the other hand, she could be of some use to him on the ship; meals had to be prepared by someone, and she could free a man for sailing if she

took over those duties. And then there were the sails
that had been badly ripped by the storm that had scup-
pered *Courageous* and that needed to be mended ... On
reflection he had to admit that she could be of
considerable use on the voyage, and at least he could be
sure that she would not cause the trouble among the
men that a woman on board usually did. It was not as
if she would expect him to go to the bother of defending
her honour, after all—if any of the men did get desperate enough to want to tumble her she would no doubt
be as happy as any of the other Kororareka women to
oblige.

At last he raised his shoulders in a shrug of acquiescence. 'All right, I'll take you with me. But it won't be
an easy trip, and I can't guarantee that where I put you
off will necessarily be much better than here. Do you
understand?' She nodded quickly. 'And what do I call
you?'

'Jara Perrault.'

He did not bother to ask what a Frenchwoman was
doing among Swedish whalers—how she got here and
why she thought she had to leave was certainly not his
concern. 'My name is Kit Bennett.' He sat back on his
heels and looked at her thoughtfully. 'Well, Jara, we'd
better get you out to the ship as soon as possible. I've
a longboat further up the beach—I didn't want to land
too close to the *whares*. The trees come down to the sea-
edge there, so it should be simple enough for you to get
in the boat without being seen. I'll take you out now
and then I'll have to come back for my men.'

He stood to go, but she reached out and touched his
wrist with a hand that startled him into recoil with its
softness. 'Thank you.'

He covered his surprise with a cynical smile. 'You have
nothing to thank me for, believe me. Out of the frying
pan ...'

'What?' she said blankly.

'An English expression. Your people will be stirring soon. We had better go.'

'They are not my people...' she started to say, but he had already gone.

An hour later Jara stood on the foredeck of the *Courageous* and looked back at the country that had been her home for all her life. From here she could clearly see the sharp contours of the land; how the emerald-green of the bush plunged down to embrace the deep, mirror-surfaced sea. Even from several hundred yards away she could clearly hear the rich bell tones of the *tuis* calling to each other in the flowering *pohutukawa* trees. It looked like paradise. But a little further around the bay the charnel houses were visible, where the ravaged carcasses of many whales lay putrefying under the sun. The stench was always noticeable, varying only in its intensity with the numbers of whales and the direction of the wind. Squatting on the red beach were the *whares* of her mother's primitive and depraved people and behind that, no longer visible from the sea, were the shallow unmarked graves of the only people who had ever cared for her. It wasn't paradise at all—it was hell.

Her eye was caught by the movement of two long-boats preparing to leave the beach. Kit must have retrieved all his men and was returning. He had given her implicit instructions to stay below decks and not to let the men see her, and so she hurried below to the cabin he had shown her and shut the door.

Quite unused to ships, she thought the cabin tiny, little bigger than a cupboard, but after living on the beach it seemed almost luxurious. There were two narrow bunks either side with a table, covered with charts and several instruments, built in under the porthole. Small cupboards under the bunks intrigued her, and she knelt to open one of them. A few items of clothing neatly folded, some books, a razor...

She shut the cupboard and sank down on one of the bunks. It was not proof, but she was suddenly as sure as she could be that this was Kit's cabin. But he had shown her here, had indicated that this was where she was to stay... Perhaps she had misunderstood him. Her English had been learned from books and from the passable English that the Perraults had spoken to their customers. Kit spoke too fast, too impatiently, for her to always understand what he was saying. But his aversion to her had been clear, she had been certain of that. He had not wanted to come anywhere near her on the beach, so why hide her here, in his own cabin...?

She heard the longboats pulling alongside the ship and felt a cold finger of fear run down her spine as for the first time the full enormity of what she had done dawned on her. Out at sea there would be no forest to run and hide in. She had thrown herself completely on the mercy of a total stranger about whom she knew nothing at all. So he was clean, so he had learned some manners somewhere, so he had not after all joined the debauchery on the beach last night. Was that recommendation enough for her to have entrusted him with her life?

He had denied being a Naval officer but he had not, she remembered now, denied Bjorn's assumption that he was a deserter or even a criminal. And as for his men...there could be no doubt but that some of them were among those with Helga last night. And now she had delivered herself utterly into their hands, with no indication whatsoever that Kit would act as her protector. She buried her head in her hands and despaired. What had she done?

She sat motionless for a long time, while there came the sound of activity on the deck above her and then the loud rattle of the anchors being raised. After a while the ship began to rock slightly and she rose to go to the porthole and look out at the islands and the harbour that had always been her home slipping past. She stood for hours, until at last she saw the Maori *pa* on the eastern tip of the island of Motu Arohia and knew that ahead of them now lay only the open sea. The silhouette of the fortified walls, of tall thin trees tied together, suddenly reminded her of skeletal ribs, and she turned away from the porthole with a shudder. As she did so her head spun, and it was only then that she remembered that she had not eaten for almost two days. She retreated to the bunk and tried hard not to think of her empty stomach.

It was late afternoon and they had been under way for several hours when she finally heard steps outside the door and then someone fumbling at the handle. She waited tensely to see who it was and was relieved to see that it was Kit who came in, moving awkwardly with the burden of a large pail of steaming water.

He shut the door behind him and looked at her.

'Are you all right?'

'I am very hungry...'

'Mmm. First things first. A meal comes later.' He went over to the porthole and opened it. 'Would you take your clothes off, please. All of them.'

'I...I beg your pardon?'

'You heard me clearly enough,' he said impatiently.

'I heard you, but I do not understand you!'

'Yes you do. Come on, now—I've got a great deal to do today without having to wait for you to do what you're told.' He leaned back against the wall, arms folded. She began to retreat from him, feeling behind her for the door-handle. For the first time she saw a hint of amusement in the level brown eyes. 'And I don't think it's a good idea to leave the cabin just now—the men don't know you're here yet, and they...don't like surprises.'

'I will not take my clothes off!' she said from between gritted teeth. 'How dare you? I should never have trusted you!'

He frowned. 'No, of course you shouldn't. What in the hell is all this reticence about anyway...?' Then he looked more closely at her frightened face and gave a short bark of incredulous laughter. 'You...you didn't think that I wanted to...? Oh, I see. No.' She was startled to see an expression very much like embarrassment on his face, and after a short silence he began again in a rather more conciliatory tone of voice. 'Look, Jara, I'm sorry if I've offended your sensibilities, but you'll have to wash. If you're going to sleep in my cabin...'

'In your cabin? But I cannot!' Her hands flew to her face in distress. 'Is there nowhere else I could stay?'

He shook his head. 'The crew have taken over the officer's quarters. There's plenty of hammock space of course, if you don't mind the lack of privacy. I just wanted to leave it for a day or two before I let the men know you're on board, because there've been a few grumbles about my not allowing them to bring other women with us. Once we're well at sea, and can't turn back, you'd be free to sleep where you please. But if washing is going to upset you that much, you're welcome to go and sleep with the men right now—in which case you needn't bother washing.' He walked past her towards the door and she threw herself against it, preventing him from opening it.

'Please! I cannot...I mean...if there is nowhere else to go... Can't *you* sleep somewhere else?'

'Yes, of course,' he said in surprise. 'I'll be catching some sleep up on the deck—I can assure you that I'm not particularly keen to share a cabin with you. But I'll want to have my cabin back later, and I don't want it smelling like a whaling station when I do. If you choose to stay here you must wash. At once.'

She blinked back the sharp tears of humiliation at his words and tried to outstare him, but this was something at which he had had considerably more practice than her. It was not long before her eyes dropped uncomfortably under his unflinching gaze.

'All right. But ... I want you to leave.'

'Certainly. After you give me your clothes. I want you to change every stitch of clothing you have on. There's a blanket on the bed you can wrap yourself in, and I'll get you a complete set of clean clothes. Come on, now!' he added irritably when she made no move to undress. 'I don't want to do it for you, for God's sake, so get a move on, woman!'

'Turn your back first!'

'With great pleasure,' he muttered, and he turned away to face the porthole.

She seized the blanket and held it around her while she struggled with the buttons of her dress and slipped off her undergarments. They fell in a pile around her feet and she bent to gather them up. She had taken great care of her clothes while at the settlement—they were, after all, the only things she had left to remind her of the life she had led before her world had gone mad. The smock and shirt were plain but of the best quality linen, and they had been exquisitely sewn for her by Marie. A careful laundering and they would be as good as ever.

Kit took them from her and bundled them out of the porthole.

'My clothes!'

'Your clothes were filthy and no doubt crawling with vermin,' he said sternly.

'No, they were not!'

'Now wash yourself, please. I'll be back later with some clean clothes.' He shut the door behind him.

'*Cochon!*' Jara spat after him before running to the porthole to vainly look for the last glimpse of her clothes sinking slowly in their wake beneath the churning green waters of the Pacific Ocean. There was suddenly a hard knot in her throat. The unfeeling brute! The clothes had been her only possessions, the only link with her past. And he had thrown them out as if they were nothing but rubbish.

She turned to look at the pail of water and for a moment thought of tipping it out to follow the last of her belongings through the porthole. But then there would only be another argument, and another pail of water. It appeared that she had no option but to do as he insisted after all. His open contempt of her appearance had stung and some perverse part of her was defiantly shouting—do as he wants, then! Let him take the consequences!

She found a basin and some soap in another cupboard and began to wash herself, paying special attention to the thickly smeared mud on her arms and face. It took a while to remove the whale oil she had combed through her hair, but at last it squeaked cleanly beneath her hands. She had no hairbrush, and so stood wrapped in the blanket by the open porthole, drying her hair with her fingers in the breeze. And it was like this that Kit found her when he rapped briefly on the door and let himself in. His jaw visibly dropped in dismay as he set eyes on her.

'Oh, bloody hell!'

The girl—for she could not have been past eighteen—turned to stare at him. As he had noticed that morning, her nose was slightly discoloured and swollen, as if from a blow, but despite that there was no disguising her good looks. Her colouring was pure Nordic, with arctic-blue eyes and thick hair that was drying to flaxen. But her facial structure was finer than those of the women he had seen at the settlement, with a small well-shaped mouth and a nose that would eventually match. As she turned to face him she raised her head in the same gesture of defiance he had found so comical in Kororareka, but now it was not in the least amusing.

She was not a small woman—only half a head shorter than himself, and statuesquely built. His eyes automatically fell to follow the generous lines of her body beneath the blanket and it was only with an almighty effort that he wrenched them away and back to her face. The stab of desire that jolted through him coincided with a surge of fury. Christ, he thought, this was the last straw! He flung the clothes he had brought her on to one of the bunks and then collapsed beside them. Jara stood motionless above him, watching his every move warily. 'So.' He found his voice at last, and addressed her toes. 'So this is what you look like. I'd no idea you'd scrub up so well.'

'Thank you,' Jara said uncertainly. It didn't sound much like a compliment.

'And before? The dirt, and...and that repulsive smell?'

'Whale oil. I almost became used to it after a while, and it did what it was meant to.'

'I see.'

'Do you?' She sat on the bunk opposite him and studied him closely. His eyes were fixed on a point on the floor and she could read no sign in his face of what he was thinking. 'I think that maybe you do not see. I was only at the whaling settlement for one week—my mother was from there but she died, and I was raised in the trading post above the harbour, by very good people. Then a Maori war party killed my family and I was brought to work at the whaling station. I...I protected myself in the only way I knew. The dirt and the oil was—camouflage? It kept me safe while I waited to get away from that place. *Now* do you see?'

Kit ran his hands distractedly through his hair. 'Jara, I don't know what to think, or what to do. I think...' He dropped his hands and looked at her again. 'I'll have to take you back to shore.'

'Not to Kororareka!' she said quickly, a desperate note in her voice. 'I cannot go back there!'

'Not there, maybe. But to another settlement...'

'I do not know where the other settlements are. My mother's people came to Kororareka just one year before I was born, and I have only heard recently of one or two other whaling stations in New Zealand. I know nothing about them except that...they will be no better.'

'Then...' His voice trailed off as he realised what he had done. A woman alone with sixteen men on a sea voyage that would take many weeks. Seventeen men, if he counted himself; he, who would have to share a cabin with her for all that time. He couldn't touch her, he couldn't trust himself... And, for entirely different reasons, he couldn't trust her.

Sudden helpless rage surged up inside him. 'I should damned well throw you overboard, then! If I'd known...'

He stood up abruptly to leave before he lashed out at something or someone and Jara caught his arm, dismayed at the abrupt change in him. The blanket around her shoulders slipped as she moved.

'Please! I will not be any trouble, I promise! Only please do not take me back to shore! I will do any-thing——'

'Will you?' he interrupted her harshly, and as she looked into his eyes she was shocked by what she saw there. Before she had a chance to move back his hands came up to her bare shoulders and he pulled her towards him, his fingers hurting her. 'Will you?'

Unsure of what answer he wanted her to give, she stood paralysed under his hands, grasping the blanket tightly around her with her elbows, holding her breath as she waited to see what he would do next. Her eyes were level with the pulse throbbing in his throat and she was so close to him that she could see the hard lines around his mouth, pale under his tan.

The moment seemed to last an age, but at last he pushed her roughly away from him and turned to walk out the door, slamming it behind him.

She sank down on to the bunk as her legs gave way. The vulnerability she had felt while in his arms, and what she had seen blazing in his eyes, had shaken her badly. Yet through her fear she still comforted herself with the fact that he had not pressed the advantage he had over her. Had he chosen to, he could easily have taken what he so obviously wanted from her, and she was in no position to defend herself. But he hadn't. Unlike every other man she had met at Kororareka, he had not exploited the defencelessness of a woman.

Had she made the right choice of man? She was beginning to think she had.

CHAPTER THREE

THE wind steady in the sails, open sea ahead, his hands on the helm—once these things were all Kit had thought he needed for complete happiness. His priorities were very different now, but despite everything he felt his spirits soar as he raised his eyes to the billowing sails above. He had heard about the legendary *kauri* trees of New Zealand, and had had no trouble whatsoever in identifying the towering giants in the dense forest. It had taken a full day and two broken axes to cut down the two trees they needed, but now the newly installed masts were fully rigged and handsome to Kit's appreciative sailor's eyes. It would take more than a hurricane to bring down *those* two beauties.

His eyes dropped to the considerably less pleasing sight of what—in lieu of anything better—he now had to resign himself to calling his crew. They were working well enough now, if still a little slowly and unsteadily after the previous night's excesses, but a filthier, more untrustworthy bunch of men he had yet to encounter, and his control over them was still very tenuous. There had been a potentially ugly scene a couple of hours earlier when he had ordered the barrels of liquor some of the men had bought in Kororareka thrown overboard. The outraged owners had objected strongly, and for a minute or two he had thought that he would be joining the barrels over the side, but he had stood his ground over this just as he had over a hundred other things. His years of command at sea had given him the skills to out-face them, even with his hands clenched so as not to betray their shaking and with a cold river of sweat trickling down his back. He didn't think they could begin to guess how afraid of them he really was.

He had had to be so very careful, especially in the beginning, but he had survived somehow—had more than survived. By sheer force of personality and strength of will he had beaten his way to the leadership of these men, and now they were at sea, and thus more dependent on him and his sailor's knowledge, he hoped that his hold over them would be even greater. Time, of course, would tell. For now, the coast of New Zealand was fast diminishing behind them and the skies ahead held no immediate danger.

'Mr Davies!' He called over the man nearest to him and explained to him how to hold his course steady at the wheel. The first stars were appearing in the darkening sky, and he wanted to get below and plot their new course carefully before he caught up on his missed night's sleep.

He was almost at the door of his cabin before he remembered who was in there, and he cursed softly. It must have been six hours since he left her, and she had been complaining then of hunger. At least she had had the sense not to come above decks—he had not yet given any thought as to how to introduce her to the men.

He detoured to the galley to collect a mug of warm tea and some hard biscuits, having to step over the sacks of food that they had brought on board that morning and which no one had had time to stow away. He was unhappy with the quantity of their supplies; the few vegetables he had been able to buy from the whaling settlement had been inordinately expensive and grudgingly spared—as a result of his earlier disagreement with Bjorn, he suspected. But they had refilled all the water barrels with pure fresh spring water and with so few men on board, and with frugality and good fishing their supplies should last them for at least four months. The charts he had of the southern Pacific gave only a rough idea of the location of the few islands on which they could obtain fresh water supplies in the event of a prolonged voyage, but that did not concern him unduly. If the girl settled down with the men she could hopefully be left safely in charge of the galley, and then the calculation of rations would become one less responsibility for him.

A first surprised glance inside his cabin made him think momentarily that the girl had changed her mind and gone to the men's quarters after all, but then he saw the huddled lump under the blankets on one of the bunks. He lit the lamp before leaning over to shake her. The face she raised to him was pale and tear-stained. He almost—but not quite—found it rather appealing.

'Are you still angry with me?' she demanded.

'What?' he said blankly, before remembering his last words to her. His was not a brooding or vindictive nature, and he had forgotten about the incident five minutes after he had walked out the door. Remembering it now, and his near-loss of self-control, brought him a fleeting but unexpected sense of shame. 'Er . . . no. I'm not angry any more. I've brought you something to eat.'

She groaned and slumped back on to the pillow. 'Nothing to eat, please. Just . . . I am a little thirsty.'

Kit knew what it was and sighed. 'You'd better try to keep something down—it must have been a long time since you've eaten anything. Come on now, sit up, there's a good girl.'

'Go away!' came the voice from beneath the blankets. 'Have you no heart? Can you not see I am dying?'

'No you're not!' he said in exasperation. 'You're just seasick. It'll pass soon, but in the meantime I want you to try to eat something.' He helped her to sit up and put the mug of by now cool tea in her hands. She sipped it gingerly and he noted with relief that it seemed to be staying down. Just in case, he pointedly pushed the basin over beside the bed. 'Do you want the biscuit?'

She shook her head and eased herself down between the blankets again, apparently falling into an immediate sleep. He sat and watched her for a moment, having to admit reluctantly that this activity gave him a certain amount of perverse pleasure. She really was a beauty, especially when she kept her mouth shut. It was just a pity that she wouldn't remain beautiful—not after the men found out that she was on board.

Kit had no illusions about how long he would be able to keep them away from her; he had been pushing what authority he had over them to the limit from the very beginning, and he knew that making them leave Kororareka so quickly had made many of them openly question his self-appointed authority over them. To insist now that they all keep their hands off the girl sleeping in his cabin would be far too much. It might take place immediately upon her discovery, or it might not happen for a day or two after that, but it was inevitable. There were elements in his crew that even he could not control. He had seen women who had been raped by many men before, and it had never failed to sicken him, but to make the girl an issue would put his command at risk, and nothing—not even the extreme distress of a woman—was worth that. Once he might have fought to protect her against any odds, simply because she was an unprotected and unwilling woman, but that had been a long time ago. He was harder now—much harder—and yet there was still a small, insistent voice of decency somewhere deep inside him that revolted against the idea of simply handing such a young and plainly inexperienced girl over to the men. She needed rest first, and to be prepared for what would happen to her.

This indisposition might mean that the girl would be kept to her bed for a few days, but at least while she was seasick he was spared from having to let the men know she was on board. If indeed it was simply seasickness and not exhaustion and delayed shock—if what she had told him was true, she had gone through just as much as he had, in an even shorter space of time. And she was so very young...

He recognised the feeling that was making him uncomfortable as pity, and angrily dismissed it. He might have made an error in judgement in letting her aboard in the first place, but it was entirely her own fault that she was here and in this situation! Whatever happened to her now was unavoidable, and she was certainly not worth jeopardising his own life for. She was as expendable as any of the others. The only person on this ship whose survival mattered was himself and under no circumstances could he allow himself to forget that.

Jara stirred slightly, as if unconsciously troubled by his thoughts, and Kit watched her irritably. The last time he had put compassion above duty he had caused destruction far beyond his wildest nightmares. He would be damned now if he would repeat the mistake!

Bending over the maps on the table, he picked up his compass and began to plot their route. He was taking a more north-westerly direction than the men suspected, in the remote hope that they might cross the path of any other Naval vessel bound for Norfolk Island. And if they didn't...

The thousands of miles of open sea that lay between New Zealand and the southern coast of China filled the table before him. He had never heard of anyone taking a ship the size of the *Courageous* to sea so undermanned. Even if by some miracle they met with no mishap, even if the winds were fair all the way, the journey would take months. And they had already spent two months refitting the *Courageous*. If he got to China at all he would still be far too late and the certain disgrace that awaited him there would only be compounded by failure.

He threw himself down on his bunk and lay staring at the ceiling for a very long time.

'But I want to go up for some fresh air!' Jara said plaintively. 'For weeks you have kept me a prisoner down here with nothing to do.'

'It's been four days,' Kit said testily. 'And if you've got nothing to do, why don't you try tidying up this cabin? The bed hasn't been made, you've left clothes lying on the floor...'

'The cabin is too small to keep tidy!'

'Rubbish! Because it's small there's all the more reason to keep it tidy. You may be used to living in a pigsty, but I am not. Now—pick those clothes up.'

She folded her arms and stared up at him provocatively. 'I will pick them up if you let me go up on deck.'

She could actually hear him grind his teeth. When he at last spoke his voice was very measured, each word precisely clipped. Jara had no idea that it was a mannerism of speech that had never failed to intimidate a recalcitrant midshipman.

'I should have thrown you out the porthole after those filthy rags you called clothes! How many times do I have to tell you that you can't go up until I tell the men that you're on board?'

'Then please tell them! Can you not understand what it is like to live in a little cupboard like this! I need to breathe some air, and to see the sun for a little time. I think I will go mad if I have to keep staring at these four walls for another minute!'

She had not realised that she had broken into French in her agitation until he stepped forward, his face white with anger, and roughly covered her mouth with his hand. 'Don't you ever speak to me in that goddamned tongue again! And for God's sake stop shouting, or you'll have everyone hearing you all over the ship.'

She wrenched his hand away. 'How dare you treat me like this? And you should not blaspheme like that! I speak French because I *am* French, and I know that you can understand me—I can see it! Why should you dislike it so?'

'Because I've spent so many of my years in fighting the French, and that, madam, is why I've no wish to hear the language in my own damned cabin! If you want your head to stay on your shoulders you'll remember to speak English at all times on this ship. Is that understood?'

Jara regarded him warily, her own anger losing intensity as she evaluated the risk of further enraging her saviour. He was probably exaggerating about pushing her out the porthole, but all the same she decided on a more conciliatory tack.

'I am sorry that my nationality should offend you so much, but you must remember that I have only ever lived in Kororareka. Our only contact was with the ships that came—French, American, English, Dutch... From all countries, and all with different stories. So many thousands of miles from Europe, no one seemed to care so much about what country another ship was from. The war was never fought in these waters, and so we never knew very much about it. There was no need, you see?' She bestowed upon him the winsome smile that had never failed to disarm her adoptive father, or the scores of officers who had had reason to call in at her parents' trading post. 'I did not mean to offend you, Captain. Please forgive me.'

Kit stared at her lovely face completely unmoved. What an impossible witch she was. Manipulative, nagging, self-centred... all the things he most detested in a female. He was by now heartily regretting that he had ever set eyes on her, and the role of protector she was insidiously forcing him into was completely out of the question. It was high time he disabused her of her blind faith in him and he had just opened his mouth to say so when the cabin door creaked open.

The head that appeared around it was shaggy and unkempt, with a matted black beard framing a curious face; Jara recognised him at once as one of the sailors she had seen drinking on the beach at Kororareka. The man stared at them both for a long moment in silence before stepping inside the cabin, carefully closing the door behind him. An odour akin to that of rotting fish filled the cabin.

He slowly surveyed Jara from head to foot and back again, seeming to take in all the smallest details of her appearance. Her hair was pulled back neatly into a single thick plait down her back, and she was wearing the men's clothing Kit had given her on her first day on board the ship; the too-large white shirt came almost to her knees and beneath that she wore brown heavy cotton trousers, rolled up at the bottoms. Whilst she was completely covered and knew that the clothes effectively hid any hint of her shape, she suddenly felt indecent and undressed under the avid eyes. She was aware of Kit standing beside her, and even then she briefly wondered why a man who was not usually lost for words was saying nothing to this unpleasant-looking person who had burst so unceremoniously into his cabin. When she glanced at him, only a clenched muscle in his cheek betrayed his anger.

'Well,' the man drawled at last, a smirk on his face. 'Ain't you the sly one, Mr Bennett? Gone and kept a nice little piece like this all cosily tucked away in yer cabin and not a word to any of us, eh? Don't seem fair, now, does it?'

Jara could not help but glance at Kit in surprise. She had supposed that he was the Captain of this vessel, but this man was hardly addressing him as such.

'Fairness doesn't come into it,' Kit said evenly. 'You haven't seen her before because she's been sick up until now. She's on board to do the cooking, but that's the extent of her duties. Do you understand that, Moody?'

The man snorted. 'I understand all right. So it's meat for the Captain's table while the rest of us poor buggers go without, eh? Well, blow that, mate—you ain't in the Navy now! No women on board—that's what you said! You go breakin' yer own rules and you know what you can expect, don't you?' He turned back to Jara and his eyes had a hard glitter as he added, 'So...welcome aboard, lass.' He stretched out his hand and for one puzzled second Jara thought he was going to formally shake her hand, despite his rough speech. She gave a small choked gasp of shock when he instead grabbed the front of her shirt and pulled her against him. She had a quick gust of his foul breath, a glimpse of his lips red against the matted beard, and then she was propelled backwards again as Kit forced his way between them.

'Get your hands off her, Moody. And get out.' He spoke firmly but quietly; much too quietly, Jara thought, to have any effect on the man who was still clutching her shirt. But there must have been something in Kit's eyes, something in his tone of voice, that she was not aware of. It took a long moment, but slowly the man's fingers loosened and she was able to tear herself free. The two men stood very still, glaring at each other, and it was Moody who dropped his eyes first, his face contorted in a snarl. 'Now get out.'

Turning on his heel, Moody obliged, slamming the cabin door behind him. Kit's shoulders dropped in a sigh of relief and he turned around to find Jara gazing up at him apprehensively.

'Are...are they all like that man?'

'Like Moody? I wouldn't have said he was the worst, but the others are...' He fell silent and then looked at her speculatively. 'Well, I would have liked a little more time, but thanks to your shouting your presence to all on board, time is something we no longer have. Your wish is about to be granted, I'm afraid, Jara. You'd better come up on deck and meet the men.' He opened the door and looked at her expectantly, but she stayed where she was, her fingers nervously fiddling with the collar of her shirt. Much as she had longed for fresh air and freedom of movement, Moody's sudden appearance had made the tiny cabin seem like a haven of safety and security. And the way he had looked at her, and what he had said... A small, and very nasty suspicion was beginning to form in her mind. Kit's air of authority had led her to believe not only that he could be trusted, but that he would also ensure her safety with the crew he commanded. Only now did she begin to realise that she might have been wrong on both counts. She began to back uncertainly away.

'Perhaps tomorrow...?'

'Why not now?' Kit said, and he could not keep the hard edge from his voice. He was bitterly sick of this damnable situation, and all he wanted now was for it all to be over—after all, she had brought it on herself, all of it. If only she'd kept her mouth shut and Moody hadn't heard her; if only she'd stayed at Kororareka! 'Weren't you complaining just a few minutes ago about my keeping you shut up in this cabin like a prisoner? Well, you're free to go now.'

Still she did not move. 'But that man... I am frightened to go up, Kit,' she said in a small voice.

He shrugged, his face still hard although he would not look at her. 'I'm sorry about this. But you must have known that it had to come to it sooner or later. There's no point in delaying—if you stay down here much longer they'll come and get you, and I think you'll agree that that would be worse.'

'Kit, will you . . . please . . . help me?'

'No.' He did not sound unkind but simply unequivocal, and she stared at him in dismay.

'You . . . you would give me to your men to . . . *appease* them?'

She knew she had struck home when he dropped his eyes and shifted his weight uncomfortably. 'Not to appease them, no. But it's inevitable that . . .' He broke off and looked at her with a scowl. 'Well, what else did you think was going to happen when you begged your way on board this ship? Or did you think they were all going to be like me?'

Having now discovered the chink in his armour, she dropped her pleading tone and instead gave him a withering glare of disdain. 'I will tell you what I thought, Mr Bennett! I thought that you were the *Captain* of this ship—I thought that *you* were in command. I realise now how wrong I was. *They* command *you*! You have such fear of this rabble that you would rather sacrifice a woman to them than stand up to them!' She ran out of breath and words then but was gratified to see that her words had stung as much as she had wanted them to. He turned his back to her, to stare out the porthole, but she could see the flush that had risen on the back of his neck.

'Being Captain means occasionally using the art of compromise. But of course I couldn't expect you to understand that.'

'Not when I am the one who is being compromised, Captain Bennett. No, I do not understand. Is this the way that you English treat a lady in your country?'

'Treat a lady . . .? A lady? Is that what you call yourself?' He flung his head back and gave a short, harsh, uneven laugh. 'Have you looked in a mirror lately? Look...' he ran his hand abstractedly through his hair '...you don't have to keep up this pretence about being some innocent, orphaned maiden—you're from Kororareka, aren't you? For pity's sake, woman, make it easier for both of us and stop acting like a nun in a brothel! You knew what to expect, surely?'

'But I have explained to you——'

'You've told me your life story, yes. But that doesn't change a thing. None of the men on this ship are going to believe that a whaling station woman from Kororareka is here for anything but their convenience. You can stand here and argue with me all day, but they'll be down any minute to get you regardless of what you tell me. I'm sorry—believe me, I really am—but nothing *I* can say or do is going to make this any easier for you.'

She bit her lip to steady its trembling. 'So you will not help me.'

'As I've said, I can't.'

She closed her eyes for a moment and to compose herself. His tone might be adamant but he was still refusing to meet her eyes. If she could shame him a little more, raise the dormant gallantry she was certain lurked below... Her voice when she spoke again surprised her by its evenness. 'Very well then. But if your men...if you let them touch me... I promise you that I will jump overboard at once. If you have a conscience, Captain Bennett, then my death will be on it.' It sounded good, even to her ears. She began to move towards the door, giving him plenty of time to think. She had begun to open the door by the time he put his hand on her arm and stopped her, roughly turning her around to face him.

'Would you really be as stupid as that?'

She kept her eyes lowered. 'I have my honour, Captain...' She let the words trail away meaningfully. There was a long silence and her confidence grew with every second. She kept her eyes on the hand that was firmly gripping her arm—a strong hand, tanned, with long, sensitive fingers. It was not the hand of a ravisher of women. Slowly his fingers unlocked and released her, and somewhere deep inside she began to exult. When she judged the moment right, she peeped up at him from under her eyelashes. He was not shame-faced or even slightly abashed. He was grinning broadly with a glint of what just might have been admiration in his narrowed eyes.

'What a little madam you are,' he said softly. 'But there's no way that you are going to make *me* take responsibility for you. If you want my advice——'

'I most certainly do not! Not if that is all you are going to give me!'

'It *is* all I'm going to give you, so shut up and listen. When you go up there, don't show them you're afraid. That's what they'll look for. Fear. If they see it, or smell it, or sense it in any way, they'll be on you like a pack of dogs. Be calm or be angry, but whatever you do don't allow yourself to be frightened. Now—do you think you can do that?'

'How would you know?' she demanded furiously. 'How would you know what it is like to be in my position? I will be alone up there, with no help from anyone...'

He took her chin in his fingers and forced her defiant, scornful face up to his even when she would have pulled away.

'I know a damned sight more about fear than you might think, Jara. Just remember what I've told you. Don't show it.'

Even through her rising panic, something in his voice reached her and she stood still, looking at him with growing curiosity and a very faint glimmering of hope. There was no unkindness or even indifference in his eyes, and she sensed that he was trying to tell her more—much more—than he was saying. If only she could understand...!

Instead, she took a deep breath and nodded. 'Thank you for the advice.'

'Don't thank me. It's only advice. But we're so short-handed that it would be damned inconvenient to lose the cook over the side before we're scarcely clear of New Zealand waters.'

'Your concern is very touching, Captain,' she flashed, furious again at his flippancy. 'Almost as touching as your total self-interest!'

He smiled again. 'My only interest, if you haven't already noticed, is in keeping this ship functioning as it should. I don't even know why I should be concerned about you; manipulative little bitches like you always survive—it's one of the laws of nature. You'll be all right.'

Above their heads came the sound of heavy feet and raised voices, and Kit moved quickly to throw open the cabin door.

'We've wasted enough time—they're not going to wait much longer. Come on now.'

He went first up the ladder to above decks and turned to help her as she came to the top, his hand on her elbow with what she took to be a sardonic gesture of courtesy. But she did not need his help; her feet were steady on the decking, the nausea of her seasickness having passed now with the gaining of what Kit had called her 'sea legs'. She stood blinking for a moment in the bright sunlight, taking in deep breaths of the tangy air, determined to stay in control of herself. She must remember what he had told her. Be calm, don't show any fear...

Her first sight of his men, however, almost served to unnerve her completely. The big man called Moody had had plenty of time to talk of what had happened, and the men had obviously been waiting for them to come on deck.

As they approached, Jara was acutely conscious that all eyes were upon her and it took every last ounce of her courage not to shrink back behind Kit's broad shoulders. She found herself wishing that he would take her arm again, or show some other sign of proprietorship, but somehow she knew he wouldn't. This was something only she could do. She threw her head back and looked each man in the eye.

'Good morning,' she addressed them as clearly as her quivering lips and dry mouth would allow. There was no reply, but she heard one of the men snigger. They continued to stare at her with hostile appraisal.

Kit cleared his throat. 'Gentlemen, this is Miss Jara Perrault, who is going to be our cook for this voyage. Miss Perrault, I'd like you to meet my crew. Mr Nathaniel Brown, Mr Patrick O'Regan, Mr Edward Moody whom you have already met . . .' He ran through the names as if formally announcing her in a gathering of polite society. The absurdity of it was not lost on the men, and there were a few grins by the time he had finished. He was used to being in control, Jara thought even as he spoke. By making them smile he had taken the first step towards defusing the situation, and the looks on their faces were—she told herself—slightly less antagonistic. The man he had introduced as Davies stepped forward.

'What I'd like to know, Mr Bennett, is why this young woman was kept in *your* cabin. And why we've not heard a word about her from you until now.'

There was a murmur of support for this and Kit said, 'Miss Perrault wasn't well, and I didn't think she'd get any better if you all knew she was on board.' He waited until the lewd guffaws that greeted this statement subsided before continuing blandly, 'As you know, there are no free cabins on this vessel, and the Captain's cabin is much more suitable for a lady——'

'I'll bet!' one of the men interjected. 'An' yer kin drop that bit about her bein' a lady, Bennett. She come from Kororareka, din't she?'

'She does, but she's the daughter of the traders there— she's not one of the whaling women. And in my book that makes her a lady, Mr Smithies,' Kit said smoothly, and Jara glanced up at him in surprise. 'I'd like her treated as such.'

'No women, you said!' Moody said in a voice that was almost a snarl. Despite what Kit had said about him being not being the worst of the men, Jara somehow found his gaze the most intense—almost desperate. His line of vision seemed locked on the rise of her breasts under her shirt, and he hadn't taken his eyes off her once.

'And I meant it. Women on board always mean trouble. But she was the only crew available in Kororareka, and I expect her to be very useful—if she's allowed to get on with her work. She'll be doing all the cooking, and I'd like Mr Davies to teach her how to mend the sails—she'll be kept busy enough without having to spend time below decks pandering to all your little perversities. If it hasn't already occurred to you, Mr Moody, it's a long way to China, and we're going to need all the help we can get.'

China? That was the first Jara had heard about that! She had of course assumed that they would be going to Australia or England or even America. But *China*? The older solidly built man called Davies burst out laughing at the look on her face.

'Looks like the new cook didn't know where we were headed, Mr Bennett! You been too busy to get round to telling her, then?' He came closer and she stood her ground, steeling herself not to flinch from the waft of his bad breath. Oddly enough, his face looked to be not at all unkind. 'What's the matter, little lady? You don't want to go to China with us?'

'No! I...I mean, I shall be happy to go to China,' Jara said hastily. 'I was...I was just a little surprised. I did not know that...trade took you to such a place.' But of course even in isolated Kororareka everyone had heard of the lucrative trading to be done with the Chinese mandarins. Silks, precious stones, and especially tea... So Kit Bennett and his dreadful crew were traders after all! A feeling much like relief swept through her. But her words had not lessened the men's amusement at her reaction. Only Kit was not laughing.

Forgetting for a moment about the others present, she turned to him anxiously. 'Wherever you are going—will it be possible for me to find a ship to France? It is very important that I go to Rouen; I am expected there.'

He shrugged. 'I imagine we should be able to find you a ship to France eventually. What's in Rouen for you? Family?'

She glanced uncertainly at the audience of men around them, hanging on her every word. 'No. I am to join the nuns there, as a novice,' she began, but her next words were drowned out by another great shout of laughter from the men. This time, even Kit looked faintly amused. She stared at them all helplessly. This must be the notorious English sense of humour—she remembered Marie speaking of it in disgust, and of how they could laugh at things that did not seem even faintly amusing to a Frenchwoman. She wished that she could understand the joke.

As the laughter subsided one of the men began to speak but Kit quickly cut through his words. 'Why don't you come with me, Miss Perrault, and I'll show you the galley?' His hand firmly under her elbow, he spun her around and propelled her back towards the ladder leading to below decks. There could be no mistaking that he was not keen on her hearing what the men's reaction was to her last words, and she was so pleased to be able to leave their company that at that moment she did not stop to wonder why.

At the bottom of the ladder Kit released his breath in a great sigh of relief and smiled at her. 'Well done! I think you'll be safe enough for the moment. And keep looking indignant—I think it confuses them.'

She was unsure whether to agree with him or to protest that her indignation had been genuine enough. Instead she kept her face impassive and turned to examine the room he had brought her to. The galley was surprisingly large, despite having such a low ceiling that Kit had to bend his head to avoid hitting it—but he seemed well used to that hazard. She had never seen the kitchen of a ship before, and she listened attentively as Kit showed her how the cooker was fired, and opened those provision cupboards which were next to the galley for her inspection. From the compact ovens to the high-sided shelves, the smallest of details seemed to have been carefully thought out and designed, and she did not think she would have much difficulty in working in there in even the highest of seas. It was also spotlessly clean and this, she was sure, had everything to do with Kit's enthusiasm for order, and very little to do with the inclinations of his crew.

She could not believe the huge number of utensils that lined the galley and counted aloud no fewer than twenty-three small iron cauldrons hanging on special hooks in the pantry.

'Go-ashore pots!' she exclaimed, picking one of them up to test the weight of the iron. 'And in such excellent condition! These would have been worth a fortune to Bjorn! Why do you have so many?'

'The original crew on this ship was very large,' Kit said briefly. Then, puzzled by her fascination with such an ordinary item, he added, 'What did you call them?'

'Go-ashore pots. The Maoris have nothing that is made of iron, and so these pots are very valuable to them. When they see any on a ship, they will not leave without them. In the end the sailors always get tired of the Maoris asking for them, and so they will thrust one at them and say "Now go ashore!" And that is what the pots are called.' She looked at him suspiciously. 'You said to me that there was nothing of value on this ship! Bjorn's men would have been very happy indeed to have seen such a fortune!'

'Believe me, I had no idea we were so wealthy,' Kit assured her, much impressed. Carefully, almost reverentially, Jara hung the pot alongside all the other gleaming treasures and Kit continued his explanations. She learned that their meals were to consist of bread, freshly caught fish or salted meat—which Kit steadfastly maintained lost much of its saltiness if it was cooked in sea water. The few precious sacks of vegetables were to be added sparingly to their diet for as long as possible. After that... Kit raised the lid of a large barrel. 'Pickled limes. They taste terrible, but are vital if we're not all to get scurvy. They're quite palatable in water and sugar, but whatever you do you must serve them up once a day—I'll ensure that they get eaten. There used to be barrels of sauerkraut, but unfortunately none of this crew could get past the smell, and they were thrown overboard a long time ago. So the limes are important. Now... I think that's about all I can tell you. Have you got any questions?'

Reluctant to tackle him at once, she opened a random jar from the dozens lined up on the shelf beside the chopping boards and looked inside. 'What is this?'

'Turmeric—for curry.'

'Curry?' she repeated blankly. It was not a word she had ever heard before.

'Curry. You mix turmeric and other spices together and cook it with fish or meat. It's an essential on a long voyage when everything gets to taste the same. It's an Indian dish, and very useful for covering up the taste of rotten meat.'

'I could never serve anyone rotten meat, ever!' she said hotly. 'Have you no fresh meat on board?'

'On this ship? At the start of the voyage there were some chickens and pigs, but they were eaten a long time ago.'

'How do you know that this ship carried livestock once?'

'Because the crates in which they were kept are still in the bow,' he said, feigning surprise at the sudden note of suspicion in her voice. 'So I'm afraid the only fresh meat you'd be able to get your hands on would be the rats—but then, they're quite tasty curried.'

Jara stared at him tight-faced for a moment before turning in silence to replace the tin, thereby missing the gleam of amusement in Kit's eyes at her repulsion. Did the girl have absolutely no sense of humour? he wondered. Or perhaps it was just her difficulty with the English language?

She picked up a rectangular pale object. 'And what is this?'

'That's bread.' When she looked at him disbelievingly, he explained. 'Biscuit, you may have heard it called. It was baked in England about nine months ago. It's the staple food on ships.'

'Nine months old!' She broke a piece off and exclaimed in disgust at the tiny insects that fell to the floor. 'It is full of weevils! How can you eat this?'

'Well you knock them out, of course, unless they're the white maggoty ones with the black heads. They've got a cold, fatty, sweetish taste, which isn't too unpleasant. It makes a change to the diet, at any rate, although the nutritional value is probably minimal.'

She put down the bread hurriedly. 'I see.'

No sense of humour, he decided, and this time he could not stop a smile at her disgust. 'Have you any more questions?'

'Yes. I have several.' She planted herself in front of him and looked up straight into his eyes. 'To begin with, who are you? What are the men on this ship? And please do not tell me the story that you told Bjorn, because I do not believe it any more than he did!'

'Oh?' Kit raised his eyebrows in surprise. 'And why not?'

'Because your men do not act as if you were their captain. And you do not act like the captain of a trading vessel.'

His smile did not drop, but it had become very cold suddenly. 'And how the hell, Miss Perrault, can you presume to know anything about crews and their captains? Just who do you think you are to question the way I run my ship? I suggest you mind your own damned business and leave me to mind mine!'

'It is my business because I am on this ship!' she said doggedly. 'And I might never have been to sea before, but I have met many captains from many ships, and I know that you have *never* been the captain of these men before. Of other men, yes. But not these men.'

'I see.' Kit seemed to have grown several inches in height. In the cramped galley he loomed over her. 'So you're still insisting that I am not in command of this ship?'

'I am not saying that, only...' She dropped her eyes, struggling against being browbeaten into silence. Her intuitive knowledge that he was experienced at intimidating others—and unused to being questioned—made it all the harder for her. 'I am saying only that you are not a captain of a trading vessel. I believe that...that Bjorn was right. This is a Naval vessel. Perhaps you were telling the truth when you said that you found her deserted and abandoned, but you know a great deal more about this ship than you are saying. You are a Naval officer—that is so clear to me that I wonder why you should even bother to deny it. But this crew is not a Naval crew—that is equally clear to me. So what are you doing here, Mr Bennett? And why are you with these men?'

There, she had said it! She took a deep breath and looked up at his face again. She couldn't even begin to read what she saw there.

After a long moment Kit leaned back against the wall, his arms crossed, his eyes not leaving hers. 'For an ignorant savage who's been living in the wilderness all her life, you presume to know one hell of a lot, Miss Perrault. All right then, I'll tell you the truth, because you may as well hear it from me as from one of the men.' He spoke almost lazily but, perhaps because English was not her first language, Jara could sense that the slowness was only to give him time to choose his words.

'You're quite right—we're not traders, and we didn't just chance upon this ship. The *Courageous* was a fighting ship during the wars against Napoleon but now that Europe is at peace once more she's been put to quite another service for her king and country. She's a convict ship, Miss Perrault. Or at least, she was—until she went aground on the shores of New Zealand and my men and I took over.' He paused, as if waiting for her to say something, but she could only stare at him, her hand over her mouth, her eyes as wide as saucers. He smiled slightly at the dramatic effect that his words were having and continued.

'We were all bound for Norfolk Island to spend the next ten or twenty years of our lives in hard labour in the penal colony there. When the ship ran aground and we were released from our chains and taken ashore, it was much too good an opportunity to miss. We overpowered the officers and crew and took control of the ship. We remasted and repaired her and...well, you know the rest. China is the destination we finally decided on because——' he shrugged '—we're a little less likely to meet up with any other ships from the British Navy. We plan to sell this ship there and split up to go wherever we care to. There's a Portuguese colony there called Macao, and that's where you'll most likely get that ship to France you're looking for.'

She shook her head impatiently—that did not seem so important at the moment. Her throat was so dry that she could barely force out the words, 'The crew? The officers? What...what happened to them? What did you do to them?'

'We killed them,' he said flatly. 'We had to.'

She shook her head disbelievingly. 'I can't believe that of you! You wouldn't! You couldn't——'

'Oh, yes, he would.' It was Moody, standing in the doorway on the bottom rung of the ladder to above decks. She jumped at the sound of his voice, shocked that he had come upon them so silently. But Kit showed no surprise at all, and she wondered if he had known that he was there all the time.

Moody swung down off the ladder and joined them in the galley, the presence of a third person seeming to fill the low room. Jara shrank as far away from him as space would allow, and he smiled belligerently at her, enjoying her reaction.

'Saw him myself, Miss Perrault. In with the rest, he was, taking his fair share of them Navy bastards, ripping their insides out, paying them back for all they'd done to us poor souls down in the bilges for three months and more——'

'Stop it, Moody,' Kit snapped as Jara blenched and began to sway slightly. 'That's quite unnecessary!' He put an arm about her waist and she leaned against him helplessly for want of any other support.

'Aw, yeah, sorry 'bout that, Mr Bennett,' Moody said laconically. 'I keep forgetting you're a gentleman and all. Ever since I watched you butchering them officers on the beach I have to keep reminding myself that you was once one of them. Until you got drummed out and took to highway robbery and assaulting the travelling public, that is. You told her about that yet, Mr Bennett?'

'I said, shut up, Moody!' But Jara had already thrown off Kit's hand and was pushing her way past the two men, towards the ladder. Moody would have stopped her but she heard Kit issue a sharp order and he dropped his arm. She sped unimpeded across the decks to the stern, and clambered quickly down the ladder to the captain's cabin. Once there she slammed the door shut behind her and crossed to the small table under the porthole. If she pushed it under the door-handle...

It was fastened securely to the floor, as were the bunks which were the only other articles of furniture in the cabin. If only there were a lock on the door! She looked around desperately for something—anything—with which to secure the door but without any success at all. She sank down on one of the bunks as the futility of her actions sank in.

If she barricaded herself in, what possible good would it do anyway? There were seventeen men out there who could break down the door whenever they chose, and besides she would need to eat at some stage over the next few months. She had to calm down, stop over-reacting...

Over-reacting? To the knowledge that she was alone on board with a crew of escaped convicts and murderers?

The behaviour of Kit's men in Kororareka seemed tame indeed to what they had done earlier. To have cold-bloodedly murdered all the officers and sailors on this accursed ship...

She jumped to her feet as the door opened and Kit walked in.

'Get out!' He made no move to do so, only looking at her carefully, plainly wondering if she was going to turn hysterical. 'Get out, I said!'

He shut the door and leaned against it. 'You can't take that attitude, Jara. Not all the way to Macao. Now you know what you've got yourself into, I suggest you come to terms with it.'

'Come to terms?' she said blankly. It was not an expression she was familiar with.

'Yes. That you accept it.' He tried to smile, but Jara continued to stare at him with loathing. 'Oh, come on, Jara!' he said at last in exasperation. 'You knew the risk you were taking in begging a complete stranger to take you off Kororareka! Why act like this now? Besides— you did surprisingly well with the men just now, and I have to admit that I'm impressed. In fact, I think you can be very proud of yourself.'

'Proud of myself?' she spat. 'Proud to be associated with animals like you and your men? How could I be! I wish I had never left Kororareka! You are less than a man! You are——'

'I'm not going to listen to this.' He had his hand on the door-handle to go out again when Jara spoke again, her voice lower and so intense that he had to hesitate.

'Do you never...never think of the man who once slept in this captain's cabin? The man whose place you have taken? The man you killed?'

Kit spun around angrily in response.

'I've told you before—we had to do it! I don't have to make excuses to you for that! If we'd done otherwise, we'd be on Norfolk Island right now, being worked and flogged to death. And what for? For such heinous crimes as stealing to feed a starving family, or vagrancy, or drunkenness!'

'And highway robbery?' Jara broke in. 'Was that not your crime, Mr Bennett? Or do you call it an excuse?'

The slamming of the door was all the response she got.

It took a long and restless night, but by the time Jara awoke the next morning she had come to the reluctant decision that Kit had been right—she had to come to terms with the men on board this ship and what they had done. To do otherwise would be not only futile but dangerous. As Kit had pointed out, she had passed her first test with the men, and that had to augur well for her survival on this ship. Besides . . . she sat bolt upright as a new thought occurred to her. If she played her cards right and she was able to convince them that their criminal actions were of no account to her, then surely she would be able to report them to the authorities at their first port of call! Yes, indeed—that would be a far more sensible course of action than showing them how much they all disgusted her!

The sky she could see through the porthole was a soft pearl-pink, and she threw back the blankets and swung her feet to the floor. She might as well start as she intended to go on—and taking over her duties as cook was as good a way of stating her new intentions as any.

She had almost drawn off the shirt she wore as a nightdress when she realised that there was someone lying in the bunk across the narrow room, and she hastily pulled the shirt down again. But it was only Kit, and he was fast asleep.

He had been clear enough before about his aversion to sharing his cabin with her, so why had he changed his mind? She had not heard him come in, and he had not touched her... He must have done the night watch, she reasoned, and so only come downstairs to sleep before dawn, an hour or so earlier. Just what was he playing at now?

Greatly daring, she leaned over to study his unconscious face. He looked very different when he was asleep. The fine network of lines around his eyes indicated that he was in fact older than she had at first thought— perhaps as old as thirty. But at the same time his mouth, which he held tense and thin-lipped when he was awake, was relaxed into a pleasant line, and the cold brown eyes of yesterday were covered with dark lashes which were almost absurdly long. His fair hair was damp with sweat across the forehead, and for the first time she saw a dark shadow of stubble on his chin. One tanned, muscular arm was thrown clear of the blankets and his fingers were curled defencelessly into his palm. He looked hot and tired and restless. He did not look in the least like a man who could cold-bloodedly murder his own fellow officers. It was just as well, she told herself, that she knew better now. How deceptive appearances could be!

She dressed quickly into a clean pair of trousers and a shirt and left the cabin, taking care to close the door silently behind her. She came on deck to a cloudless dawn, with already more than a promise of heat in the air. As far as the eye could see there was nothing but the misty horizon of the sea. The myriad sails above her head were billowing gently in a light breeze and despite everything she could not help her body's instinctive response to such a beautiful day. She put her arms above her head and stretched like a cat in the pure pleasure of being alive, turning around quickly at the short laugh behind her. Davies was at the wheel, his face creased with amusement.

'Good morning, little lady. It's a grand morning to wake up to, isn't it? Going to make breakfast, are you?' he asked hopefully.

She had already smiled back before she remembered that he, too was a convict and a murderer, just like all the others. But she could not help but feel that the kindly twinkle in his eyes was genuine, and so she answered politely, 'Good morning, Mr Davies. It *is* a beautiful morning and yes—I am going to try to make breakfast for you.'

The smile on her face died as she walked to the fore of the ship to where the hatch to the galley was situated. Moody was sitting there alone, filleting a number of the large silver fish the Maoris called *terakihi*. The long sharp filleting knife ran expertly over the fish in his hands, making a rainbow spray of scales across the top of the barrel he was working on. His expressionless eyes dropped to her breasts and the swing of her hips as she walked past him, and she looked away quickly, feeling unclean.

She hurried down to the galley and lit the oven before setting about preparing a meal. The 'bread' that was lying in a wicker container on the floor could go over the side, as far as she was concerned. She was not sure that Kit had been speaking the truth when he told her about the weevils and maggots and the rat curry—he did have a very strange sense of humour—but the very thought of having such things in the kitchen was disgusting. And that anyone could bring themselves to actually *eat* them! She shook her head in dismay. Marie Perrault had had the Frenchwoman's inherent love of good cooking, and she had passed it on to Jara while the girl was still in her infancy. Jara had grown up in the kitchen, and knew that her culinary skills were more than adequate. But there was very little at all that she could do with the limited range of foodstuffs in the store

and the time available to her, so she had to be content
with making several loaves of fresh unleavened bread
with the unweeviled flour and oatmeal she found,
flavoured with a pinch of caraway seed. That, and a large
can of the tea which she had heard that all Englishmen
were addicted to, would have to suffice for now.

One of the men heard her struggling up the ladder
with her load and hurried down to help her with it. To
her surprise they did not eat below decks in the great
cabin, but on the deck, so that they hardly needed to
stop what they were doing while they ate. A ship this
size required almost constant setting and resetting of the
sails, as well as the less demanding but time-consuming
tasks of scrubbing the salt off the decks, tending to the
fishing lines... every man on deck seemed to be busy
and—assuming that few if any of the men were sailors—
they were oddly disciplined about it. Perhaps she had
been a little hasty in criticising Kit over his mastery of
his crew; especially so when even she could see how
undermanned the ship was. *Someone* had taught these
men how to sail, and it could only have been the man
who called himself their captain. But of Kit himself there
was no sign.

The men wolfed the bread down and several actually
thought to mutter a word of thanks for it. It was interesting, she thought as she watched them demolish the
last loaf, how important food was to men. While they
were eating—and enjoying it—not one of them stared
at her in the way they had yesterday, or made any personal comments that she could hear. Even Moody kept
his eyes off her and on the warm fragrant bread he was
intently cramming into his mouth. She decided that there
was a valuable lesson to be drawn from this. 'Men think
through their stomachs,' Marie had told her many times,
and in this—as in everything else—Jara acknowledged
that her adoptive mother had been right.

It was several hours later, and she had a pot of herbed vegetables and dumplings bubbling away for dinner when Kit at last appeared. He plummeted below in his disconcerting fashion—hands either side of the ladder, feet barely touching the rungs in what was almost a leap. He grinned at her startled face. 'Sorry to alarm you—standard Navy descent. I've only just woken up, I'm afraid. Is there any chance of some breakfast?'

Silently she handed him one of the loaves she had saved from that morning and poured him a mug of the tea she kept to one side of the stove. He accepted it with thanks and ate it standing where he was, watching her. His presence annoyed her, but she refused to lower herself to saying anything, busying herself instead with breading fish fillets for sautéing later.

'Thank you, Jara,' he said again when he had finished. 'That was very good.'

'Better than rat curry, Mr Bennett?' she said tartly, and he ruminated on that for a moment.

'Not quite, but it comes close. No wonder the men are all in such a good mood this morning. Do you know, I'm beginning to think that if you stay down here for the next four months and keep cooking like this you might just come through this unscathed?'

She looked at him then, and frowned. 'I think you are serious!'

'Absolutely.' He flashed her a quick and unexpected grin before climbing back up the ladder. 'Keep cooking as if your life depends on it, Jara. Because it just might.'

CHAPTER FOUR

KIT'S advice might have been of dubious value but, much as she hated to admit it, Jara found herself following it all the same. She awoke at dawn every morning and went to the galley to prepare as much of the day's food as she could before most of the men were up. Davies was invariably at the wheel then, and his cheery greetings always made her smile.

After serving breakfast she would clean up, set out the food for the midday meal, and then go straight to her cabin, there to spend the next few hours in solitude until it was time to return to the galley for the evening meal. The days were monotonous and lonely but, as she kept reminding herself, it was a small price to pay for transport out of Kororareka.

Kit took the night watch and so did not come to the cabin until an hour or so before she rose, and by the time she had finished her morning's duties some three hours later he was on deck again. That they never spoke alone suited her perfectly, especially when she at last realised why he had taken to sleeping in her cabin.

It was on the fourth day of her duties, and she had gone down to get a bucket of water from the barrels stored on top of the ballast in the hold. There were three sets of ladders to negotiate to get to the upper deck, and she was struggling by the time she got to the top of the last one.

'Mr Barker!' she heard Kit shout from the stern.

'Eh? What?' The tall thin young man seated repairing a sail on the deck beside the hatch looked up blankly.

'Mr Barker, there is a lady standing beside you who needs assistance!' Kit bellowed, and a scarlet-faced Barker jumped to his feet at once and took the bucket from her.

'Thank you,' Jara said in flustered surprise, and glanced down towards Kit. But he was watching the sails, his hands on the wheel as usual. Barker took the bucket down the steps to the galley and went back on deck, but he was back again within the minute.

'Please, miss, Mr Bennett wants to know if you want some more water.'

'Oh . . . no, thank you. But I will a little later.'

'Yes, miss. Mr Bennett says you're just to ask, and one of us will get it. And anything else you need from the hold or the steward's stores. Just you ask.'

Jara blinked at this. Could this possibly be one of the same men who had so terrified her just days before? Why, he seemed almost human now! She smiled brightly.

'Thank you very much, Mr Barker. That is very kind of you.'

'Don't mention it miss. And . . . and I'm sorry if we were . . . a bit rude, like, when you came aboard. We shouldn't have treated the Captain's woman like that. Sorry miss.'

He shot back up the steps then, leaving Jara with her mouth open. *The Captain's woman?* Was that what they all thought she was? So *that* was why Kit had taken to sleeping in the cabin again! But it hardly seemed necessary now, when she was slowly coming to know each of the men and was finding most of them reasonably amicable. She resolved to speak to him about it at the first opportunity.

The opportunity did not arise until Kit crept quietly into the cabin in the half-light of the next morning. Jara had deliberately awoken early and was sitting fully dressed on her bunk when he came in. 'Why are you sleeping in this cabin?' she demanded even before he had a chance to shut the door. He took off his jacket before he answered.

'I've got to sleep somewhere, Jara.'

'Why in this cabin with me? You slept elsewhere before your men knew I was here, so why do you have to sleep here now?'

He sat down on his bunk and began to pull off his boots. 'I'd have thought that was bloody obvious even to you.'

She jumped up and stood over him, her voice as low and angry as his. 'Do you know what Mr Barker called me today? "The Captain's woman!" I think that you want the men to think that you...you share my bed. That I am a woman of no morals. That I would stoop to...to let a murderer touch me! Am I right?'

Kit sighed heavily and lay down on the bunk. 'Yes, you're right. For once. Now, will you shut up and let me get some sleep?' He went to roll over towards the wall but Jara dropped on to the floor beside him, pulling his arm back roughly so that he faced her.

'But that is a lie! A deceit...to say such things!'

He looked up into her face. In the soft light of dawn he could clearly see the fury in the ice-blue eyes, the outraged set of her lips, and he smiled slightly. 'What's the matter? Are you so troubled *at* the deceit—or because it *is* a deceit?' Such semantics were quite beyond her, and she stared at him in silence for a moment, trying to work through what he had said. His smile widened and he raised himself on one elbow, bringing his face close to her. 'You're taking an uncommonly long time to answer me, Jara,' he said softly.

'I am not sure that I understand...' she began. But as his hand left the bed to begin an ascent up her arm she suddenly understood very well what he meant. She threw off his hand with a hiss of disgust and stood up in one rapid motion. The door to the cabin slammed resoundingly behind her.

'Thank God for that,' Kit muttered, and fell asleep almost immediately.

She must have made her objection very clear to him, Jara reflected some days later when they had still not exchanged a single word. It was surprisingly easy to avoid conversation if one so wished, even sharing the one cabin—he rarely woke her when he came to his bunk in the morning, and if he was awake when she slipped out in the morning he gave no sign. Dressing with him in the cabin had concerned her at first, but he always seemed to sleep with his back turned to her, and she did not think her modesty was at risk.

She did have to take care with the rest of the crew, however—they had what she regarded as an unfortunate habit of breaking into the cabin unannounced at irregular intervals and demanding Kit's assistance or advice. It could be a problem with the resetting of the sails or an adjustment to their course or just another squabble among the men that had come to blows... Sometimes it seemed to her that it was as if Kit were in command of a group of nursery brats rather than a crew of grown men. But every time he was called upon Kit would rise and go up on deck, exhibiting a seemingly inexhaustible level of tolerance for his men's failings. Perhaps, she thought in a more charitable moment, that was what it took to be a captain and—even with her lack of experience of the sea—she could see that he was a good captain. To the men he was an imperturbable commander whose unflagging confidence in his own knowledge and abilities made them obey him without question. It would seem that only she had seen the other side of him—the mercurial, uncertain side—and he seemed determined not to let his guard down with her again. She longed to know why he had been court-martialled, but would not have dreamed of lowering herself to ask him.

Her days ran slowly into weeks, and there was little interruption to the rigid routine she had set herself. Breakfast, luncheon and then dinner. Bread, meat, fish, vegetables...on and on it went. The most ingenious cook in the world could not have done more with the limited foodstuffs she had to prepare, and the men—after many months of prison-ship food—were completely uncritical of whatever she prepared. But it was tedious work all the same, and gave her a new respect for ships' cooks. It was not a profession she would ever have chosen.

She was slowly coming to know the men and, far from all being evil murdering convicts, they were beginning to become individuals to her. Some, like Moody, she learned to avoid at all costs. But some—like Davies and Barker—she came perilously close to liking.

Davies told her that he had once been a tailor and now Kit was putting his tailor's skills to good use on the sails, of which there were always some in need of repair. During the midday heat she took to coming up on deck to sit cross-legged next to him in the cool breezy shadows of the bow and learn how to repair the sails. Although he did not speak very much, what he did say was always congenial and she found that she was convincing herself that it was impossible that he had ever had anything to do with murdering the first crew of this ship.

The younger man, Barker, she found quite different. He was no less friendly, but more talkative. He had been a porter until he had volunteered for service in the Navy during the last years of the war against Napoleon. His experiences had given him a deep and abiding hatred of all things Naval, especially the officers.

'Cruel bastards they was, miss. Have you whipped for anything you care to mention, they would. See me hand, miss?' He held up his left hand for her inspection, and she saw that all the fingers save the thumb and index finger were missing. 'Didn't lose them in the war; no, miss. Lost them to the cat-o'-nine-tails. You're s'posed to be tied up proper when they whip you, you see, so it's just your back what gets hit. But I served on a ship where the Captain didn't fuss himself with such details. They took all the flesh off my hand and then they had to amputate when it went septic. And all because I dropped the Captain's dinner one night, miss.'

'How...dreadful!' Jara was moved to quick sympathy by such tangible evidence of cruelty. 'I did not know... The Naval officers that I met when they came to my parents' home were so well-mannered. I cannot imagine them ever doing such things...'

'No?' Barker shook his head at her. 'You'd no doubt think that if you met them on shore—they're all fine gentlemen there, when they're with ladies and such. No, I reckon they're all the same, if you don't mind me disagreeing, miss. Take Mr Bennett over there—I sided with him right from the very beginning, after we'd run aground and...well, when we were trying to figure out who was going to lead us. I've seen him in a fight, and I can tell you he can fight as dirty as any of them, for all his fine ways. He's as hard a bastard as I've ever met in Newgate Prison, and I don't see that he wouldn't have been no different when he were in the Navy either. But I don't hold it against him. At least he got himself drummed out, so that's his saving grace in my eyes.'

'Drummed out? What does that mean?'

'Means he were court-martialled, miss. Don't know what he did, but it must have been quite something— he escaped from custody, he says, and took to the roads, thieving and the like till they caught him again. S'pose it goes to show that we're all the same under the skin, whether you're a gentleman or a pauper, eh?'

'Mr Barker, will you stop gossiping and get aloft with Mr Smithies! I want those topsails brought down at once!' Kit roared from the other end of the ship, and Barker ducked his head and scurried off to obey. Jara stared with narrowed eyes at the man standing at the stern. Yes, it was very easy to imagine him in a Naval officer's uniform, strutting about on the quarterdeck pompously barking out orders like some kind of a demi-god! It had been that very arrogance and sense of self-control that had marked him as different from all the others even on the beach at Kororareka. As if he were aware of her thoughts he looked up suddenly and caught her eyes.

'Get below at once, please, Miss Perrault.'

Dear Lord, she thought resentfully, that's not a request but an order! How could he be so unreasonable? She had spent all morning in the galley in a clammy heat so intense that she came close to dropping everything because of her wet hands. She had come on deck for some respite in the afternoon but had found little even there. The sky was heavy and there was a strange orange tinge to the clouds that she had never seen before, but there was not a breath of wind and the sea was mirror-smooth. Within the last few minutes a light refreshing wind had at last sprung up and the sails were beginning to fill again. And he chose *now* to order her below to her muggy little cabin?

Instead she stayed where she was, lifting the heavy plait from the nape of her neck to let the cooling wind reach there. It felt marvellous after the the still humidity of the morning.

However, it seemed that she was the only one re-laxing, as Kit had almost every man clambering about up in the rigging, taking down all the sails. That struck her as odd; they had been all but becalmed these last two days—shouldn't he be trying to make the most of the wind that was now blowing steadily?

She quickly scrambled out of the way as a coil of rope slipped from the hands of one of the men in the foremast and fell to the deck beside her, and the movement caught Kit's attention.

'Miss Perrault!' he bellowed.

'Yes, Mr Bennett!' she shouted back just as rudely.

'Are you deaf or just stupid?'

'I am neither, Mr Bennett! But I do not know why I cannot stay on deck!' She heard him curse and then he was striding down the deck towards her, his fists clenched. He paused to give a quick order to one of the men who was fastening some barrels together and then he was at her side, gripping her arm painfully as he half walked and half dragged her along the deck.

'You're a member of the crew, Miss Perrault, just like everyone else on board. So when I give an order, I expect you to follow it. Now will you damned well get below or do I have to kick you down the hatch myself?'

She wrenched her arm free. 'There is no need for you...ohh!' Her words ended in a small scream as the ship suddenly lurched to one side, and she would have lost her footing had it not been for Kit's grip. He thrust her down the hatch to the cabins and then slammed the hatch down hard above her head, as if to forestall any ideas she might have had about returning to the decks.

Furious, she went into the cabin and threw herself down on the bunk. That man grew more obnoxious with every passing day! She mentally added extreme rudeness to Mr Bennett's ever-growing list of sins. And thoughtlessness—it was like an oven in the cramped cabin.

Resigning herself to a hot and sticky confinement, she took out her sewing. She had discovered that the thick, waxed cotton used to sew the sails gave good results when separated and used on a finer weight of material. One of the shirts Kit had given her to wear was of fine good-quality linen—she did not like to think of what had happened to its previous owner—and she had begun to stitch it into a nightdress, more out of boredom than any real desire to wear it. She had created a bodice with hardanger work, and was now embroidering small flowers on the collar. She had cut the sleeves off for comfort in the increasingly hot nights, and so the nightgown was now far too immodest for any but her own eyes. Still, the work gave her some pleasure and helped to fill in the hours.

But it was not long before she had to break off the thread in irritation—the light had gone completely, although it could only be mid-afternoon, and the boat was pitching so much that it was becoming impossible to place her needle accurately. For the first time she became aware that the creaking and groaning of the timbers—a sound to which she had become very accustomed over the past few weeks—was now so loud as to be almost alarming. She stood up, finding that she was forced to hold on to the chart table in order to keep her feet, and carefully made her way across the cabin to the porthole.

The change in the scene that met her eyes was so dramatic that she had to blink hard several times to ensure that she was not dreaming. The sea was very heavy now, with the sort of sharp-peaked waves that were causing the boat to lurch rather than roll. But the sky was what startled her most—it was almost pitch-black to the west. There was a crashing and rustling from outside the door and then Kit burst in, wearing the sealskin garments the men wore for wet weather.

'All right down here? For God's sake, Jara, shut that porthole or you'll be awash.'

She quickly did as he said, and he was almost out the door again when she said, 'I am sorry—about before. I did not realise that there was a storm coming. Is it so very bad?'

He smiled briefly, but she could see the tightness in his face. 'I honestly don't know—it hasn't hit us yet. It's a typhoon, and we've no way of knowing whether it'll miss us or if we'll get the full force.'

'That is why you took down the sails?'

'Yes. I can't afford any fancy sailwork and risk losing the masts; I haven't the men to do more than concentrate on keeping us upright. I'd better go—I'll be needed on deck. The others are manning the pumps.'

She knew about the pumps—Barker had told her how on the Naval ships he had served on it took teams of eight men in fifteen-minute shifts to keep the bilge from rising in an emergency. 'The worst job in the world,' he had called it. The *Courageous* had been holed when she had been run aground in New Zealand and, while she had been repaired and thoroughly caulked, Jara had heard Kit complain that the ship leaked like a sieve and required several hours pumping a day even in light seas. In this kind of heavy weather...

'Let me help!' she said quickly. 'You will need everyone on the pumps, and I cannot stay here in my cabin like this!'

'Don't be so bloody silly, woman!' Kit snarled, and slammed the door in her face.

She gave him time to get up the ladder to the deck and then left the cabin. From there she found her way through the rabbit-warren of passages 'tween decks to the ladder which led down to the lower deck and the rest of the crew. Seven men were working four pumps, stripped to the waist and slick with sweat as they forced the heavy handles up and down as quickly as they could.

The other eight were slumped exhaustedly against the walls, having obviously just come off their shift.

They stared at her in surprise but she did not allow them time to make any comment, moving immediately to where one of the men was struggling with the third pump. To her relief it was Davies, and he gave her a tired smile.

'You better get back, little lady, before the Captain sets eyes on you.' In answer she placed her hands alongside his and applied her full weight to pulling down the pump handle. At once she felt her muscles stretch and ache, and realised why the men who had finished their shift looked so shattered. But she could feel that even her puny effort had helped a little, and after a moment Davies stopped grumbling about her leaving the safety of her cabin and moved his hands to one side, to allow her a better grip.

Pull...release. Pull...release. Each movement seemed to tear every muscle and sinew in her body but she kept going by sheer determination. After five minutes she knew, with a fierce surge of triumph, that her strength was needed, as the speed of the pump she was helping to man came close to that of the others.

The sweat was pouring from her hair-line and down into her eyes, and she was unaware of the other shift coming to replace hers until she was tapped on the shoulder and the pump taken from her hands. She sank to the floor, her back against the wall, her chest heaving as she struggled for breath. There were the men on either side of her, no less exhausted, and a couple of them gave her encouraging grins. But none of them had the energy to speak.

After a few minutes, when her heart was no longer threatening to break through her ribs, she began to look around her. She had never been to this part of the ship before, and she wondered what it was normally used for.

There were no portholes, and no source of fresh air that she could ascertain; the air here felt heavy and foetid. Lamps had been lit to enable them to fit the pump handles and work, but the large area of deck was quite empty save for an occasional gush of blackish water running across it.

She became aware of regular fittings along the walls and turned to examine the one nearest to her. It consisted of a heavy metal plate riveted to the wall, with a chain hanging from it and a circular band attached to that.

'A manacle!' she could not help but exclaim aloud, and Davies chuckled drily at the look on her face.

'That's right, little lady. This is where we all spent the longest fourteen weeks of our lives, shackled to each other in lines across the deck there. Hundred and fifty men, with five feet by eighteen inches each. Though we ended up with more room than that, of course; each time a man died we could all stretch out a little easier. I reckon hell couldn't be any worse than this place—that's why none of us feels easy about coming down here, even if it is to save this tub from sinking. Ready to start again?'

She had only just got unsteadily to her feet when the deck seemed to disappear from beneath her and she fell heavily to her side, sliding across the sheet of water across the deck and slamming into the opposite wall. One of the men cannoned into her, winding her, and through salt-stung eyes she could see that only the men clinging on to the pump handles had managed to retain their feet. For one horrible moment it seemed as if the world was about to turn upside down and then with an audible creak the ship righted herself.

'That was an almighty one,' one of the men said as they struggled upright. 'Hope Bennett knows what the hell he's doin' up there.'

'He knows what he's doing, all right,' Barker said tersely. 'I've served under a fair few and he's one of the best. But maybe the best isn't good enough when you've got no crew to speak of in a leaking ship in a typhoon.'

They had almost made it back to the pumps when another wave hit and once again the deck moved from under their feet. This time Jara was more prepared, and took the fall on her shoulder, throwing her arms protectively over her head as she was thrown against the wall. It was almost with relief that she took over the pump this time—clinging to it at least saved her from being flung all over the deck. Water was rising from the bilge now, coming up past the wooden cylinders of the shafts, hissing and splashing around their feet. Although she needed no further reminders of the danger they were in she worked like a maniac, her teeth clenched with determination, cutting off that part of her mind that was screaming with pain and with panic. If the next wave was even bigger...if they capsized...if they couldn't hold the water...

She lost count of the number of times she pumped...the times she slumped on the wet floor to gain her breath before the next shift...but hours must have passed. None of them spoke any more, but she could hear a few of them muttering prayers in snatches of caught breath and she silently joined in.

Her back felt as if it were on fire, her hands were raw, but still she carried on somehow. And then at last Davies stopped pumping and said quietly to her, 'Listen!'

She stopped and he shouted over his shoulder to the others to do the same. They were still, listening intently, the loudest sound the harsh rasping of their breathing.

'The bilge water,' Jara said slowly. 'I...I can hardly hear it! Does that mean...?'

There was a ragged cheer from everyone and even Jara got a tired slap of congratulation on the back. They resumed pumping then, but with an easier rhythm, their pain lessened with the diminishing danger of flooding. The ship was still pitching steeply but it occurred to Jara that it had been some time since one of the huge waves had sent them all flying. Could they possibly have come through the worst of it?

The hatch from the deck above opened and Kit came skidding down in a wash of water. As he reached the bottom of the ladder he removed his sealskin hat and Jara was annoyed to see that he looked as cool and unflustered as ever. She pushed her wet strands of hair back behind her ear with stiff fingers and wondered if he had ever known the meaning of hard work.

'I think we're going to make it, gentlemen,' he announced. 'We've just got the tail of it now, and it's still a little rough, but we've still got our masts. How's the bilge?'

'Manageable now, sir,' Barker responded, and Jara glanced at him in quick surprise. She had never heard any of the men call Kit *that* before and no one seemed to object to Barker's use of the title.

Then Kit saw her and was at her side in a few angry strides, his eyes glittering. 'I thought I told you to stay in your cabin! What the hell have you been doing down here besides getting in everyone's way? Get out of here at once!' She opened her mouth to protest vehemently, but she was so enraged at his words that nothing came out. Instead she released the pump abruptly and ran past him to the ladder.

Back in her cabin she dragged off her saturated clothing and dried off her hair. Buttoning her dry trousers was difficult, and she noticed that her hands were shaking. She felt like crying. It wasn't exhaustion, or the pain, she told herself—it was *him*! Him and his stinging, sarcastic tongue! All the time he told her she was stupid, that she was a nuisance, that she was in the way! It wasn't fair! *He* wasn't fair!

There was a rap on the door. 'Jara?'

'One minute, please.' She pulled on her shirt and brushed the hair out of her eyes. 'What do you want now?'

He didn't answer and so she opened the door wide with a sigh of exasperation. 'What do you want?'

'Just...to apologise for what I said down there. It came as a shock to see you with the men like that. But they've told me what you did; to hear them talk, you'd think you'd saved the ship single-handed!'

She had to smile at that, but then she remembered how angry she was with him and said briefly, 'Is that all?'

'Yes—apart from asking you to get these on.' He thrust a set of sealskins into her arms. 'It's still too rough to light the stove, but I'd appreciate it if you could get us all something to eat. I'll wait outside.'

'I can get to the galley myself, thank you, Mr Bennett!'

Kit shook his head. 'I'll wait.'

She got into the cumbersome clothing and went out to the ladder. Kit tied a rope around her waist and then lifted the hatch to the upper deck. She was halfway out when what felt like a bucket of salt water was thrown in her face. Kit closed the hatch behind her and she gazed about her in amazement. At first glance the ship seemed awash—the decks were covered with inches of water, and at times the bow disappeared beneath the huge crashing waves that were tossing the boat about. The spray thrown up by the waves filled the air with a thick grey drizzle.

'Kit!' she cried in terror, but he had his back to her and couldn't hear her. She flung herself against him, putting her hands on his shoulders to make him bring his head down close to hers. 'Kit—are we sinking?'

Under the cover of his hat she saw the whiteness of his teeth as he laughed. 'Sinking? Good Lord, no! This is just a bit of rough weather after the hurricane. Don't worry—the old girl might be riding a bit low, but she's been through a lot worse than this in her time.'

He put a reassuring arm around her and hugged her and she found herself melting against him, wet and cold and nasty-feeling as they both were in their wet-weather clothing. How did he always manage to make her feel so safe and secure whenever he was with her? She raised her head and laughed back at him in relief and even pleasure. 'Now I *do* feel like a member of your crew!'

Kit shook his head. 'I can assure you I'd never do that to any of my crew, Jara. Or this.' He bent his head and swiftly kissed her lips. It was over in a second, almost before she had time to realise what he was doing, but it was a kiss for all that. She took in her breath in astonishment but already he had stepped back and his hand was on her waist to guide her along the wet, angled deck to the galley hatch. The safety rope, she saw now, was essential, with the very real danger of being washed overboard every time the ship reeled sideways.

He saw her safely down to the galley and left her there. Thanks to the careful design of the galley there had been very few things up-ended, but there was—as Kit had said—no chance of her being able to light the stove. She found a container of lime-juice that she had made up the previous day, together with some day-old bread and dried meat. It was not much, but it would be the first meal any of them had had in almost twenty-four hours.

Halfway through her preparations she found herself smiling and she stopped to reprimand herself sternly. How *could* she feel so pleased with her life right now? Every muscle in her body ached, beneath the sealskins she was still wet and chilled to the bone, and the raw blisters on her hands would take days to heal. She was on a storm-tossed ship with sixteen convicts, and their self-appointed captain—who was not only a disgraced officer, but a highwayman and a murderer—had just had the temerity to kiss her. She put her fingers to her mouth, remembering how warm and firm and salt-tasting his lips had been. Oh, but she was foolish to feel so happy about that!

CHAPTER FIVE

THE rough weather lasted another twenty-four hours and then disappeared as abruptly as it had come upon them. Jara awoke on the third day at dawn as Kit came into the cabin, literally staggering with weariness. She watched him from under the shelter of her blanket as he took off his sealskin jacket and went straight to the chart table, but after only a moment he put down his compass and passed his hand over his face.

'Are you all right?' she asked quietly.

He turned slowly. 'I'm sorry, I didn't mean to wake you. I've got to work out where we are now, and...and I can't seem to see what I'm doing...'

He was swaying slightly and Jara leaped out of bed and led him to his bunk. 'It has been three days since you had any sleep,' she scolded him gently. 'No wonder your eyes will not stay open. Go to bed now. Then later you can find where we are.'

She pushed him down and then bent to take off his boots. Kit half-heartedly tried to fight her off but she persevered, pressing his head back down on to the pillow when he made an attempt to sit upright again. She was drawing the sheet over him when he grasped her wrists. 'What on earth is that you're wearing?'

She looked down. 'One of your shirts. I have made it into a nightgown. I hope you do not mind?'

'No,' he muttered. 'It's very pretty. It's...' His eyes slowly closed and his hands slipped from her wrists. She guessed that he would be asleep for quite some time.

Moving quietly, she dressed and then checked on him again. His breathing was slow and shallow, that of a man in deepest sleep. The surge of tenderness she felt as she looked down on him was so strong that it shocked her—she really had to stop feeling like this about him! But it was so hard to remember what he was, what he had done, when he looked like this...

On the deck she almost bumped into Smithies, on his way down to Kit's cabin. She put out a hand to stop him. 'Please let him sleep, Mr Smithies; he is so very tired.'

'I know he is, but Moody's just seen a ship to the south, and Mr Bennett always said to tell him at once if we ever saw one. I think he'd want to know, miss.'

She hesitated, watching as Moody clambered down the rigging from the main mast, telescope under his arm. Smithies stayed where he was, as if waiting for her opinion. Since the storm she had noticed a perceptible change in the men's attitude to her; she felt more accepted by them now, almost respected. No doubt much of it was due to Kit's insistence that she be treated with respect by them all, but she also suspected that her help on the pumps during the storm had helped immeasurably. She could face them all with greater confidence now—all except for Moody of course, who was now on the deck, speaking over her head to Smithies.

'Might be English. Long ways off, though, and not likely to catch up with us the speed we're going now. You going to wake his lordship then and tell him?'

A ship...perhaps with decent civilised people on board, people who were not violent criminals and who could take her to safety with them...

'There is no point in waking him,' Jara said, unsure as to what decision she was making. 'If there is no chance that it will catch up with us...'

Moody's belligerent gaze fell on her. 'No chance. But his lordship said to let him know. You telling me not to?'

She took a deep breath. 'Yes. I do not think he should be woken.'

'Suit yourself.' He spat deliberately at her feet and moved off. Jara stared in repulsion at the huge blob of sputum and knew that she still had one implacable opponent on this ship. She walked to the stern of the *Courageous* and stood for a time looking out at the sea they had just crossed. Far, far away on the southern horizon she thought she could make out a sail and she concentrated hard on that tiny image as she tried to make sense of the battle raging within her.

Before going below Kit had put the ship under full sail, and she was slicing rapidly through the waves, sending sheets of silver spray high in the strong wind. It would take a miracle for the other ship to catch up with them now, even if it had reason to. If it did, and if it happened to be a Naval vessel, then Jara should have the opportunity to speak to its commander and convince him to put the men back in captivity where they belonged. If, if, if... But none of it was probable, and in some perverse way she was happy that it was so. In just a few more weeks this long journey would be over, and while she had given considerable thought to what exactly she would do when they landed at Macao she had not as yet reached any decisions. She knew exactly what she *should* do, but the thought of turning Kit and his men over to whatever authorities there were in Macao no longer sustained her as it once had. It was one thing to stand in judgement of men when you did not know them or anything about them, but when you *did* come to know them, and one of them was Kit...then it became a great deal more difficult. The thought of him in irons was intolerable now.

It was approaching midnight, and she was almost asleep herself, when Kit at last awoke. She sat up as he did, and in the light of the moon streaming through the porthole, they smiled at each other.

'Are you feeling better?' she asked softly.

'Mmm. Much better.' He ran his fingers through his hair. 'Anything happen while I was asleep?'

'Nothing very much. We have made excellent time, I think. And...and Moody saw a ship on the horizon.'

She started as he dropped his hands and leaned forward suddenly. 'What?'

'A ship...an English ship, Moody thought. It was a long way behind us, and——'

'Then why wasn't I woken?' He jumped to his feet and glared down at her. 'I've given explicit instructions—if ever any man saw another ship I was to be told *immediately*! So why the hell wasn't I?'

His rage was as frightening as it was unexpected, and Jara could not help but start to stumble over her words. 'You...were so tired, and...and it was not pursuing us. I...I thought——'

'*You* thought? So you were the one responsible, were you? When are you going to give up trying to exercise that minuscule brain of yours and leave the thinking to someone else? You stupid, ignorant little...' Words seemed to fail him, and he could only shake his head in furious disbelief at her. He picked up his boots and she winced as the door slammed behind him.

She slowly lay down again on her pillow, all thoughts of sleep gone. Since the typhoon he had begun to treat her a little differently. He had not kissed her again, or touched her, but when he spoke or looked at her there had been a warmth in his voice, a look in his eyes that had not been there before. And now...what had she done that was so wrong? Why was it so important that he had to know about some ship that had only been

glimpsed on the far horizon? She had not been stupid—
she had used her common sense, and he had no right to
be so brutal about that. It was as if he could brook no
deviation from his total authority, and that was something Jara thought was unfair and unreasonable. No,
she would never understand him!

There were subtle but distinct differences in the air
and the sea around them these days; the fish they brought
up on their lines were like no other that she had ever
seen before—larger and more brightly coloured. The
dolphins and the whales that were so numerous in the
New Zealand seas had given way to more sinister species,
and on several occasions they had been forced to cut
their fishing lines when one of the large grey sharks that
seemed to be following the ship took the bait.

The winds were more predictable at this latitude, and
they were making better time than they had before, but
the breezes seemed to do little to lessen the increasingly
hot temperatures. The sun stood directly overhead now
and the heat was sometimes almost debilitating, with the
nights only slightly more comfortable than the days. Jara
did not know whether it had anything to do with the
ship they had evaded earlier, but Kit had taken to having
someone on watch regularly, giving as a reason that the
Spanish islands of the Philippines were not distant now.

She spent the cooler mornings working in the galley
before joining Mr Davies on the shadiest part of the deck
in the heat of the day to help in the never-ending task
of making and repairing the sails. She enjoyed this time
the most, listening to whatever snippets of information
about his earlier life in England that the taciturn Davies
let drop, and at the same time practising her English on
him. She wanted to sound more colloquial in that language, and after just a few weeks found that she was
speaking more fluidly and that the slang expressions Mr
Davies taught her came tripping quite readily off her

tongue. She did not copy her teacher in all things however; after Kit complained that she was beginning to sound like a fishwife—and she was too embarrassed to ask Mr Davies what *that* was—she made a strenuous effort to adopt Kit's own, clipped, precise vowels.

After putting away the mended sails in the afternoon, she always went below to sew in her cabin or read one of the books she had found in the cupboard under Kit's bunk. She assumed that the books had once belonged to one of the unfortunate men who had earlier occupied this cabin; they were mostly geographical books, but several of them consisted of essays of a morally improving nature. With the exception of a well-thumbed copy of *A System of Naval Tactics*, none of them looked as if they had been read at all, and she was not surprised as she found them uniformly boring and tedious to read. But they served to keep her mind occupied, and books in whatever form they came had always been one of her greatest sources of pleasure.

Kit kept a log book on the chart table and she was leafing through it one day, wondering at the strange hieroglyphics written there, when she saw the last date he had written and was surprised to find that it was now almost three months since they had left Kororareka. She looked to find some estimation of how many thousands of miles they had travelled, but the numbers Kit had scrawled in his bold distinctive hand made no sense at all. But she did discover something else in the book which gave her considerable food for thought.

It was just a day later that Kit announced that they were within a few days of landfall at Macao, and there was a rising sense of excitement among the men at the prospect of leaving the ship for good. They had all heard of each other's plans many times over—the Americas were a common choice of destination, with only a few brave souls deciding to attempt a return to England under

a new name. Only Kit did not speak of his plans and—
in the light of what Jara had just discovered about him—
she was not altogether surprised.

For several days she wrestled with her new knowledge,
wondering how she should approach him with it, if at
all. She had a fair idea of what his reaction was likely
to be, but balanced against that was the thought of how
satisfying it would be to have the upper hand over him
for once...

Kit knew that the dream was going to come again even
before he fell asleep. It always did on nights like these.
It probably always would for the rest of his life.

It was intolerably hot in the cabin, even in these coolest
hours before dawn. He had stripped and had a cold wash
but still he found it hard to fall asleep. Perhaps it was
just as well. He glanced across at the other bunk and
saw Jara lying flat on her back on top of her sheets, her
arms and legs thrown wide, her nightgown as usual barely
covering her. Even as he watched she stirred restlessly
and the nightgown rode higher up her thighs...

He looked away again quickly, wondering why he tor-
tured himself like that. Sometimes the pain of wanting
her was so bad that he would take to leaving the cabin
to sleep on the deck, but that was not something he
wanted to do too often, in case the others discovered
that Jara was regularly sleeping alone. The heat was such
tonight though that he thought he would risk it...until
he remembered that Moody was taking the watch. He
didn't trust that bastard an inch, especially where Jara
was concerned.

He closed his eyes and emptied his mind for sleep, and
it came at last. But just as he had known he would, he
was back on the beach, lying on the sand, his legs in the
water...

No! He woke himself with a mighty effort and lay staring wide-eyed at the ceiling. Not that nightmare again! Think of something else, for God's sake. Home...his family...an English winter... Yes, that was it. Christmas with his family. Snow falling outside, a roaring fire in the hearth...no, forget the fire. Concentrate on the snow...

But he was back on that beach again, and this time he couldn't wake himself up. The sun was warm on his wet back, the sand was gritty beneath his fingers. And George was beside him, his chest heaving with the effort of having swum a quarter of a mile still clad in breeches and shirt. George had never been much of a swimmer.

'Where are they all?' George had asked plaintively. 'Dammit, these breeches are ruined! Why couldn't they have sent back just one of the longboats?'

Kit had laughed and got to his feet. 'They must have landed further up the coast. Let's go and see if they're in the next cove along. On your feet, man.'

'Ooof!' George collapsed back on the sand. 'Just a minute, Kit. Have a heart, will you—I'm exhausted after all that swimming!'

'I'll go then, you lazy beggar. You've got ten minutes to lie in the sun and try to look like an officer again. Understood?'

'Aye aye, Captain.' George threw a handful of pebbles at his departing back and rolled over with a groan.

Kit had left the beach and entered the dense greenness of the forest, struggling sometimes to pass through undergrowth so thick that it was clear no man ever walked these parts. On the top of the hill he had been able to look down into the next bay. One of the longboats was there but from where he was standing he could see no sign of life.

Well, they couldn't be far. He turned to go back to where he had left George. They'd have sought shelter for the night of course, either deeper in the forest or in another more sheltered bay. But the high seas had passed some time ago, and he had waited for hours past the time that he would have expected some signal from the shore. He would certainly have something to say to his officers when he saw them again.

He was halfway down to the beach when his stride slowed and he paused to really look about him for the first time. He had heard about this place, but he had never been to New Zealand before. Lord, but this was a beautiful country! The forest smelt...green. He grinned to himself. He had not thought of a colour as having a scent before now. The birds over his head were like none he had ever seen before, and so patently unused to men that some of them were fluttering within his arm's reach. Eden must have been like this, he thought. This might be an unscheduled call, but he suspected he might enjoy it, just the same. They would be a little later to Norfolk Island than planned, but he at least still had plenty of time.

The *Courageous* was visible from up here, listing to one side on the sandbar where he'd run her aground the previous night. With the tide out the damage to her underside was just visible. He'd gone down to inspect it with George that morning, and he had been heartened at how little work would be required by the carpenters to repair her hull. The masts and spars and rudder would take longer, of course, but the forest seemed full of suitable timber, and at least he had managed to mini-mise the damage. And, even more importantly, he had managed to safely beach her without the loss of a single life. Although he would never admit it to anyone, he felt quietly proud of that.

He had almost come to the beach when he heard the sound of raised voices, and his innate caution had made him drop to his knees and crawl forward to where he could see what was going on unobserved.

What was going on had stopped his heart for one horrified second. George was lying very much where he had left him, but he was on his side now, curled into a tight ball in an effort to protect his vital organs from the kicks and blows of the ragged men who were gathered around him. The men were cursing him, laughing at his agony, but George was silent except for an occasional stifled moan of pain.

'Thought we'd got all your lot,' one of the men was saying. He was a big man, about Kit's height, and fair. 'Anyone else come ashore with you, you slimy scum? Eh? Anyone else?' He kicked George brutally in the head and it was all Kit could do not to throw himself forward and attack him. All the instincts of friendship, of decency, were propelling him to do just that, but the older, deeper instincts of self-preservation kept him where he was. Coward! he abused himself. Fool! another part shouted back. There must be at least thirty men down there, and some of them were armed with weapons he recognised from the ship's armoury—he wouldn't stand a chance!

'No one else,' he had heard George gasp out. 'I came ashore alone. For pity's sake...'

The fair man had knelt beside him. 'Turn him over.' They had forced George on to his back and then the fair-haired man had picked up a heavy rock and held it high over George's face...

Kit had turned away to vomit silently into the ferns. He had seen many men killed before, but not like this, and not as close a friend as George... of all men, not George! His stomach had contracted again and again, as the scene remained etched forever on his eyes. And it was all his fault...everything was his fault...

'No!' He sat bolt upright on the bunk, his eyes wide and staring, his chest heaving with great laboured gasps. In seconds Jara was beside him, her hands on his shoulders.

'Kit, are you all right? Kit!'

He looked at her blindly at first, still seeing the sun and the sea and that blood-soaked beach... But then his pulse gradually slowed and his breathing no longer constricted his throat and he saw before him nothing but the strangely reassuring sight of Jara's concerned face, her hair loose and white over her shoulders in the moonlight.

'Jara? Oh, Christ, Jara, hold me...' He took her in his arms and she was so surprised that she did not push away and instead let him lie her down beside him on the bunk.

He was hot to touch, and wet, and she could not help but notice now that he was wearing very little, if anything at all. But she was also acutely aware that his unmistakable need for her, his need to be touched and reassured by her, would make any protest she thought of making seem not only impolite but indeed heartless. Her heart pounding uncomfortably, she lay still and suffered his caresses.

'You're so soft...so sweet...' he muttered into her hair. He turned her face to meet his and kissed her gently. She kept her mouth firmly closed under his, wondering how she was going to get up at this stage without hurting his feelings. One of his hands was leaving her face and travelling down over her shoulder.

Oh! Her mouth opened in a gasp as he brushed his fingers across the tip of her breast and at once Kit kissed her again, still gently, exploring her mouth as slowly and thoroughly as his hand was exploring her body. He was unbuttoning her nightdress now, and she put her hand on his to stop him, but somehow her concentration became all taken up with the sweet sensations his mouth was creating around the sensitive areas of her neck and her restraining hand instead slid unconsciously around his back.

His mouth, harder and bolder, was on her breasts now, and she had to clamp her lips together to stifle the small cry that nearly escaped her. But she could not stop the involuntary arching of her back to meet his demanding hands and mouth. She had never suspected that her body was capable of such delight, of such a response! Then his mouth was travelling inexorably lower and the low animal growl of pure pleasure that she heard herself make brought her at least part way to her senses.

'No! This is wrong!' She pulled his head up and tried to make him look at her. 'This is wrong! You mustn't!'

'Oh, no, it's not wrong,' he whispered urgently, kissing her again, 'it's not wrong at all. And I must, Jara, please...'

He tried to guide her hand but she wrung it free and turned her head away from his mouth and all the wonderful, wild chain of responses it was arousing in her. 'Don't do this, Kit, please, I beg you!'

He didn't answer in words. Unable to reach her mouth, he started now on her inner arm which was trapped beneath him, kissing her with tiny softly nipping kisses, working his way up from her wrist while she lay helpless and gasping under the assault of her senses. By the time he had reached the soft side of her breast she had very little resistance left. 'Kit...please. You are frightening me...'

At once his hands stopped their maddening journey of exploration. He raised himself on straightened forearms to look down at her, and she saw the struggle in his face as he fought to control impulses that she realised now were much stronger than hers. At last his breathing slowed.

'I'm sorry,' he said slowly, his voice thick. 'I didn't mean to frighten you. And...you're right. This *is* wrong.'

He moved himself away to allow her to leave his bunk. But as soon as she felt that freedom, as soon as she felt his weight leave her, she found herself hesitating. Just as her mind warned to get up and leave him *now*, something—some deep and frighteningly irrational compulsion—was holding her there just as securely as Kit's arms had done minutes before. As if the same blind need had belatedly transferred itself from him to her, she felt the blood begin to pound thickly through her veins, she felt the urgency to hold him close against her again. *Now. At once.* Scarcely able to believe her daring and her madness, she reached up and placed her hands against his chest. For a long time, an eternity, they looked at each other, and then Kit breathed her name in a groan of surrender. He bent his head to claim her lips again just as the sound came of someone coming down the ladder to 'tween decks at great speed. They both froze, waiting to see if the man was going down to the other cabins, but almost immediately there was a mighty thump on their cabin door.

'Mr Bennett! Man overboard!'

Before she even had time to realise what had happened Kit had thrust himself away from her and was on his feet and pulling on his trousers. The door opened and it was Moody she saw in the ragged pool of lamplight.

'Who?' Kit demanded.

'Davies. He was up on the rigging and must have slipped or something. We threw him a spar but don't know if he got to it. Don't even know if the poor old sod can swim...'

Kit pushed past him and was up on the deck by the end of Moody's explanation. Moody followed him but not before he had taken a long look at Jara lying naked and scarlet-faced on Kit's bunk, vainly trying to pull the sheet over herself. The expression on his face was one which stayed in Jara's memory long after he had closed the door.

She quickly pulled on some clothes and followed them on deck. The men were all up there now, either finding and lighting every lantern that they had, or in the rigging trimming the sails. To turn a ship this size around took time and it took skill, she knew. Kit might have the skill, but not the time...

Dawn was beginning to break sullenly in the east but it was still dark upon the water. By the time they had achieved a turn-around all the lamps had been lit and hung on the side of the ship, throwing long oily streaks upon the almost flat water. They lined up at the bow, looking and listening as hard as they could for a shape in the water, or a response to their calls. There was nothing.

Kit tacked again, and yet again, as the sun began to slip above the horizon and the sea turned a blinding silver. An hour after they had begun their search they found the spar that Moody had thrown to Davies, but that was all that they found.

Jara ran up to the quarterdeck, where Kit was at the wheel, and said bluntly, 'Will we find him?'

He shook his head. 'No, not now. It's nigh on impossible to find a man overboard at any time, let alone one that can't swim. I'll tack once more, and then we'll have to go on.'

'Oh, poor Mr Davies—he was such...a kind man.' She could not control the throb in her voice. 'What if he is still out there somewhere, waiting for us? Please let us stay longer.'

She put a hand of appeal on his arm but was taken aback by the abrupt manner in which he removed it.

'Don't do that, Jara. Don't touch me. Especially not up here.'

She was so taken aback by this that for the moment she forgot even Mr Davies. 'But . . . why not?'

His mouth tightened in annoyance. 'Didn't you see the look on Moody's face when he came into the cabin and saw you in my bed? Just don't touch me in front of the men, no matter how . . . innocently you intend it.'

She could hardly believe her ears. 'You're so unfair! You're making it sound as if it was me who . . . started that . . .'

'I might have started it, but I don't remember you stopping it,' he said tersely. 'I apologise for forgetting myself, and you have my word that it will never happen again—but unfortunately it's too late to undo the damage that it's done. Moody's not going to forget what he saw.'

'But you have gone to so much trouble to ensure that everyone on this ship knows that you sleep in my cabin at night . . .'

'Knowing and seeing are two completely different things. I'm simply warning you, Jara—stay away from me in front of the men, and watch everything you say and do from now on. Do you understand that?'

'Oh, yes,' she muttered from between gritted teeth. She understood very well. She turned away, too over-wrought and angry to continue arguing, but then her eyes were caught by a sharp diagonal point cutting smoothly and silently through the sea alongside the ship and despite his admonitions she unthinkingly seized his arm again with a gasp of horror. 'Kit! Look, do you see? Do you think . . .?'

'Go below, Jara,' Kit said quietly, not taking his eyes off the course before them. 'There's nothing more you can do here.'

She went, moving stiffly back to the hatch to 'tween decks. The black fin had been joined by others now, and they were travelling at exactly the speed of the ship, as if waiting for something. Something else...

Back down in the sanctuary of her cabin she curled up on her bunk and wept for Mr Davies.

They all missed Samuel Davies. Kit held a short memorial service for him in the afternoon, and Jara stood silent alongside the others, blinking back the tears as she remembered all the tiny kindnesses he had ever done for her. If ever she had tried to thank him he had backed away quickly, with a smile and some self-deprecatory comment. He had never allowed her or anyone else to break through his reserved exterior, and yet he had touched her heart for all that. What a horrible end to a hard, unfair life, she thought.

She retired to her cabin after the service, to sew and to remember Mr Davies in private. The latest project she had devised to fill in her long hours of tedium was yet another shirt, which she had cut down to her own proportions. She was working on the hem, and the long sailmaker's needle she was using darted evenly in and out of the material on her lap. The monotony of it soothed her as her thoughts kept veering from Mr Davies' demise to the man who slept at night in the bunk a few feet from her, and what had happened there hours before. The passion he had awoken in her had taken her by surprise and had shaken her deeply, and she had to make a conscious effort to clear her mind of emotion in order to decide what to do about this unexpected complication. But, she thought, whatever she did would not be easy...

So engrossed was she in her thoughts that it was a time before she became aware that she was no longer alone. Moody was standing inside the cabin door watching her.

She started violently. 'Mr Moody! What is it? Does Mr Bennett want me?'

Moody's mouth stretched into a laugh, but his eyes remained cold and unblinkingly on her. 'No doubt he does want you, Miss Perrault. No doubt he does. But the thing is, if Mr Bennett wants you, he can have you, can't he? Not like the rest of us, eh? Not like the rest of us.'

'I think that you had better leave this cabin at once, Mr Moody,' Jara said as firmly as she could, although she knew that he would not. He had been building up to this ever since she had come on board, she realised now, and seeing her in Kit's bed had lifted the final restraint. He would not go quietly this time. She needed to summon Kit immediately.

'No, you don't!' Moody lunged forward and thrust his hand over her mouth. 'Don't you go screaming for help, 'cos if you do, you'll be dead by the time your pretty boy gets down here. You understand?' He moved his other hand to her neck and easily found the vulnerable spot there. 'If I just squeeze here, hard, you're dead, woman. Dead! You understand that?'

She managed to nod and he slowly took his hand from her mouth, watching her face intently. He stank, and his filthy beard and clothes filled her with revulsion. Her every instinct told her to get as far away from his person as possible, but while he had his hand on her throat she could not risk making any sudden moves.

'Right,' he whispered hoarsely. 'Now I want you to take off your clothes, just like you do for his lordship. All of them. Every last stitch.'

She took a deep breath to steady herself. It was not a matter of *if* she could do it—she *had* to do it... 'My clothes? Very well...' His hand grabbed her arm painfully as she went to rise from the bed and she looked at him levelly. 'You wish to see me take off my clothes, Mr

Moody? Then let me stand up. You will see more then, much more...'

His eyes flicked from her face to the cabin door and back to her again. She did not drop her eyes, and indeed tried to attain what she hoped was an inviting expression, lowering her eyelids and throwing her head back slightly. Then she parted her lips and slowly ran her tongue over them. It seemed to her to be a ridiculous thing to do, but she had seen for herself how successful the whores of Kororareka had been with such tricks when they were touting for business, and she hoped she was doing it correctly. She must have, because all at once he grinned gap-toothedly and settled himself back on the bunk.

'Why not? Go on, then.'

She put her hand down beside her as if to push herself off the bunk, and under the cover of her loose shirt her fingers closed on the sailmaker's needle lying on top of her sewing. Slowly, slowly, she drew it free of the waxed cotton and hid it in the palm of her hand as she stood. Then she turned and stood looking down at Moody.

'Come on, get on with it,' he growled impatiently. 'The shirt first.' She raised her free hand to the collar of her shirt, pressing hard against her throat until her hand had stopped shaking. Then she slowly and deliberately undid the top button, then the second, and the third, her eyes holding his all the while. She undid the final button and dropped her hand to her side, leaving her shirt hanging loose. Moody's tongue flickered over his lips nervously. She noticed that he was sweating heavily now, his small avid eyes narrowed, his breathing hoarse and uneven. *Bon Dieu*, she thought wildly, how can I have this much effect on a man when I feel nothing but disgust for him inside?

'Take it off...'

She forced herself to give a short laugh and tossed her hair back over her shoulders. He glimpsed a curve of breast and would have reached out for her but she stepped back and put out a playfully restraining hand.

'Oh, no, Mr Moody. The Captain doesn't make love to me with his boots on. Now it is your turn. Take them off, please.'

He was grinning up at her now, his eyes glittering. 'I knew it. I knew all the time what you was like underneath all your pretty ways. Going to a nunnery, eh? Yeah, going to hell, more like. You're ripe for it, aren't you? I can tell. I should have done this a long time ago...shown you what a real man is like...'

You loathsome creature, she thought. 'Yes,' she breathed. 'And I need a man, Mr Moody, a *real* man...'

He made a strangled noise and looked down to fumble with his belt. He had his trousers down to his knees and was trying to kick off his boots at the same time when Jara opened the cabin door and made a dash for the ladder. Behind her she heard a crash as Moody fell over, and a curse. She was almost up to the top of the ladder to the top deck when he grasped her ankle and the force of his wrench made her think for a moment that he would break it. Clinging to the rail with one hand, she spun around and wildly stabbed the needle in his direction. It made contact with something and he yelped and withdrew his hand immediately. She scrambled on to the deck and flew across it to almost crash into Kit on the quarterdeck.

'What the...?' But a quick glance at her frightened face and dishevelled clothing told him exactly what had been going on. 'Do your shirt up,' he said under his breath. 'Who was it? Moody?'

She nodded and then moved around behind Kit as Moody came slowly across the deck towards them, shaking his hand as if to rid himself of the pain Jara's needle had inflicted on it. The look on his face was murderous.

He stopped in front of them and surveyed them for a long moment. The others, aware now that something was amiss, slowly joined them from the rigging and the far decks, coming to stand behind Moody. No one spoke. Kit looked to be standing at ease, his feet firmly braced on the deck as he met Moody's eyes squarely, but from where she stood behind him Jara could see that his hands were clenched so tightly that they were white. Not since that first time he had brought her on deck had she seen him like this, and she knew that this was going to be a greater test of Kit's authority than any that had gone before. There were undercurrents here that it seemed she alone had never been aware of—until now.

Moody spoke first. 'Hand her over, Bennett. You've had her to yourself for long enough.'

'I see.' Kit gave a long cool stare to each of the men lined up behind Moody. 'This looks as if it's been a mutual decision, gentlemen. Does every one of you feel the same way?'

Some of the men muttered agreement and others, like Barker and Smithies, dropped their eyes uncomfortably. But none of them moved from Moody's side. Moody smiled cynically. 'Looks like we do, Captain. So why don't you just be sensible now and step aside? We mean no harm to you—or her. You've brought us safe this far, and we're grateful for that. But it ain't fair what you've been doing, and you know it. We're only asking you to share her around a bit, that's all.'

His speech brought forth a louder muttered agreement this time, and a couple of the men stepped forward. Kit held up his hand and they fell silent. 'We're within two weeks of Macao port...'

'Aye, and we're three months out of Kororareka. Damned if I'm going to wait any longer, Bennett.' Moody came closer.

As Kit hesitated, Jara stared at him in growing dismay. She had automatically turned to him for protection, and yet the debate going on in his mind was painfully clear even to her. He was actually thinking of turning her over to these animals! He had said once before that he would if he had to, but that had been months ago, long before...all that had happened between them. And now, to save his command, he was thinking of doing it again! Kit turned to her and she could not read what was on his face. 'Get below, Jara.'

She stared at him, wondering what he was planning, but then he mouthed the words 'Be careful' at her and with a great gush of relief she knew. Slowly and deliberately she left his side and began to walk back down the deck, careful not to look at or come anywhere near the group of men.

'Leave her!' Kit shouted suddenly, and without looking behind her Jara instinctively threw herself back against the railing, missing Moody's grasping hand by inches. The look on his face was so evil that she cringed back from him, stifling the scream that came to her lips. To her surprise he did not touch her, but slowly bent over to untie one of the grappling-hooks from the rail beside her. Then, with a smile that showed his yellowed, sharp front teeth, he walked back towards Kit, the hook swinging from his hand. As if at a prearranged signal, the others all shuffled back to leave an area of empty deck between the two men.

Kit watched him approach in silence, his face impassive. The grappling-hook made a barbarous weapon. Two feet in length, splaying out into eight sharply barbed hooks... Jara closed her eyes and struggled with the tightness in her throat as she imagined just one of those vicious hooks clawing into Kit's flesh.

Still Kit did not move, although Moody crouched slightly as he came nearer, the hook poised. Not until

Moody slashed lightly, almost teasingly at the air before Kit's face did he step back. He bent down swiftly, his hand brushed his boot, and when he stood again there was an unsheathed knife in his right hand. He transferred it to his natural hand, his left, and held it up as if for Moody's inspection. It was not long, but it looked very sharp, and at least Kit was no longer unarmed.

Moody looked taken aback, but only for a moment. Then he laughed. 'Didn't trust us after all, did you? So much for your authority, *Captain*! And how long d'you think you'll last with *that* toothpick, you cack-handed bugger? Eh?'

'Put down the hook, Moody.'

In answer Moody swung the hook wide at Kit, missing his face by a fraction of an inch. Kit ducked easily and as he came up again he thrust his knife into Moody's upper right arm. It was done so quickly and casually that Jara was surprised to see Moody stagger back, his hand over his wound as blood began to seep at once through his shirt.

'Why, you . . .' He lunged again at Kit and again Kit jumped back and slashed with the knife, only this time both of them missed. They stood back, Moody glaring and Kit smiling slightly, but both breathing tightly. Not one of the other men moved except to stand back to give them more room.

'Stop it!' Jara shouted, but no one heard her, lost as they were in the vicious excitement of the fight. Moody was bleeding heavily, and there were splatters of dark red blood all over the area of deck that had become the arena. She realised now that the men were watching Kit with different eyes. He was slighter in height and build but much faster on his feet than the other man, and his left-handedness appeared to be undeniably to his advantage. Despite the disparity of the weapons, the match was not as uneven as it had seemed at first. If

Kit won, she had no doubt but that the men would at once fall back under his command like a pack of dogs. If Moody won, then the dogs would have a new leader. And her as a reward.

She stepped quickly to one side to avoid Kit as Moody came at him again. This time Moody's advantage of a longer reach showed, and the point of the grappling-hook cut through the loose fabric of Kit's sleeve with a small rapid ripping sound. Kit spun around, unable to place his knife, and jumped away. A small wooden bucket was in his way and he kicked it clear and into Moody's legs as he moved, not taking his eyes off the other man for an instant. It was not the most sporting of gestures, but it succeeded in making Moody lose his balance for a moment and he almost cannoned into Jara.

'Stop it! Stop it!' Jara screamed almost in his ear at the top of her voice. Why did they not listen to her? She was not worth this! Nothing was worth this senseless fighting. Not if Kit died.

Moody had his back to her now and her face was within inches of his heaving shoulders, of the blood dripping thickly on to the deck. It was then that the fear that had paralysed her turned to angry frustration. As Moody moved forward she kicked the bucket away from her and back under his feet. Taken by surprise he staggered, slipping on the bloody deck, and fell heavily face forward.

For a long moment no one moved, and then Kit stepped forward and, with the toe of his boot, turned over his opponent's prone body. An almost inaudible sigh went up from the assembled men at the sight of his unconscious, bloodied face. The leader of the pack has kept his place, Jara thought in disgust. But when Kit raised his eyes to hers she did not see the gratitude for her timely intervention that she might have expected, but unmistakable fury blazing there instead. Her own anger abruptly boiled up out of her.

'You stupid, stupid men! Can't you think of anything but fighting each other?'

'You shouldn't have interfered——' Kit began, his face rigid, but she sliced through his words.

'Should I not interfere? Should I not interfere when . . . when *this*——' she indicated the prone body at her feet with a hand shaking with rage '—*this* is all because of me?'

'It wasn't all because of you!'

'It began with me and who I belonged to! Well, I will tell you—and you—and you—that I belong to no one. Do you hear me? I belong to no man! You are nothing better than a pack of savage animals, and you all make me sick. You can all go to hell!' She turned on her heel and went straight to her cabin.

CHAPTER SIX

IT WAS night before Jara came out again. No one had disturbed her and it had been very quiet on the deck all day. A few hours before she had heard the men climbing down the 'tween decks ladder to go to their cabins for the night, but then there had been silence. Blessed silence.

She changed her shirt before tying her hair into a smooth plait at her back. Then taking her courage and a small leather-bound book in her hands, she went up to the deck. Just as she had hoped, there was no sign of anyone above deck but Kit, on the quarterdeck as usual. He had tied the wheel and was leaning against the rail, looking down at the waves hissing quietly away from the side of the ship. Apart from the navigation lamp on the stern there was no light but that from the stars in the crowded sky, and a clear slim crescent moon. Kit had long since discarded his jacket in these warmer temperatures, and his white open-necked shirt gleamed palely in the dark. He raised his head as she approached and his face was unsmiling. Keeping her distance, she perched uneasily on a coil of rope beside him. 'I think that we should talk,' she said without preamble.

His eyes flickered over her and then away. 'Can't it wait until I come down to the cabin in the morning?'

She pointed looked up and down the deserted, dark decks. 'There is no one here to overhear us. Besides—I do not want you to sleep in my cabin any more. I know, I know——' she raised her hand as he began to speak '—it is *your* cabin, as you have often told me. But

111

after...this morning...I do not think you should sleep there any more.'

He was silent for a moment, his eyes narrow, and then she heard him slowly release his breath. 'Very well. I'll sleep on the deck from now on. I think you'll be safe enough alone now.'

'Safer I think than with you,' she could not help but retort tartly, and the corners of his mouth lifted in amusement.

'By God, you could be right there. But you're a hot-blooded wench, Jara Perrault—I can't help but think that the sooner you get to your nunnery the better. Although for the life of me I can't imagine you in a habit and wimple, mouthing your prayers——'

'Can you not?' she snapped back, furious that he should laugh at her and her response to his own passion. 'I can assure you that I will be happier there than living here with you foul-mouthed, brawling men! You were like animals today, fighting like that!'

'It wasn't the first time I've fought some of these men and won. You shouldn't have interfered——'

'But Moody could have killed you!' she gasped indignantly.

'Never! Not Moody! Not in a month of Sundays.'

'Then you could have killed *him*!'

Kit threw back his head and laughed again. 'You came a hell of a lot closer to doing that than I would have. Oh, and by the way——' he fumbled in his shirt pocket '—I've got something to give you. A memento of this morning.'

He tossed her something. She caught it in both hands and looked at in the faint light. It was small and irregularly shaped and pale in colour. 'For me? But what is it?'

'One of Moody's few remaining teeth that you knocked out of his mouth this morning.'

'Aaah!' She dropped the tiny object with a scream of disgust and kicked it away with her bare foot while Kit doubled over with laughter. 'You are disgusting! You have a very strange sense of humour!'

'And you have none at all.' His face was abruptly sober again. 'So why don't you go back down to your solitary cabin and stay there? I can promise you won't be disturbed tonight—by me at least.'

'About...what happened this morning...' she began.

'Yes?' he said coldly.

'I ... I think we should talk about it.'

'Why?'

'Because...' She sought for the right words, her face scarlet with embarrassment. How could she ask him? The passionate man who had taken her to his bed was not the same man as that standing before her now, waiting indifferently to hear what she would say. She gave up, shrugging her shoulders in a silent expression of helplessness.

'I wouldn't give this morning a second's thought,' Kit said at last. 'I'm only a man, like any of the others. And I've been more months without a woman than I care to remember. When you came to my bed like that...well, I'm sorry, but how else do you expect me to react? As I've said—it won't happen again.'

His cold face swam before her eyes and she clenched her fists so hard that her nails broke the skin of her palms. How could he do this to her? He was humiliating her, once more putting the blame for what he had started back on to her shoulders...

He said nothing more, turning away to the binnacle to check the compasses. Her dismay gave way to sudden anger, and then was swept aside by an overwhelming urge for revenge. And what a weapon she had now...

'Kit, I have something to show you.' She picked up the book she had brought from the cabin and raised it high, almost in triumph. 'It is this.'

He looked up and she saw his eyes suddenly widen. He didn't answer, but from his stillness she could tell that he knew exactly what she was going to say. Savouring the moment, she slowly opened the book at the frontispiece.

'There is a name in this book. And a . . . a message?'

'An inscription,' he supplied tonelessly.

'An inscription. Thank you. The name is that of Captain Christopher James Montgomery. And the inscription reads: ''To my dearest Kit. On the occasion of his commission to the captaincy of *HMS Courageous*, June 1813. With fondest love, Emily.''' She closed the book carefully and looked at him. 'Well?' she prompted him.

She could hear him breathing. 'Well, what? It's a conventional enough inscription. Is the book worth reading?'

'It is your book, Kit.'

'Like hell it is!' He turned on her angrily. 'Just what are you trying to say? Give me that damned book!'

'No!' She twisted away from his hand and tried to put the book behind her, but he was too fast. 'Kit, please—you are hurting me!' He pulled the book from her hand and threw it over the side of the ship, pushing her down at the same time. Her back hit the deck with a thud that left her breathless for a moment and then Kit was over her, his knee across her legs, her wrists caught viciously in one of his hands. Powerless to move, terrified at his sudden and violent reaction, she lay gasping in great shaking gulps. She could not see his face in the shadow, but she did not need to.

His own breathing was harsh and measured. It was some time before he spoke. 'All right, Jara. You can't move. And if you try screaming for help I'll have you over the side long before anyone else gets up here. So I want you to tell me—just what little fantasies have been going through that tiny brain of yours? What is it that you're claiming to know about me?'

Her mouth and throat were so dry the words caught like sand in them. 'Please...let me sit up...'

'Shut up!' He shook her and her head banged against the hard wooden deck. 'Just tell me—what do you know?'

She licked her lips and tried to speak clearly, although her words were shaky and disjointed. 'I...I didn't think you were like the others. There were...things that you said and did. You know this ship very well, and you know how to sail her. You said in the storm that she had been in worse——'

'That was pure conjecture, woman!' he snarled. 'How the hell can you read more into it than that?'

'—and then I began to read that book that you have on the chart table—the log book? And...I saw that the entries for the days before the *Courageous* was ship-wrecked were written in your hand. You were the Captain then. You have always been the Captain. Your name is not Bennett—it is Montgomery.' She ended in a rush.

Neither of them spoke or moved for a long time and then Kit let out his breath in an explosion of sound. The pressure on her hands and legs did not lessen.

'All right, Jara. Now *I* have something to show *you*.' He lifted himself off her and pulled her to her feet. As she staggered against him he led her to the rail and stood close behind her, his arms around her body like a lover's. Directly below her the water churned, white frothy lace over black oily waves. Terrified, she pressed back against him, vainly trying to take a hold on the fabric of his shirt.

'Do you remember Davies? Remember the sharks? They're still out there, Jara—I saw them this afternoon. Do you remember?' His voice was low, a savage whisper, and when she did not respond he shook her. 'Remember?'

'Y...yes...' She managed to nod against his chest.

'Yes, I thought you would. We'll be in Macao in just a day or two now, Jara. If it were going to be any longer than that, I swear you'd be over the side now. But I'm going to give you a chance to save your worthless skin. Just keep your mouth shut for a little bit longer, and when we're safe in Macao I'll make sure you get your ship to France. But if you say anything—*anything*— about that book or about me, then—God help me—I'll kill you. I'd be a dead man—but I'd take you with me, Jara. Believe that.'

She nodded again jerkily. She believed it. His hands slowly released her and she turned around to face him, edging away at the same time from the rail and the unseen horrors below.

'I...would not have told them, Kit... Never...'

'Of course not.' He was watching her closely, poised to spring upon her again if she should say the wrong thing. And this was the man she would have trusted with her life an hour ago! Disbelief at what had just occurred threatened to overwhelm her. This was the man who just that morning had seduced her with his tenderness and gentleness; who had contained his own desires rather than frighten her... She had believed in him then—just as she had always believed in him—and even now that trust was hard to put from her. She could not help herself as she put her hands out to him, the palms upwards in pleading. 'Kit...?'

'Get out of my sight,' he said harshly, and this time she did not need his urging to escape back to their cabin—*her* cabin now. Behind her she heard the sound of his fist meeting the rail and his voice swearing low and fluently, and she was not to know that it was not directed at her.

CHAPTER SEVEN

KIT Montgomery was like a chameleon, Jara thought to herself the following morning. One night he was a violent stranger fully prepared to murder her, and the next day he was just as agreeable and unruffled as he had ever been. She found the contrast as frightening as it had been unexpected. He would have thrown her overboard last night without a moment's qualm, she was sure, and all to protect his identity! The measure of trust—and even affection—she thought that they had shared had been proven to be nothing but an illusion, fostered by him to protect himself and shattered in a few violent minutes. And yet here he was, sauntering about, acting for all the world as if nothing had happened last night!

The previous day there had been seabirds in their wake, and occasional clumps of seaweed. And today there was land on the horizon, low and brown across the sea, a scattering of islands. The atmosphere on the decks was veering between euphoria and anxiety as the end of their voyage drew near, and Kit was driving the men hard, not allowing anyone the leisure to watch their nearing destination. She walked up to the quarterdeck where he was standing alone by the wheel, looking out to sea through the telescope. He appeared to ignore her, spinning around to bark out an order to the men below. 'Brace up. At once.'

'Brace up, Mr Bennett?' One of the men stopped and looked up at him doubtfully. 'It's a fair wind, and we've a way to go...?'

'Don't question me, Mr Trent. We don't want to go into Macao under full sail, do we? Come on, get a move on, man.'

The men seemed more than happy with this reasoning and, besides, they seemed more amenable to Kit's demands for total obedience since the fight with Moody the previous day. A pack of dogs indeed, Jara thought grimly. As the men scurried up the rigging to trim the yards Kit checked the compasses one more time. 'Did you want me, Miss Perrault?' he said flatly, without looking up at her.

'I am concerned about Mr Moody's arm,' she said quietly, determined to match his calm detachment. 'It is giving him even more pain than yesterday, he says, but he will let no one look at it. Also, he has a fever.'

'I'm not surprised.' Kit glanced up at her sardonically. 'He keeps it covered with those filthy rags and won't wash it. It'll no doubt become gangrenous and will have to be amputated in a few days.'

'Yes. He said you had offered to cut it off for him,' she retorted, and she could not keep the accusation from her voice this time. 'You lack all compassion, Mr Bennett!'

'Far from it—often it's the only remedy, and if you'd ever been on a battleship in wartime you'd understand. The gun-deck on this ship used to be painted red, so that when it was covered with blood—and it frequently was, in a close battle—it didn't deter the men so much. It might surprise you to know that I've assisted in at least a dozen amputations, and invariably been thanked by the man for saving his life. Besides, it's a fine old Naval tradition, cutting bits and pieces off sailors when they get infected. Leave the Navy an entire man and you can't say you've earned your pay.'

'I have not seen any such injuries on yourself!' Jara said indignantly, remembering Barker's poor mangled hand.

'Of course not—I was an officer,' Kit said in what might have been genuine surprise at her ignorance, and turned to make an adjustment to the wheel. Jara watched his profile with more than a touch of resentment. Mr Barker's horrific stories about the cruelty of the Naval officers all seemed personified in this newly revealed Kit; he was no different after all from the cruel tyrants dispensing harsh justice from the quarterdeck that she had heard so much about over the past months. And he had been the captain of a convict ship as well! No wonder the prisoners had rebelled so violently... She mentally stopped herself there. There could be no justification for what the men had done, just as there could be no justification for the cruelty of men like Kit Montgomery.

He was scanning the horizon through the telescope again, she noticed, and again the small adjustment to the wheel... They must be coming very close to the end of their journey. Feeling oddly heavy inside, she went down to the galley and poured a quantity of water and lime-juice into a mug. Then, balancing it carefully, she made her way to the forecastle to where Moody had been laid in the coolest and shadiest part of the deck. He watched her approach with no lessening of his old belligerence, for all that he was prostrated on a pile of bedding on the deck, barely able to move now for the fever and the pain that racked him.

'What do you want now?' he growled. 'Come to gloat, have you? Eh? Come to see what your pretty boy's gone and done? He wants to cut me arm off, you know—he said so.'

She knelt beside him and held out the lime-juice to him. 'He said that he may have to...amputate—but only if you do not keep the wound clean. Please, Mr Moody, will you let me clean it for you?'

He flung out his uninjured arm and the mug in her hand went flying down the deck. 'You touch me and I'll kill you, you hear? You and his lordship—right pair you are. But I'll see you gets what's coming to you...' He broke off, gasping for breath and she saw the fresh perspiration breaking out on his face.

'Mr Moody, you must rest and have more water——'

He broke in with a foul curse that was so colloquially explicit that Jara was fortunately unable to understand anything but the most general meaning of it. She would have risen and left him then, but he reached over and grasped her sleeve. 'I'll tell you something, you little whore. You think you've got that bastard where you want him, but you haven't. No—not by a long chalk. He's planning on selling you in Macao, you know...to some Chinee. Heard him say so once, I did. Good-looking white woman like you'd bring him a fortune—and no better than you deserve...'

He collapsed back, drained by the exertion of so much hate, and lay muttering obscenities at her in a harsh monotone. She stood up, feeling nothing but pity now for this deranged, suffering soul. The ugly words leaving his lips meant nothing to her, but Kit had come forward to see what was going on. He prodded Moody so hard with his boot that the injured man groaned.

'I'll amputate your other arm for you as well if you don't shut up,' he said brutally, and it was only then that Moody subsided into a sullen silence. Distressed by this barbarity, Jara bit her lip and moved away, resolving to say nothing more. The coast of China was only hours away, and soon she would be able to leave this ship, and the man who captained it...

'Ship ahoy!' The shout from the man up in the rigging overhead made her start.

'Where?'

'Port bow, Mr Bennett.'

Kit moved to the rail and put the telescope to his eye. But even without its aid Jara could see the white sail on the horizon. He had spent all day scanning the sea—he *must* have seen it long before! It occurred to her then that he had, and perhaps had even been steering them towards just such an encounter. Even as she watched the sails became substantially larger.

'Shouldn't we put up more sail, Mr Bennett?' Smithies asked, his face worried.

'No time. If we run we'll likely be pursued, and we don't want that. We've no cannons, remember—we had to offload them in New Zealand to get off that sandbar.'

Everyone was standing beside them now, staring in silence at the ship that was inexorably drawing closer. No one needed to make the observation that it looked so much like the *Courageous* that it could have been a sister-ship; tall and graceful, moving with a leisurely speed that was deceptive under full sail, like some huge white bird of prey. No, that was not how she should feel about it, she reminded herself—Kit had planned this, and had done all he could to stall the *Courageous*. But the fear she could sense and almost smell on the men around her was so infectious that she could not help the tight knot gathering in her stomach.

'They're puttin' up flags now—what do they mean?' someone asked. Kit was silent for a moment.

'They want to know who we are.' He turned to look at them all and Jara wondered why the others did not seem to see the exultant gleam in his eyes. 'And we can't oblige them, can we? Jara—will you go below? And don't come out until I send for you.'

She went below without argument, realising that in a way she was glad to be leaving that dreadful scene on the deck. The men might be convicts and murderers, but there had been times when most of them had shown her some gesture of friendliness. And in her life there had been very few people who had done that. It seemed intolerably unjust now that Kit should betray them all like this, after he had led them all the way across the Pacific. There was no doubt in her mind but that the ship he had led them to was of the British Navy—he had been planning this for so long that it was unlikely to be anything else.

She had not, up until now, worried about herself. Kit had told her once before that she would be safe, and she had had no reason then not to believe him. But the way he was leading the men who had served his purposes to their fate, and his behaviour of the previous night, made her wonder now. Who else was there on this ship who knew who she was and why she was on board? What if he found it more convenient to have her treated as just another of the convicts? Perhaps he would—she no longer felt able to predict anything he would say or do.

Her cabin was on the starboard side, and she could see nothing of the other ship approaching, but after a time she felt the shudder as it came alongside, and heard the thud of the grapling-irons as the two ships were secured to each other. Her heart pounding she waited for shouts, for any sound of fighting, even for the sound of gunfire. But all she could hear was the sound of foot-steps above her head, and muffled voices.

Much as she wanted to leave the cabin she disciplined herself to stay where she was, trying to concentrate on the sewing on her lap instead, sewing blindly with wide, stabbing stitches. At least the relative quiet was a sign that there was little or no violence, and she could only be grateful that the men had had the sense not to fight against the inevitable. Oh, but Kit Montgomery had a lot to answer for!

It was hours before she became aware that the *Courageous* was picking up speed again. She dropped her sewing and hurried to the porthole. The other ship was behind them now, tacking to take a parallel course. She caught a glimpse of the name—the *Eagle*—with the British ensign flying from the stern, and she rested her head against the wall as a great wave of emotion washed over her. *It was over.* The men would all be in custody now, and Kit would be among his own kind once more. But why had he not come? What did he intend for her?

There was the sound of footsteps outside the door and she spun around, Kit's name on her lips. But the door opened to a younger man, with dark curly hair and a grave expression. He wore the dark blue coat, spotless white breeches and highly polished black boots of an officer of the British Navy. He said nothing for a moment, taking in her over-sized shirt and trousers and her bare feet, and when at last he spoke his manner was curt. 'Stay in this cabin. You will be taken ashore on our arrival at Macao.'

'Where is Kit?' she demanded. He ignored her and went to shut the door, but she was there before he could. 'I demand to know where he is! You must tell me! Where is Captain Montgomery?'

He was apparently not quite rude enough to slam the door on a woman, and he hesitated. 'Captain Montgomery is following on the *Eagle*. I've orders to keep you in this cabin until we reach Macao,' he said at last. 'Now will you kindly stand back from the door...?'

'And the others?' She stood her ground, despite his exasperated effort to push her back into the cabin. 'Where are they? Can I see them?'

He scowled at her. 'Certainly not. I don't know if you'll be seeing your friends again when we reach Macao, but I do know that you're to remain here. I must warn you that if you leave this cabin, or create any disturbance, I shall be forced to restrain you. Is that understood?' He did not wait for an answer but shut the door firmly in her stunned face.

As if in a trance she sank back down on to her bunk. So much for Kit's promise that she would be safe! She should never have trusted him for a second! It was clear enough now that she was to be treated as if she were just as much a criminal as any of the others of his unfortunate crew! And there would be no one else to speak for her, no one to believe her... She curled up on her bunk in a miserable huddle and worried.

'Kit, what a delightful surprise! What has it been—two years since I last saw you? Please—sit down. Can I get you a drink?'

Admiral Sir Walter Ashley finished heartily shaking Kit's hand and went to pour two measures of brandy from the decanter on the sideboard. Kit took the seat Sir Walter had indicated and looked at his surroundings appreciatively.

Outside the walls of this house were streets filled with Europeans and Chinese, lush gardens and all the sights, sounds and scents of the multinational colony of Macao. But within these walls one could easily be convinced that one had never left England's shores. From the carved fireplace to the mullioned windows, from the vibrant Persian rugs on the polished floors to the fine furnishings, this house was intrinsically English. That it was by reason of its design and materials also most impractical in this climate—and as hot as hell—did not matter, Kit reflected. Its somewhat eccentric nostalgia was both welcoming and relaxing.

So was the brandy he was handed. It was not until Sir Walter enquired politely whether he would like another that Kit realised that he had downed the entire drink in one gulp.

Sir Walter gave him another brandy and sat opposite him, the smile on his kindly face masking his concern. He and his wife had always taken seriously their responsibilities as godparents to Kit. They had taken his part in his battles with his parents when he had wanted to go to sea at the tender age of fourteen, and Sir Walter had watched the younger man's meteoric rise up the ranks with a mixture of pleasure and quiet pride. Lieutenant at nineteen, post-captain at twenty-one, captain at twenty-three, and at the age of twenty-five he had been given command of the seventy-four-gun barque *Courageous*.

His rise had not been without its problems, and one of those had been the enemies he had made on his way up—Kit was considered a brilliant commander by some and unconventional by many. He had a tendency to interpret even the most pedestrian of orders in a manner which could only be described as unique, and whether his many successes at sea in the last war against Napoleon were due to skill or luck was sometimes held to be debatable. But every one of his men would have faced the jaws of hell for him—and frequently did—and those friends he did make were his for life.

If he had ever been blessed with a son, Sir Walter thought now, he could not have wished for anyone different. He could only be thankful that he was here in Macao at this time. For Kit to turn up like this, dressed in the roughest of seaman's clothes in a ship he no longer commanded, the scanty crew on board all in chains... From all appearances he was in deep trouble this time.

'Well, young man,' the Admiral said at last, when Kit's second glass rested empty on his knee. 'I gather you're in something of a scrape. Care to tell me about it?'

'It'll be a positive relief to tell you about it, sir. I'm afraid...it's rather worse than a scrape. I'll have to make a written report to the Admiralty immediately.'

'Oh, yes, the Admiralty.' Sir Walter's expression was frankly curious. 'The last I heard, you'd been seconded to the Admiralty office in London after the war ended. It was seen as a promotion, I understand, although I must admit I was surprised that you'd willingly leave the sea. I wasn't aware you'd been given another commission on the *Courageous*.'

'I wasn't. I...oh, hell.' Kit broke off and looked away to the empty fireplace. Sir Walter studied him discreetly, thinking how much his godson had aged in these past two years. Kit's had always been a cheerful, irrepressibly self-assured personality, and yet now he looked as if he was struggling with some unbearable inner agony. What on earth had happened to take this young man's youth from him?

Kit appeared to brace himself. 'It's a long story, I'm afraid, sir,' he said calmly. 'I'd be obliged if you could obtain a clerk to write it down for me—it's likely to be clearer if I dictate it.'

Surprised, Sir Walter rang for his secretary and requested that he prepare pen and paper. 'Another drink?' he asked, as they waited.

Kit sprang to his feet as the sound of a commotion erupting outside in the hallway met their ears. The door opened and Lieutenant Lewis of the *Eagle* appeared, unusually flustered and with a look of mortification on his handsome features as he held the arm of a struggling woman with some difficulty.

As soon as the woman saw Kit she stood stock still and glowered at him in silence. Sir Walter was about to demand of the Lieutenant why he had seen fit to bring such a disreputable hoyden into his drawing-room but Kit spoke first.

'For pity's sake, Lewis!' He was across the floor in a couple of long strides and raised the girl's hands with a look of disgust. '*Manacles!* What the hell are these for! I told you to treat this lady with care and consideration—not like a common *criminal*! Take these off at once!'

Lieutenant Lewis flushed. 'I'm sorry, sir, but she tried to get away from me when we disembarked.'

'I thought I'd given you very clear instructions as to the treatment I wished this young lady to receive. They didn't include manhandling her, manacling her, or keeping her in ignorance as to why she was being brought here. Would you unlock her immediately and offer your sincerest apologies for your gross abuse of her person?' Kit spoke quietly but every word was angrily bitten off. With unsteady hands Lieutenant Lewis did as he was ordered, muttered an apology that was as graceless as it was patently insincere, and took his leave.

Sir Walter stood as Kit led Jara to a seat, and his sharp eyes missed nothing. He saw the mistrust and fear on the girl's face, but he also saw the concern and unmistakable affection with which Kit treated her. So his godson had lost his heart at last! It was high time too, although Sir Walter hoped that it would not be a lasting affair—even in her scruffy men's clothing and bare feet the girl was clearly lovely, but she was by no stretch of the imagination a lady, no matter what Kit insisted upon calling her. Still, he and his wife had given up years ago on Kit ever taking more than a passing interest in the fair sex, and it was nice to be proved wrong on occasion.

Kit introduced them flatly, giving no explanations. Sir Walter cleared his throat. 'May I suggest a cup of tea, Miss Perrault? You look rather in need of some refreshment after your...ah...recent ordeal.'

He did not wait for an answer but rang for a servant. Jara sat very still in the armchair where Kit had placed

her, her eyes darting from Kit to the man he had introduced as his godfather. The elderly man had a kind-
looking face and manner, but she had seen his face when
the Lieutenant had brought her in, and knew that the
courtesy with which he was treating her now was only
for Kit's benefit. He could be quite intimidating, she
decided. No doubt he was also a sailor—he had the
weathered skin and the deep-etched lines around his eyes
that she thought to be common to all men of the sea.
And he had the same clipped, precise way of talking as
Kit, as if he was also a man used to giving orders and
having them obeyed. So it surprised her to see how
obviously ill-at-ease Kit looked here, and from the way
in which he was avoiding looking at her she understood
that he did not want her to ask any questions. In any
case, under the politely relentless scrutiny of his godfather she would never have had the courage.

She looked surreptitiously around her while a Chinese
maid served them all tea in a service of the most
exquisitely delicate china Jara had ever seen. Many of
the books she had read in Kororareka had described the
interior and furnishings of a European house of quality,
but never in her wildest imaginings had Jara ever thought
they could be like this! There was such a quantity of
real glass in the windows, and so much light in the room
that she looked at first for the lamp that must be the
source of it. The rug under her bare feet felt as soft and
thick as a pelt, and yet was made up of a multitude of
bright colours. And the furniture looked strange; all
curves and padding, and so light that she was surprised
that it could stand the weight of so substantial a man
as Sir Walter. The armchair she sat in felt hot and prickly,
and she ran her fingers experimentally over the seat,
guessing the pale blue material to be wool.

'Thank you, Soo Lin,' Sir Walter said when the maid
had finished serving them. 'Would you tell Mr Barry

that we are ready for him, please?' The maid bobbed a
curtsy and left, with Jara staring curiously after her; how
pretty she looked with her sleek black hair and golden
skin. Her clothes were dark and foreign-looking—a long
tunic over trousers—and she moved noiselessly and with
immense grace on slippered feet. Jara had never seen a
Chinese man or woman before until Lieutenant Lewis
had led her through the streets in manacles, with
everyone stopping to stare at her as she tried to hide her
face in humiliation and fear. There were so many people
and houses, and everything was so confusing and frightening! She was startled when Kit at last caught her eye
and winked in patent reassurance.

'Would you like something to eat, Miss Perrault?' Sir
Walter indicated an elaborate silver tiered stand, covered
with assorted sweet things. She shook her head. How
could she tell him that not one of the things there looked
edible? They were so delicate and beautiful that it would
be a crime to eat one even if she were able to get it up
to her mouth intact. Besides, she noticed that Kit had
not touched anything.

Sir Walter's secretary, Mr Barry, came in and sat at
the desk by the window, preparing his pen. Kit abandoned all pretence of drinking his tea and sat forward
on his seat. 'May I begin now?'

Sir Walter glanced at Jara. 'If the young lady would
like to leave us for a moment or two—I'm sure that my
good wife is around somewhere...'

'If you don't mind, sir,' Kit said firmly, 'I'd like her
to stay. Miss Perrault has no idea of how, or why, she
ended up in the situation in which she found herself, and
I feel the least I owe her is an explanation.' He turned
to her as she stared at him open-mouthed. 'And I'll per-
sonally vouch for her loyalty and discretion.' Jara blinked
at that, but said nothing—Kit had surprised her too often

over the last few days for her to question him any more. Sir Walter hesitated and then nodded.

Kit began to speak, enunciating clearly and slowly so that the secretary could keep up. 'I am Captain Christopher Montgomery of the Admiralty Office. On orders from the Lord Admiral I took passage on the convict ship *Courageous*, leaving from Portsmouth on the sixth day of August, 1817, under the command of Captain Williams, for the penal colony and Naval base at Norfolk Island, where I was to give certain information to Admiral Buckler.

'By the time we had been ten weeks at sea we'd buried a full third of the crew, and fifty-one of the prisoners. All died from an unidentified sickness which affected almost everyone on board and due to the shortage of crew I was asked to take over the duties of the First Lieutenant. It became clear that Captain Williams was incapable of command. Possibly as a result of his illness, he began to drink, and his judgement became increasingly unsound. He was rarely above decks, and when he was his temper was uncertain. He was ordering at least one flogging a day, for the most minor of offences, on both the prisoners and the crew who were in some cases so weak that they could barely perform their duties. When I intervened, I was ordered off the quarterdeck, and relieved of my position.

'Three hundred miles from Norfolk we ran into foul weather. Captain Williams was unprepared and the mizzen and main mast went down almost at once. We also lost our rudder. At this stage I took command with the support of acting Second Lieutenant George Gables.'

'Just a minute, Mr Barry.' Sir Walter held up his hand and the soft scratching of the secretary's pen stopped. Sir Walter turned back to Kit. 'Now, think hard about what you're saying here. It sounds very much like . . .'

'Mutiny?' Kit smiled bleakly. 'Perhaps, although I regarded it as relieving a grossly inept officer of his command. His reaction was to drink himself unconscious. And it might have been his command, but I outranked him. Does that qualify as mutiny?'

Sir Walter hesitated and then sat back. 'Go on, Kit.'

'We were adrift for three days in severe storm conditions before we sighted the north coast of New Zealand. We tried to anchor offshore, but our anchors dragged and we ran aground on a sandbar. This resulted in damage to the hull and as the lower decks began to fill with water I believed there was real danger to the lives of the prisoners who were chained there. I gave orders to abandon ship, and the prisoners were taken ashore under guard. They were manacled, and the officers carried weapons. I remained on board with Lieutenant Gables. I...I thought I had taken all the necessary precautions.'

He stopped and took a deep breath. 'The landing was accomplished under difficult conditions, and one of the longboats overturned. In the resulting confusion the officers were overcome and those muskets which had not become wet were taken by the prisoners. They freed themselves and...and murdered the entire crew of the *Courageous*.'

Sir Walter would have spoken then, but had to hold his silence as Kit continued relentlessly in his narrative. 'Lieutenant Gables and I came ashore the next morning to see why there had been no signal from shore. While I went inland, a group of convicts murdered Lieutenant Gables.'

This time Sir Walter did stop him. 'George? Kit, I *am* sorry. I know...how close you were. He was engaged to one of your sisters, wasn't he?'

'Yes, sir.' Kit was very pale under his tan, Jara noticed, and his hands were knotted into tight fists. But this was something he had prepared himself to do for a long time, and he was not going to be deflected now. 'I hid in the forest until I grew a beard and...looked much as the convicts did. They broke into the ship's supplies of grog and there was much brawling among them. I killed one of them—a man of about my build and colouring, and took his clothes——'

'Kit!' It was Jara this time who could not help the exclamation of horror. 'You killed a man...?'

'One man. The man who had killed Lieutenant Gables. And I can't say that I felt the slightest remorse for that action. He was drunk at the time, and I doubt he felt a fraction of what George did when he died. I took his clothes and then presented myself to the others as one of their number, a disgraced Naval officer turned criminal. It was surprisingly easy. I convinced forty of the men to help me repair the ship and make our way to China. The others had either disappeared or decided to stay where they were. There was a disagreement over our leaving with the ship and what supplies were by then left in her...and all but sixteen of the men who were to come with me died in the fighting. I called in at Kororareka in an attempt to replenish crew numbers but was unsuccessful. I did however take on Miss Perrault, who had been left unprotected when her parents were murdered by Maoris. She acted as cook and sail-maker on the voyage. And...that is all.'

'I wish it were,' the Admiral said after a silence. 'I suppose you know what this report will mean?'

'Yes, sir.'

'You've broken at least three of the Navy's Rules and Instructions. Your insurrection can only be construed as mutiny. You must know full well that it is against all rules to release convicted criminals before landing at the point of destination. And it is also forbidden to let a female on board a Naval vessel, no matter what her

situation, without prior permission from the Admiralty.
You know all that, Kit. What defence can you offer?'

'None, sir. I take full responsibility for all my actions
and...I would do it again should the situation arise.
And you can write that down, Mr Barry.'

'My boy...' Sir Walter got heavily to his feet and laid
a gentle hand on his shoulder. 'Don't be hasty about this
report—the Admiralty can wait a little longer for it. If
you should choose to reword this, it would be clear that
no blame can be attached to you and you'll be able to
resume your Naval career. Whatever interpretation the
Admiralty put on it, it seems to me that you've acted in
a most heroic fashion throughout—why not take some
of the credit for that?'

Kit shook his head firmly. 'I'm sorry, sir. I can't submit
a report that is less than the truth. Forty-three crewmen
and officers died because of my actions and I have to
hold myself responsible to their families and the
Admiralty for their deaths. If I'd not taken the decision
to abandon ship——'

'But you had to! Otherwise the prisoners would have
died!' Jara broke in. She came to kneel beside him and
pushed her hands into his in a gesture of support and
appeal. 'That wasn't the wrong decision!'

Kit's hands tightened over hers for a second. 'It will
be, as far as the Admiralty is concerned. There's a rule
of thumb for officers, Jara: if you succeed, no questions
are asked, but if you fail, no answer is sufficient. And
I'm afraid I've failed quite spectacularly.'

'A spectacular end to a spectacular career,' Sir Walter
murmured, and Kit gave a brief and humourless laugh.

'Yes, sir.'

Sir Walter sighed heavily and returned to his chair. 'If
you won't listen to me, Kit... Miss Perrault, perhaps
you could convince this young man to reconsider? You'd

likely have more influence than an old codger like myself.'

'Oh, no, Sir Walter!' Jara was aghast at the very idea. 'Kit does not listen to me—ever!'

The admiral raised a cynical eyebrow at this, but was saved from answering by the lady who opened the door at that point and exclaimed, 'Kit! Darling boy! What are you doing here, and in those dreadful clothes!'

She was an older woman, comfortably plump, with a still-beautiful face, whom Jara guessed, quite correctly, to be Sir Walter's wife. Kit stood to be embraced in a swirl of dove-grey satin and lavender scent, and then the woman turned her forget-me-not-blue eyes towards Jara. 'So. You must be Kit's little friend whom Soo Lin has been telling me about. Jane, isn't it?'

'Jara.' The woman's hostility beneath her smile was so evident and so sudden that Jara could hardly mutter her own name.

'Jara? What a peculiar name. Well, why don't you come with me, and we will find you something a little more decent, shall we? And leave the men to their tedious Naval chatter.'

Without time to utter so much as a word of protest, Jara was bustled off out of the room. Kit caught a glimpse of her anxious face and nodded encouragingly. Sir Walter did not miss the exchange. 'She's in good hands, my boy. Another drink?'

Kit frowned and shook his head. 'No, thank you, sir. I . . . I'm concerned about Jara. Perhaps I should . . .'

'Constance will be fitting her out and taking good care of her. Don't fret yourself about her, Kit—you have far more serious problems to concern you.'

Still Kit hesitated and his godfather gave him a wry smile. 'Yes, I know. My wife has a heart of gold but even I have to admit she's a little inclined to snobbishness. Although I don't think for one moment that your young woman would notice that once Constance starts making her more presentable. You know what women are—a pretty dress and a few baubles and she'll be as right as rain again.'

'She is neither my "little friend", nor my "young woman", sir,' Kit said abruptly. 'She was brought up in a Christian home and her experience of life has been—to put it mildly—extremely limited. She's worthy of my protection and respect, and I'd appreciate it if others would extend her the same courtesy!'

'Calm down, my boy, calm down! I had no idea of her situation, I assure you!' Or of how far this has gone, Sir Walter thought as he watched Kit pace restlessly up and down the long, sun-lit room. From Constance's chatter he had gathered the lad was considered quite a catch in the marriage market, and it was only to be assumed that he would marry someone of his own social position. That he had not married yet had not concerned anyone—he was not quite thirty, and unlikely to look about for a bride until he resigned his commission and settled down. But from the little that Sir Walter had seen, his godson's attachment to this young person was rather more than merely chivalrous.

No doubt the perils of the voyage had forged some kind of emotional bond between them—and the last thing Kit needed now was the added strain of a romance. Sir Walter would have to talk to his wife about what to do, but he was quite confident that a few days of civilisation would bring his godson back to reality. If Kit was being quite truthful, and if indeed he had not touched the girl, then it would be all the easier. He was a healthy young man, after all, and if Sir Walter knew anything at all about the deprivations of sea life—which he did—then the subtle delights of Macao's numerous houses of pleasure would soon be proving rather more interesting than the dubious charms of this entirely unsuitable young female.

He cleared his throat. 'Admiral Buckler is due any day now from Norfolk Island, Kit. As the senior representative of the Admiralty in the Pacific it will be up to him to decide what—if any—charges should be brought against you. In the meantime, I suggest you take up residence in the Hatfields' house. They've gone home for a year, and there are only the servants there now. In fact, didn't you stay there last time you were in Macao? It's rather primitive, but you'll be comfortable enough. And of course Miss Perrault is welcome to stay with us.'

Kit stopped his pacing for a moment. 'Thank you, sir, but I'll have to ask Jara about that. All this will be quite bewildering for her, and it's likely she will want to stay close to me. If need be I'll take her to the Hatfields' house with me.'

Sir Walter gave him a stern look. 'Will you, indeed? The remarkable circumstances under which you arrived here will cause enough speculation, Kit, without you adding fuel to the fire by living openly with this young woman. You could hardly expect society to recognise her if you did that, could you?'

Kit ran his fingers through his hair and gave a short and uneven laugh. 'With all due respect, sir, after what the two of us have been through, the opinion of other people seems completely irrelevant at the moment. But as far as Jara is concerned, she wants to travel to Rouen to join a nunnery there—it was what her mother had always had planned for her. I've asked to be notified of any French ships in harbour, and I intend her to leave Macao in the next couple of days.'

'A nunnery, eh? Well, well.' Sir Walter's face smoothed out. It seemed a little unlikely, but he wasn't about to contradict the lad. His wife would be relieved to hear about this!

*   *   *

'Now, then,' Lady Ashley said thoughtfully. 'I think I may have something to fit you here . . . ah, yes, I thought so.'

Jara watched her ladyship sorting through the huge camphorwood trunk that stood at the end of her bed. The bedroom was just as astounding to Jara's eyes as the drawing-room had been. There seemed to be lace everywhere—on the bed and at the windows and on all the tiny cushions scattered about on the chaise-longue. The furniture was in the same ornate style as the other rooms, and there was even a fireplace with an embroidered screen. Completely overawed, Jara could only stand and stare.

'Here you are.' Lady Ashley laid out two dresses on the bed for her inspection. 'These belonged to a niece of mine, and I've always meant to pass them on to someone. I'm afraid they are a little out of fashion, but you should look well enough in them. Would you like to try one on?'

Jara put out a tentative hand and touched the garment nearest to her. It was of jade green, with a lace collar and cuffs. The other one was plainer, of pale blue with tiny white flowers. Never having been allowed any adornment on her clothes other than a little embroidery, she could hardly believe that they were for her. How did one cook or clean in such impractical clothes? The material would be ruined in no time at all!

She became aware that Lady Ashley was waiting impatiently for her to speak and looked up, embarrassed. The older woman misinterpreted her flushed face. 'Oh dear, I don't even know if you speak English . . .'

'Yes, Lady Ashley, I do. I . . . I am sorry but . . . I have never seen such . . . dresses.' She was going to say nightdresses, for that was what she had at first thought them to be, but on closer inspection of Lady Ashley's own clothes Jara had realised that this must be the fashion. 'They...are lovely,' she finished lamely.

'Then you must try them on,' Lady Ashley said with a smile of relief that her charity was not, after all, going to be wasted on an unappreciative subject. 'Do take off that dreadful shirt, my dear.'

Jara shook her head. 'I...I would rather I did not. I do not...possess any undergarments, and...' her voice failed her at the look of horror on the other woman's face.

'None at all? But...you must have had some once? What happened to them?'

'Kit threw them out of the porthole,' Jara answered in complete honesty, and at once sensed that it had been the wrong thing to say. Lady Ashley pursed her lips in silence for a moment and then turned around to the trunk once more. When she stood it was with a small pile of white garments.

'These should do you for the time being, although I don't have any stays that would fit you. But with your figure they should not be immediately necessary. Now put those on and I shall see what we can do for you in the way of shoes. Have you ever worn shoes before?' She was no longer even bothering to conceal her dislike with a smile, and Jara was not sure why. She struggled out of her old clothes and into the new, the silky fabric feeling strange against her skin. Soo Lin came in and removed her discarded clothes, pointedly holding them from her at arm's length, and Jara found herself wishing that the ground would open and swallow her up.

When Lady Ashley turned her to face the long mirror in the corner Jara's mouth dropped open in shock. Was that really her? Marie Perrault had permitted no mirrors in her house, and there had been nothing but a tiny square of mirror on the ship that Kit had kept for shaving. Used to a life without the vanity of mirrors, the only idea Jara had of her own appearance was in her rippled reflection in the pool near her home in Kororareka.

Now here she was reflected with amazing clarity in Lady Ashley's full-length mirror. Whether she was beautiful or not Jara had no way of telling—that the fair-haired, sunburnt stranger in the curious dress, staring back at her from the mirror with wide blue eyes, should be herself was astounding enough. She raised one hand to her hair and then dropped it—and the person in the mirror did the same. It really was her!

Lady Ashley saw the rapt look on Jara's face and found herself disliking the girl more with every second that passed. Not only was she an ignorant little wanton, she was also insufferably vain! The sooner Kit was rid of this young person, the better for all concerned. If his poor mother only knew what manner of female he had been dragging across the Pacific with him... Lady Ashley had had enough experience as a Naval wife to know how lonely a young officer could get on a long foreign posting, but she had not thought Kit particularly susceptible that way. Apparently it was high time the young man took himself a wife. Or at the very least, a suitable mistress. She tugged at the fabric drawn tightly across Jara's midriff.

'You are a big girl, aren't you? So very tall and big-boned—my niece is considerably...slimmer than you are. I'm not sure what I have that would fit you, after all; this dress barely covers your ankles. Try the shoes, please.'

Jara thought the shoes as attractive as the dresses, but they pinched unbearably, and elicited another comment from Lady Ashley on Jara's large feet. By now Jara was flushing with humiliation, all her pleasure in the novelty of having new clothes gone. If only she could take her old shirt and trousers and run back to...where? There was nowhere she could go, and only Kit who seemed to care a little about what happened to her. And she could not even trust him as she had once thought she could...

Lady Ashley had picked up a brush but the thought of this woman laying her hands on her hair panicked Jara into backing away. 'Please... I must find Kit now. Excuse me.'

'You can't interrupt the gentlemen when they are busy,' Lady Ashley began, but Jara had already left the room, picking her skirts up out of the way as she ran over the polished floors back to the drawing room. Kit got to his feet at her entrance.

'Jara...?'

'Please, Kit, I want to go back to the ship! Please... I want...' To her consternation she burst into tears and at once felt Kit's arms warm and strong around her. Ashamed and yet strangely relieved, she buried her face in his shirt, and he felt her trembling like a terrified animal.

He looked over her head to where his godparents stood watching them both in dismay. It took very little imagination to work out what had been happening. 'Thank you for your help, Lady Constance, but I'd better take her with me. I think she'll be a great deal happier at the Hatfields' house.'

'But Kit, what will people think? You have no chaperon and besides, she has no hat, or shawl...' Lady Constance said weakly, as he drew Jara towards the door.

'I'll make sure she gets all those things. Thank you again for all your help. Sir—I'll call again tomorrow morning to discuss that other matter if that is convenient?' Only the speed with which Kit shut the door behind him betrayed the fact that he was very annoyed indeed.

*   *   *

Once more Jara found herself walking down a Macao street, but this time she was not manacled and struggling, but instead holding tightly to Kit's arm as if it were a lifeline.

She could not reconcile herself to the vast numbers of people around them, both Chinese and European. And the noise that assailed her ears like a physical wave of sound! Everywhere people talking together or shouting their wares, with the shops and street-side stalls filled with goods the like of which she had never seen before. A large box-like apparatus came rumbling through the throngs of people, with the biggest animal drawing it that Jara had ever imagined. She clutched at Kit's arm even more tightly in her anxiety and he looked down at her with amused surprise. 'I don't suppose you've ever seen a horse before, have you? Lord, Jara, this must be an entirely new world for you!'

She managed a wavering smile back and slowly released her grip on his hand. 'I have seen pictures of horses before, of course—but I did not know they could be so big! And the houses, Kit—why are they built one on top of the other? How do people get up to the top of them?'

Kit tried to hide the surprise on his face at her question as he realised that he had no real conception of just how strange the simplest of things must be for her. He kept his voice carefully neutral as he replied, 'They have a staircase that connects them. You can't see them because they're inside.'

'A staircase? Oh, yes, of course, I have read of them. Can I see one? What does it look like exactly? Is it safe?'

'Like a ladder, but bigger. And yes, it's completely safe.' Jara nodded, accepting his explanation, and stared up in amazement at the buildings as high as trees, lining the sides of the street down which they were walking. Kit's face grew tighter as they continued on their way.

Introducing Jara to his godparents' house had been taking her from one extreme to another—she had been hopelessly out of her depth in their company, and her reaction was only what he should have expected. But even here in the street she was painfully different. With her ill-fitting dress, limping along in shoes that were patently too small for her, staring wide-eyed at everything they passed... She would never fit in here. He should never have let her leave Kororareka.

But he had, the small persistent voice of reason reminded him. And now this terrified little misfit was entirely his responsibility. For a time, on the ship, he had thought briefly about taking her back to England with him, but reason had quickly prevailed. It would be cruel to expect her to live in the sophisticated society of Macao, let alone that of the circles in which he moved in England, and Jara had surely had enough cruelty in her short life. Putting her on the first available sailing to France would not only be the kindest thing to do, but would also take the burden of responsibility for her from his shoulders. At any rate, if the Admiralty's reaction to his report was only half as bad as Sir Walter had thought it would be, he would soon be in no position to provide her with the protection she needed.

Thank God that episode in his cabin had ended as it had, and that he hadn't... He thrust that intense memory from his mind at once. That was all over. Now he had to deal with the present, and that meant getting Jara out of Macao as soon as possible.

He led her through a gate and up a rather overgrown garden path to the door of a low and spacious-looking house which opened even before he could knock on the heavy panelled door. Once inside Jara caught her breath in delight.

It was a low-ceilinged house, with the sparsest of furnishings, but it was cool and filled with light. Instead of being of paned glass, the windows were open to the elements, with rattan blinds above. Everywhere she looked Jara could see the luxuriant garden that surrounded the house, seemingly trying to come in the windows, and the air was heavy with the scent of exotic flowers.

The Chinese servants had been informed of their arrival and the elderly man who had admitted them bowed as they stood in the entrance-hall. His long pig-tail and high, smooth, plucked hair-line transfixed Jara. He spoke in a strange, sing-song pidgin English that was completely alien to her ears, but Kit appeared to comprehend it perfectly.

'Wei! What a coincidence! How are you?'

'Cap'n sir.' He bowed again, his eyes twinkling. 'Lon' time I see you. You welcome. An' lady.'

'But what are you doing here? I thought...?'

'I here now, sir,' Wei interrupted him.

There was a moment's silence and then Kit nodded. 'Thank you. And...I'm glad it's you.'

When Wei went before them down the hallway, Jara looked at Kit curiously. 'What did you mean by that? Why are you glad that it is Wei?'

'Only that I knew Wei from that last time I was in Macao,' he said just a little too quickly, giving her a gentle push to follow Wei. 'I was posted here for a year, when I was no more than a lad, and I've been here on a number of occasions since, over the years. Wei tells me that they were only expecting me, and that it'll take a little while to get another bedroom ready. This will be your room.'

It was light and airy, with simple cane furniture and a big window through which the sun was streaming through on to the polished floorboards. She sat and bounced on the bed in delight. 'A real bed! Oh, Kit, I think I will like it here!'

Kit, leaning against the doorway, smiled at her pleasure. 'I'll feel happier about leaving you for a while, then. I want to arrange for a few things to be taken off the *Courageous*. Would you like me to order you a cold drink before I go?'

She bounced off the bed and came to stand in front of him, her face suddenly serious. 'Please do not go away just now. There is so much you have to tell me . . . so much I need to know.'

He hesitated, torn between his desire to complete the hundred and one other things he had to do and the acknowledgement that he did owe her at least a few minutes of his time. At last he sighed and went to sit in the cane chair by the window. He stretched out, crossed his ankles and smiled briefly at her. 'Ask away.'

She sat back on the bed, her fingers twisting nervously in her lap. 'The men . . .?'

'In custody. Moody isn't expected to live, I'm afraid, not unless he allows his arm to get medical attention. If it sets your mind at ease, I've put in a strong plea for leniency for them. I've no personal knowledge of any of them being directly responsible for the murder of the crew of the *Courageous*, and . . . well, I've had worse men serve under me. I've suggested a long spell in His Majesty's Navy might be a more appropriate sentence, and I hope that will be accepted.'

Jara's shoulders sagged in relief. 'Thank you, Kit. That is fair, I think, especially when I think of how difficult it must have been for you alone on that ship . . . I wish that I had known—that you had told me! I am so sorry . . .'

'I couldn't have told you—it was far too dangerous. And no apologies are necessary.'

He spoke abruptly, and she was aware that he wanted to leave. She took a deep breath as she prepared to ask the hardest question of all. 'Kit, that night...on the deck. Would you really have...thrown me overboard?'

He did not answer her at first, studying an area of polished floor just past his boots instead. She held her breath, willing him desperately to deny it even as she knew what his silence meant. At last he said quietly, 'I would have done anything to stop you telling the men what you knew. There was something I'd been entrusted to give Admiral Buckler on Norfolk Island or—failing that—to bring here to Macao. If you'd given me away to the others, I would have failed. I had my orders to follow. It was a question of duty, do you see?'

The defensiveness in his voice made his words seem less ominous than they sounded, and she repeated, 'Yes. But would you really have gone so far as to throw me overboard?'

He met her eyes levelly but she found it impossible to read them. 'I can't answer that, because the situation never arose. Did it?'

She thought of the man he had killed in cold blood. She thought of the ruthlessness and single-mindedness it had taken to get his ship across the Pacific to Macao. His professionalism chilled her to the marrow of her bones, and she could not stop the small shiver that ran through her. She should hate him! Once she had thought she did, but now... Now everything was different. And she was entirely at his mercy. 'And...me, Kit. What happens to me?'

He visibly relaxed at the change of topic. 'I thought we'd always agreed on that—you take the first possible ship to France. But you've had a hell of a time recently, Jara. I'd like you to rest first, take a few days to see Macao, get some decent clothes...'

'Clothes?' She plucked at the dress she was wearing. 'Lady Ashley gave me these...'

'*New* clothes,' Kit said firmly. 'And new shoes, hats . . . whatever. Even a girl on her way to a nunnery needs to be decently attired. And with all due respect to Lady Constance, that dress should have remained in the rag-bag where she undoubtedly got it from.'

'Lady Ashley was very kind to me . . .' Jara defended her benefactress faintly, but as Kit continued to smile at her cynically she faltered and looked down at her hands. 'She did not like me, did she? Nor her husband. Why was that?'

Kit frowned. 'For a number of reasons that aren't important and certainly aren't your fault. But you needn't worry—you don't have to meet them again if you don't want to. Now—I must get back to the docks and clear up all the loose ends. Just ask Wei if you want anything—he understands English perfectly, and he's the very best of men, besides. Do you need anything before I go?'

She shook her head and let him go at last. She wanted a wash, she decided, and then she would explore the garden, but in the meantime she was so tired . . . She took off the dress and wrenched off the pinching shoes, and then fell on top of the bed in her chemise and petticoat. It was so soft and comfortable and cool that she could not resist the sensation of such utter bliss. Just for a few minutes.

But it was much later when she awoke. She had fallen asleep to the slanting sun of a late afternoon, and woke to a soft, muted light and a different feeling in the house.

Someone had covered her with a light coverlet and she threw it off to walk to the window and raise the rattan blind. It was early morning. How could she have slept for so long? She must have been a great deal more tired than she had thought.

What a beautiful room this was! In wonder she ran her hand over the heavy chest of dark wood that stood at the end of the bed. It was ornately carved, with tiny, delicate patterns of flowers in what could only be gold. She had never seen anything like it before. And on the polished floor stood a thick multi-coloured rug like those she had seen in the Ashleys' home. She dug her toes into it and sighed. She had never even dreamed of such beauty and luxury in her life. There was a garment that looked like a dressing-robe lying across the foot of her bed, obviously intended for her to wear. She put it on and smoothed the vibrant, peacock-blue silk against her skin. It was beautiful to look at and feel, but like everything else here it made her feel like an interloper.

She tidied her bed and was at the door of the bedroom before she heard a woman's voice coming from another room, and Kit's answering her. Lady Ashley was here! She stepped back into the sanctuary of her bedroom even as she cursed her cowardice.

Kit had called her an ignorant savage on more than one occasion and after yesterday—having now seen something of the world in which he lived—she had to admit that he had not been inaccurate. It was true that she knew Latin and Greek, as well as being fluent in French, English and Maori. She was also well-read in geography and history, and she could solve most mathematical problems set before her. But in the ways of the world—*Kit's* world—she had to admit that she was hopelessly illiterate.

She knew that she was an embarrassment to Kit; she could see it in his face yesterday at the Ashleys' when she had run away from that horrible woman and her hairbrush. It seemed whatever she said and did here would cause offence; these people—Kit's people— thought and acted and dressed in a manner that was completely alien to her. A few years before she had read

Gulliver's Travels, and thought she knew now how Gulliver had felt in the land of the Houyhnhnms. Uncouth, unlovely and unwanted.

So what was left for her? The nunnery at Rouen? She had never pretended to herself that she had any religious vocation—she had agreed to go to please her mother and because she had never been given any other choice. But it had taken just a few minutes in Kit's arms for her to suddenly understand that there was more to life than duty. She had never been so overwhelmed by an emotion in her life, and even now she had only to close her eyes to remember his face close to hers, and how his lips had felt and the texture of his skin. And how he had made her feel...

Was she in love with him? The phrase was one she had read in books, but there had been too little romantic love in her own life for her to fully appreciate what it meant. Marriage had never been considered for her, and her adoptive parents' own marriage had been an austere, businesslike arrangement in which any displays of joy and affection had long been extinguished by hardship and deprivation. The only other couples Jara had seen had been among the whalers, but their casual exchange of women for money was no basis for her to make comparisons. It seemed that she knew quite a lot about physical desire. But love? Real, lasting love that could bind a man and a woman together for a lifetime? Perhaps it only existed in books after all.

Whatever she felt about Kit, she knew that his own feelings about her were far from loving. She could never forget how he had deliberately terrified her to assure himself of her silence on the ship, and the harshness that always lay beneath his pleasant exterior. Lately he was being so kind to her, so concerned about her welfare... But he could afford to be when she would soon cease to be his responsibility. She could imagine the sigh of relief he would give when he at last saw her off to France—he would have done his *duty*. And duty seemed to be the tenet by which Kit ran his life.

She understood him better now that she had met Lady Ashley; so soft, beautiful and pampered, like a being from another world. Was that the sort of woman who filled Kit's life? His *real* life, in the faraway country of England?

She turned and caught sight of herself in the mirror of the dressing table. The way she felt was reflected on her face—and what a bedraggled, sad-looking creature she had become! No wonder Kit felt sorry for her. But pity was the last thing she wanted from him. If she was going to have to leave him, then she would do so with her head held high, and without giving either him or Lady Ashley the satisfaction of knowing how much she ached inside.

Throwing her shoulders back and drawing the dressing-gown around her, she left the room, little guessing that help was just a few steps away.

CHAPTER EIGHT

LIFE had not been good to Eustacia Ashley. Like many women who had spent their youth nursing sick and elderly parents, her chances at romantic happiness had been very limited. There had been one or two gentlemen who had paid their attentions to the quiet, plain Miss Ashley, but whose interest had invariably wandered to fresher fields, leaving her hopes dashed and her heart to slowly wither.

The death of the second of her parents meant that she was finally free to make her own way in the world, but she soon found that it was a severely restricted world for a spinster of modest means and no beauty. For a few years she eked out a miserable existence in genteel poverty in a small house in Lewisham, until she received an invitation from her dear brother's wife to accompany them to Macao. Unable to resist an opportunity to see the world at last, Eustacia had come eagerly—only to discover that she had exchanged one prison for another. She was Constance's companion, maid and nurse, but never anything more. The sparkling social occasions she had dreamed of were unattainable because she never had anything suitable to wear and because Constance always seemed to need her in the kitchen, or in the powder-room to repair a rip in an evening dress, or to provide refreshments for any lady who might become fatigued by the dancing...

Not that she had ever had reason to complain about Constance, of course, Eustacia kept telling herself staunchly—she was the very soul of kindness, with never

a cruel word about anyone. It was simply that Constance
did not think of her sister-in-law as an equal, or even as
a woman. She was just another pair of hands—essential
for the smooth running of the household, but of no more
importance than that.

So when Constance informed her that she was to go
immediately to the Hatfields' house to protect her godson's good name by chaperoning the female he had
brought with him, Eustacia did not object to the duty.
To be able to leave the Ashley household for a while was
treat enough, and the added bonus of new faces—and
even a touch of scandal—was positively thrilling.

She arrived on the doorstep of the Hatfields' house
in the early evening with a bag of her belongings at her
side; a small neat woman, with severely dressed grey hair
and sharp intelligent features. She was shown into the
drawing-room and while she waited she looked about
her curiously. It was a nice enough little house, and did
not in the least look like a den of iniquity. That, she had
to admit, was a trifle disappointing.

She stopped feeling disappointed the moment she set
eyes on the man who walked into the room. He looked
a great deal younger than the thirty years Constance had
claimed for him. Tall, fair and well-built, and with a
face that could almost have been called beautiful if it
were not so wholly masculine... He quite took her breath
away. She regained it in time to thrust out her hand and
say quickly, 'Captain Montgomery, I am Eustacia
Ashley, Sir Walter's sister. Constance has sent me to
chaperon the young lady you have living here with you.'

He took her hand. 'Thank you, Miss Ashley, but I
can assure you that your kind offer is not necessary. Will
you join me in a cup of tea before you leave?' She
allowed him to seat her and ring for tea, watching him
carefully all the while. Constance had impressed upon
her the importance of her mission—the Captain was of

an excellent family, and his welfare was dear to the hearts of both the Ashleys. But he had also spent most of his life at sea and this, Constance explained, was why he was sometimes inclined to flout the conventions of society. Eustacia's orders were to be tactful, but to be firm.

The Captain sat opposite her and met her eyes unflinchingly. 'Well, Miss Ashley. I'm sorry you've had a wasted trip, but I've no need or wish for any interference in my private life. And neither has Miss Perrault.'

Eustacia sat back in her chair at that. 'I do understand.'

'Do you?'

'Yes, I do. And I also agree that everyone is entitled to a degree of privacy, Captain Montgomery, but not in matters such as these. Lady Constance is deeply distressed at the impropriety of this situation and there is Miss Perrault herself to think of. I believe you have been in Macao before? You must know how people in such a small community gossip. Everyone knows exactly what you've done before you've even thought of doing it.'

The fair eyebrows met in a frown. 'That shouldn't concern Miss Perrault. She will be leaving the colony in two or three days.'

'And yourself? Your reputation?'

'Quite honestly, Miss Ashley, what other people have chosen to think of me has never unduly concerned me. I'm not about to start losing sleep over it now.'

'Oh, dear.' Eustacia bit her lip as she thought of her next move. Then she sighed. 'In that case, I'd better go now, Captain Montgomery. The only things I can think of to say to you would sound dreadfully pompous after such a declaration.'

A gleam of laughter appeared in his dark eyes. 'Shame on you, Miss Ashley. You can't go back to my godmother without saying you put up a better fight than that. Stay for tea, at least.' When he smiled at her Eustacia felt her long-dormant heart turn over. Surely he must have *some* idea of the devastating effect he had on women? she wondered, and yet—to judge by his complete lack of self-consciousness—it would seem not. But then Eustacia remembered. There were nine girls in that family. Ah, yes, that would explain it; no man, no matter how handsome, could possibly grow up with an inflated idea of his own masculine attractiveness with that many sisters on hand to disillusion him.

The tea he had ordered was by some coincidence also her own favourite—the rich Black Congou—and it was served perfectly: brewed rather than stewed. They sipped their tea for a while, each of them quietly assessing the other over the rim of their cup. They both rather liked the conclusions they drew. At last Eustacia put her cup and saucer back on to the table. 'And Miss Perrault? Where is she now?' she enquired, determined to make one last attempt at what she had been sent here to do.

'She was fast asleep when I last looked in on her. She's had a long and . . . very trying day. I thought it best that she rest as long as she needs to.' Eustacia did not miss the change in his expression as he spoke. It was just a slight softening of his expression and his voice, but it was still perceptible. She wondered again what sort of girl it was who could be planning to commit herself to a nunnery when at the same time she so obviously had the Captain firmly in her toils. Curiosity, as well as a genuine liking for this young man, gave her an audacity she generally lacked.

She leaned forward. 'Captain Montgomery, may I speak bluntly? You may not welcome my presence here, but don't you think you should ask Miss Perrault's opinion on this?'

'If she is the hoyden my godmother has obviously portrayed her as, she's hardly likely to welcome a chaperon, Miss Ashley,' Kit replied evenly, but the look in his eyes was daunting. Eustacia ignored it and ploughed on.

'If she were a hoyden, Captain, I don't believe you would be as protective of her as you are. And if what I understand is correct, she is a young woman who has not only lost her family and home, but has had a very difficult journey here. Don't you feel she might need some feminine company? Even if it is only for a few days, might she not need another woman to talk to, to help her...adjust...?'

Kit put his head to one side and looked at her appraisingly. 'Would you do that?' he said at last. 'Would you help her adjust? With no moral strictures, no lectures...?' He broke off at the indignant look on her face and put up his hand in a gesture of amused apology. 'I shouldn't have asked! In that case, Miss Ashley, you are welcome. And...thank you.'

And so it was Eustacia that Jara found at the breakfast table the next morning, so deeply in conversation with Kit that Jara was able to watch them unseen for a moment. The small woman was talking animatedly, her plain brown dress and sharp features making her look like a cheerful sparrow. Kit was listening attentively to her anecdote and it was his appearance which unnerved Jara much more than that of the visitor.

He was wearing his uniform for the first time since she had known him, and he looked entirely and alarmingly at ease in the dark blue coat with its gold epaulettes. His face above the lace jabot was leaner than she remembered, the lines more severely planed, and she thought at first that it was because he had had his hair cut since she had last seen him. But as she watched him

laugh at something the strange woman said, she realised
that it was much more than that. The authority and confidence that he had always worn was made substantial
now by the uniform. If she had had the courage, she
would have ripped it from his shoulders.

The stranger who used to be Kit Montgomery looked
up to see her standing transfixed in the doorway, and he
was at once on his feet. 'Miss Ashley, this is Miss
Perrault. Jara, Miss Ashley is my godfather's sister. She
has offered to stay here to help you, and to keep you
company until you leave. That is ... if that is what you
want?'

Jara looked at the little woman smiling encouragingly
at her from the breakfast table, and then at Kit. Clearly
he wanted this, and she was in no position to disagree
with anything he wanted. She nodded stiffly to Miss
Ashley. 'Thank you.'

She had no sooner taken the chair that Kit had pulled
out for her when Wei came in to tell Kit that he was
required with some urgency at the docks. Even then he
hesitated, but after receiving affirmation from Miss
Ashley that she and Jara would do just as well without
his presence, he excused himself. As the door closed
behind him, Jara stared woodenly at the fruit so exquisitely arranged on a plate before her, her spirits plum-
meting even further as she saw not a single item of food
on the table that she recognised.

'May I pour you some coffee, Jara?' Miss Ashley
broke the awkward silence. 'You don't mind me calling
you by your Christian name, do you? And you must call
me Eustacia. Captain Montgomery has told me so much
about you that I already feel that I know you very well
indeed.'

Jara kept her eyes on the table, wondering just what
exactly this statement might mean. Oh, dear, Eustacia
thought, Constance certainly did her work on this poor

little thing. Impulsively she took the girl's hand, holding it tightly even when Jara would have withdrawn it.

'I am not my sister-in-law, Jara. I am here to help you, and I would very much like to be your friend.'

'Why? Why...would you want to help me?' Her voice was low, and with an attractive and unmistakably French accent. Eustacia squeezed the captive fingers in her hand gently.

'Because I think you need help, and you need a friend. Am I right?'

Jara nodded, her eyes still wary. 'Thank you.' Eustacia released her hand and Jara pulled the plate of fruit towards her. 'I...know that I will need a great deal of help, Miss...Eustacia. For example—what...is this fruit called?'

Forewarned by Kit, Eustacia matter-of-factly named the pineapple, peaches and lychees, and deftly demonstrated the correct techniques for eating each one. Then she busied herself with pouring out the coffee. At least the child had good table manners, Eustacia thought, watching her out of the corner of her eye as Jara dealt efficiently enough with the peach, savouring each deliciously unaccustomed mouthful. She was also aware that Jara in turn was watching her serving of the coffee; she was obviously very eager to learn. Well, if the child wanted to learn, she was quite prepared to teach her.

A previously vague suspicion began to slowly clarify in her mind. She cleared her throat. 'I hope you are completely rested now,' she said carefully, 'as I believe we have rather a busy day ahead of us. The Captain has arranged for a dressmaker to call this morning, so you may as well not bother dressing until she arrives. I understand the clothes that you were given yesterday are not a good fit, so we will have to see what can be done immediately. And you will need shoes, I am told——'

'Clothes?' Jara's knife clattered against her plate. 'Oh, I don't think so... The expense...'

'Oh, forget the expense,' Eustacia said with a gay little laugh. 'The Captain said to buy you whatever you needed, and whatever you liked, and he didn't say one single word about expense! And you do *need* a decent wardrobe, my dear, even if it is just to see you through the voyage to Rouen. If you prefer, of course, you can select materials in the darker colours...' Her words trailed off as she perceived and correctly analysed the expression on Jara's face. Nunnery, my foot! she thought. It's the dashing young Captain you're after, you poor child, and who can blame you? It was on the tip of her tongue to say so, but she restrained herself. But Jara was surprised when Eustacia suddenly took her hand again and gave her a smile of pure understanding.

Jara had to keep asking herself repeatedly whether she was awake during the next few hours. Surely the fabrics, the laces and fashion sketches that the dressmaker scattered about the bedroom for her to choose from were some wonderful figment of an imagination gone wild? The laces, and the satins and the lustrous cottons, and above all the silks—as soft and as light as a rose-petal—draped and pinned about her... It was only Eustacia's down-to-earth presence that served to remind her that this was really happening to her.

She was not sure if Kit had done so deliberately, but he had chosen a French modiste, and the woman's chatter as she smoothed and tucked and pinned was in the language that Jara had grown up with. Jara found herself at first smiling and then laughing aloud at Madame Fouchard's extravagant compliments, and it was a delight to be able to answer in her native tongue. *Mademoiselle's* bones gave her an enviably Junoesque figure; she had the height to carry the high-waisted fashions;

she had no need of stays and so could wear a bodice draped *à la Greque*... Jara did not believe a word of it, but enjoyed the flattery all the same, and Eustacia— whose French was adequate enough to comprehend what the modiste was telling her charge—took pleasure in Jara's enjoyment.

The modiste dismissed Lady Ashley's donations as too unworthy to even be remade. *Mademoiselle*, she insisted, must avoid the ribbons and laces that smaller, less well-endowed women required to enhance their beauty and, after she had demonstrated what she meant, Jara had to agree. The only disagreement between the three women was over the colours Jara chose for an evening dress. Contrary to Eustacia's expectations, and rather to her alarm, Jara insisted on deep dramatic colours, whereas the older woman tried to steer her in the direction of the soft pastels which were much more appropriate for a young girl. The modiste wisely remained impartial.

They had reached loggerheads over the choice of a pale lilac and a deep, vibrant peacock-blue silk when Jara suddenly took up both bolts of cloth. 'I hear that Kit is home. I shall ask him.'

'Oh, no, my dear,' Eustacia remonstrated. 'Men know absolutely nothing about ladies' fashions, believe me.'

'Kit will know,' Jara said firmly, and to Eustacia's surprise he did. He was seated in an armchair in the study, reading one of the letters from the packet of mail on his knee, but he rose politely to his feet as Jara burst in and listened patiently enough as she explained the dilemma and demanded his decision. 'The blue,' he adjudicated. 'Absolutely. But the lilac will make a very smart morning-dress.'

'*Certainement, monsieur*, exactly as I would have chosen,' the modiste contributed, knowing very well who was going to pay her bills. Eustacia sighed.

'Very well then, Jara. Captain Montgomery must, after all, be accepted as something of an expert on what we ladies wear. We apologise for interrupting you, Captain. Is that your mail from home?'

Kit looked down at the letter in his hand. 'Yes. Including a letter from Emily.' At the sound of that name Jara's head snapped up from her contemplation of the fabrics, but no one else seemed to notice her reaction.

'Oh, dear! How very difficult for you,' Eustacia sympathised. 'Come along, Jara, we should leave the Captain to his correspondence. We still have the hats to decide upon...'

'Please—I will be with you in a minute.' Jara turned her back on Eustacia's frown of disapproval and waited until the door had closed behind them before she perched herself on the edge of the chaise-longue and indicated that Kit should do likewise. 'You look troubled. What is the matter? Can I help?'

He smiled briefly. 'No, but thank you. I have a letter to reply to that is going to be very difficult, that's all.'

'From Emily?' Jara took a deep breath, not really wanting to hear the answer to her next question. 'Who is Emily? Is she your... wife?'

'Good grief, no!' he spluttered in amazement. 'Whatever gave you the idea I was married? It wouldn't be fair on any wife to have a husband who was never home.'

'Then... is she a... fiancée? A sweetheart?'

Kit leaned back and regarded her with cool interest. 'And what if she were? It should mean nothing to you.'

Her mouth tightened. 'And it does not. I am merely... curious. Eustacia says that you are an expert on ladies' fashions. You have a book given to you by this woman. I am merely...'

'Curious. Yes, so you said.' There was a glint in his eye that warned Jara that he was playing with her yet again, but she kept the irritation from showing on her face and after a moment he shrugged. 'I suppose you also want me to confess all about Annabel, and Mary, and Catherine, and Elizabeth and Juliana—they're the twins—and Miranda...' He saw the stricken look on her face and relented. 'They're my younger sisters—all nine of them. Have you never wondered why I felt compelled to run away to sea?'

'Nine sisters!' She exclaimed, torn between relief and amazement that anyone could have so many siblings. 'And you have no brothers?'

'No, but I've plenty of brothers-in-law—all but four of the girls are married with families now. Emily was engaged to my best friend George Gables, who——' He stopped abruptly and put the letter down. 'They were to be married this June. She's sent me a letter full of instructions about keeping him safe.'

There was an edge of pain in his voice and Jara could not restrain the hand that stretched out to comfort him, but he evaded it, instead swiftly standing up and walking away to the wide, open window. The birds had fallen silent in the heat of the midday sun, and the warm, scented air was filled with the sound of the crickets in the garden.

'But tell me—how do you find it here?' he said too abruptly to sound sincerely interested. 'Are you enjoying yourself?'

A little hurt by his action, she heard herself admitting, 'Some things I enjoy, yes. But some things I do not.'

'Such as?'

'Such as . . . the way that you live here. So many servants! At sea we were able to do everything for ourselves, and yet here it seems that one cannot even serve oneself at the table without assistance. Why is that? Why does one need so many servants?'

He paid her the compliment of considering that seriously. 'Well, in our society one's status is judged in part by the number of servants one employs. There are only four servants in this house, and that is not considered to be so very many here. And employing them does mean that one has more time...'

'Time? But time to do what? This morning I wanted to see the house, and when I went into the kitchen everyone looked most surprised, and Eustacia tells me that I should not have done so! I am not even permitted to prepare a meal myself! Why should I need more time? What shall I do with it?'

'Well, my sisters used to visit friends, or read, or embroider—much as you like to do. And then, of course, they'd spend a great deal of time on their appearance and their clothes. Fittings with a dressmaker, for instance...'

'And that is all that they do all day?' she demanded aghast.

'No, it's not all. Most of my sisters are wives and mothers, with households to run, and they all seem very happy with their lot in life. Is that such a bad thing, Jara?'

'But they do not cook or clean or do any work?'

'No. They don't have to.'

'I see. So that is what Eustacia means when she tells me to behave like a lady. I should be idle. Useless.'

Kit sighed. 'I can see you're determined to be difficult about this. What is it that is really upsetting you? And don't tell me it's boredom, Jara, because I don't believe you.'

'I... I don't know what you mean.'

'Yes, you do. Something is worrying you and I'd like to know what it is.' He watched her closely for a moment. 'Is it the dresses? Are you unhappy with Madame

Fouchard? I had hoped that another Frenchwoman might have made you feel more at ease...'

'No! The dresses are beautiful, thank you, and *Madame* is very kind. Although...the cost, Kit! I cannot accept such generosity from you...'

'But why not?' he frowned. 'It's the least I can do for you.'

'The least?' Jara frowned back, trying to understand him. 'You talk as if you owed me something...'

'Well, I do, in a way. And I am responsible for your welfare now.' He picked up the packet of mail from the chair and began to shuffle through it, and she sensed that he was suddenly uncomfortable. 'Is that all, Jara? I've got a fair amount to do today.'

'I did not think that a Naval captain earned so much...' she began.

'What?' He threw himself down on the chair again and scowled at her. 'Oh—you're still on about the dresses? Look, if you're worried that I can't afford it, don't be. Just wear them and look beautiful and enjoy it. All right? Now can I please——?'

'Do you really think I will look beautiful?' Jara demanded excitedly. This was too good an opportunity to miss. There was a mirror hanging over the fireplace and she jumped up to stand before it, preening at her reflection. Kit looked pained.

'What the hell has brought this on? One of your few saving graces was your innocence of mirrors—so for God's sake don't end up like all my sisters and live with one literally plastered to the end of your nose!'

She spun around angrily. 'I am asking you a simple question! Am I beautiful? Moody said once to me that because I am...beautiful...that you would sell me to a Chinese...'

'Now that's an idea,' Kit said thoughtfully. 'But not, I think, to a Chinese merchant. The Portuguese, now—

I understand they do a flourishing trade with the sheikhs of Arabia. You'd fetch a high price there, I'm sure.' He slapped his knee in resolution. 'All my money problems solved with one simple sale! Thank you, Jara, very sporting of you to mention it.'

She stared at him suspiciously, searching for what she knew must be levity but—as ever—his boyish face was ingenuous. 'Why...why not to a Chinese merchant?' was all she could think to say, lamely.

'Because the Chinese aren't too keen on European women. They claim they're too hairy and they smell bad. Can't say I always disagree with them either. Now, was there anything else you wanted? I'm very busy, so if you'd please leave...'

'How rude you are!' she gasped. 'Yes, I believe that I will leave, and with pleasure! I thought you would behave like a gentleman here, but it seems that that officer's coat turns you into even more of an objectionable, self-opinionated monster! You and all your type make me sick to my stomach!'

'Then it's just as well you're going to a goddamned nunnery, isn't it?' Kit yelled back over the slamming of the door.

She reopened the door and put her head around it, 'And do not blaspheme, you foul-mouthed brute!'

'And don't slam the door on me, you stupid little savage!'

She slammed it shut so hard that the tiny china ornaments on the heavy carved table in the hallway shook, and then she stood still for a moment, her chest tight with the anger still churning hard inside her. She would leave this place immediately. She would go to the docks and beg a place on the first ship out of Macao. She would... Her eye was caught by Eustacia's anxious face as that kindly soul hovered by the bedroom door, convinced that murder would be done any minute. No,

she decided. There was a way—a very satisfying way—
of extracting revenge on Captain Montgomery. She flew
into the bedroom past the quivering Miss Ashley to where
the modiste was hurriedly packing away her materials.

'Are you going already, *madame*? But we have only
just begun!' Jara trilled. 'What have we ordered? Five
dresses only? But I think I need at least twice—three
times—as many! And that beautiful silk that Miss Ashley
thought was too expensive—may I see it again, please?
And I do not believe I have seen your selection of hats,
madame...'

A little less confidently this time, Madame Fouchard
began to lay out her materials, while Eustacia sank
quietly on to a chair and regarded Jara warily. Where
was the timid child who had so touchingly requested her
help just a few hours before? She had been as sure then
of Jara's affection for the Captain as she was of his for
her. And now... How could she have been so wrong?
She was forced to dismiss all her entrancing notions of
bringing two star-crossed lovers together, and to review
the situation.

Perhaps Constance was right—perhaps this little minx
prancing about the bedroom swathed in several hundred
guineas' worth of fabrics *was* a greater threat to her
godson than the massed Navy of Napoleon had ever
been. But she was such a pretty girl... Despite herself,
Eustacia found that she was nodding approval of the
mint-green crêpe de Chine that Jara was holding up, together with some exquisite silk roses in a paler green.
The colours did so bring up the child's delicate colouring. And the Captain was so very handsome...
Eustacia sighed over her confused heart. Perhaps after
all it had been no more than a particularly virulent lovers'
tiff; she did hope so!

She put her hand to her head and gasped as a sharp
pain shot through her temples. When it had passed she

looked up at Jara's worried face. 'I am sorry, my dear,' she sighed. 'A slight megrim—it takes me now and then... Do you think you can manage for a little while if I were to lie down quietly in my room?'

'Oh, yes, certainly.' Jara was all sympathy as she helped Eustacia to the door. 'Please rest for as long as you need to. I know I shall have no trouble selecting what I want by myself!'

Several hours later Eustacia was still abed, recovering from her headache, and Jara was tensely pacing the length of the sitting room. Damn Kit Montgomery! Shortly after their argument of that morning he had left the house without indicating how long he would be gone, and had thus deprived Jara of the pleasure she had so eagerly anticipated when he saw her in her new clothes. She ran her hand down the silky length of the peach-coloured dress that she was wearing. It was one of three new ready-made garments the modiste had been able to alter to fit her, and the rest of her extensive new wardrobe was to be delivered over the next few days. It was beautiful, and she felt beautiful wearing it. All she needed was for Kit to assure her of that fact, and to receive the bill for her day's extravagance. Despite her earlier defiance, she was beginning to regret her impulsiveness—Kit's temper was not likely to be sweetened by the cost of her revenge that morning.

She spun around at the sound of voices in the hallway. He was back at last! She took up a position of what she hoped was graceful indolence by the fireplace and waited.

After a full half-minute Kit had still not appeared, and so she abandoned her posture and went out into the hallway. To her dismay the gentleman talking with Wei was not Kit but Lieutenant Lewis. She stopped in her tracks, the memory of his ignominious treatment of her the previous day still very fresh in her mind, but he looked up at the rustle of her skirts, and the look of surprised appreciation in his widened eyes was so gratifying that against all her better judgement she hesitated. He came to stand before her and bowed low, looking charmingly embarrassed.

'Lieutenant,' she acknowledged him coldly. 'Are you looking for Captain Montgomery?'

'I...I understood that he was here,' he said, after taking a moment to recollect himself. 'I apologise if I have disturbed you...'

He was a handsome young man, with his dark curls and sky-blue eyes, and his disconcertion was so obvious that Jara very nearly took pity on him. She shook her head slightly and turned again to return to the sitting-room, but he cleared his throat as if he wanted to say more, and politeness made her wait.

'Miss...ah...'

'Miss Perrault.'

'Miss Perrault, I would like to apologise for my...appalling behaviour of yesterday. I misunderstood Captain Montgomery's orders, and had no idea that you...' He dropped his eyes. 'I can only offer you my sincerest apologies and hope that you did not suffer too much from your ordeal.'

She was conscious of Wei hovering in the background and, as much to avoid the servants overhearing them as to spare the Lieutenant's feelings, she opened the door to the sitting-room.

'Perhaps you would care to come in here, Lieutenant.' He obliged with alacrity, closing the door behind them when she would have left it open. At once she was aware of a change in him, and it took only a moment to identify it as the recovery of the same arrogance and assurance that seemed common to all the Naval officers she had met thus far. It was that dratted uniform, she was sure of it! Perhaps they sewed something into the lining.

He sat opposite her, drawing his chair only a little too close for her comfort, and inclining his head confidentially. 'I do appreciate your understanding, Miss Perrault. What I did was quite unforgivable.'

While she privately agreed with him, she did want to leave this difficult subject as quickly as possible, and so waved her hand with a dismissiveness she did not feel. 'Please forget that it happened. I'm sorry that the Captain is not here...'

'Oh, but I'm not,' the Lieutenant rejoined smoothly. 'I would much rather see you! But I must confess to being somewhat surprised.'

'Surprised?' He seemed to be getting closer, and she moved back a fraction in her chair.

'Yes, surprised that the Captain would leave such a lovely young lady as yourself alone like this. If you were under *my* protection I wouldn't leave your side for a single second.'

Jara blinked in surprise. She had become used to the gallantry of the many young officers who had visited her parents' store in Kororareka, but it still astounded her to hear it from Lieutenant Lewis. However, his flattery was a welcome balm to the injured feelings she still nursed from Kit's criticism that morning, and besides— he was right. Kit *was* neglecting her. She lowered her eyes and smoothed out an invisible wrinkle from her skirts. 'Thank you, Lieutenant,' she murmured.

She presented such a charming picture that the young officer was obliged to study her in admiring silence for a moment. What a difference from the grubby trollop he had brought ashore yesterday! She looked most fetching in a decent dress, and the single plait hanging down back was a piquant reminder of just how young she was. No wonder Montgomery had risked the wrath of the Admiralty by bringing her with him. He had heard a rumour or two about that, for all that the Admiralty

seemed keen to hush it all up, and it was common
knowledge now that the Captain's days as a commis-
sioned officer were numbered. It was hard for him to
feel much sympathy for the man—Montgomery's
reputation as a commander had been unimpeachable
until now, but he had always struck the Lieutenant as
something of an arrogant moralist. And yet, here he was
now openly living with this pretty little piece... Captain
Montgomery would be leaving Macao soon enough, and
then his Miss Perrault would be looking for a new
protector. The Lieutenant smiled and leaned forward,
but at once Jara pushed her chair back noisily and leapt
to her feet.

'Shall I . . . go and make us some tea . . . ?'

He laughed up at her, with the smile that he knew
made him especially attractive to women. 'Good heavens,
no! That's what servants are for! But I have a much
better idea. Have you had an opportunity to see Macao
yet? Properly?' She shook her head and he feigned surprise. 'But you absolutely must, Miss Perrault. The
praças, the gardens . . . you must see them. And I would
consider it an honour if you would permit me to show
them to you. By way of reparation.'

'No, I could not, really . . .' Jara hesitated, torn between an instinctive wariness of this man and an overwhelming desire to explore her new surroundings. She
knew she should wake Eustacia and ask her advice, but
it would be so unfair to do so when the poor lady was
so unwell. Her eyes went to the sunlight streaming in
through the windows, and the colour and sounds beyond.
She would be here for only a few days more, after all,
and if Kit could not be bothered showing her Macao . . .

She smiled shyly at the Lieutenant. 'Thank you. That
would be most pleasant.'

She was soon ready to leave, with one of her new hats
on her head, and the strange contraption called a parasol

held in the graceful manner Eustacia had demonstrated, over one shoulder. The Lieutenant offered her his arm, and she slipped one gloved hand through it, just as she had with Kit the previous day.

They walked slowly down the *Praya Grande* and the *praças*, past the beautiful churches and the elegant houses of the Portuguese, and into a small but intensely florid park. The formally laid-out gardens, the ornate rotunda, the Chinese-style bridges over the ornamental stream, all elicited exclamations of delight from Jara. She felt as if she was having the magical experience of walking through a painting.

The Lieutenant was a fluent conversationalist, interspersing his knowledgeable commentary on Macao's highlights with charming comments on her beauty, and she found herself by turns enthralled and amused. But she could not be comfortable with him—he had a tendency to press her hand tightly against his side in a way she found rather too familiar, and he would insist on standing a little too close to her whenever they stopped.

They ventured into the area Lieutenant Lewis called the Chinese quarter, and he showed her the fascinating, bustling markets, and spoke of the pawnshops, the gambling dens and the opium divans. He even took her to the great, well-guarded gate that led into the mysterious empire of China. Utterly fascinated, she stood staring at the great red and gold iron doors, trying to imagine what it was like on the other side where only a handful of Europeans had ever been.

'The only trading we English are allowed to carry on with the Chinese takes place in a tiny settlement just outside Canton, called Jackass Point, and then only for the six months of the tea trade season,' Lieutenant Lewis explained. 'Europeans aren't allowed any further inland than that, and even to go to Canton one needs special

permission from the Chinese authorities here in Macao.
We buy their tea in copious quantities—the Honourable
East India Company has a monopoly on that—and we
have to pay them in silver, or *sycee*, as the Chinese call
it. The Emperor insists that we Europeans have nothing
that the Chinese want or need. The arrogance of the
man! Do you know, our own King's ambassador to his
court, Lord Ambury, was expected to kow-tow to him—
that means he had to lie on his stomach and bang his
head three times on the floor, or some such rubbish. He
didn't, of course, which is why trade with this country
of backward heathens has remained in exactly the same
state as it was a hundred years ago. We can't deal with
them on anything like equal terms—our requests are
called petitions; we have to deal with a group of Chinese
business men called the Co-hong, and never with the
mandarins themselves... Dashed stupid set-up all
around.'

'Then why do the British stay here?' she asked.

'Oh, it's all still very lucrative, because of the opium
we smuggle in. That goes a long way towards evening
out the Honourable Company's balance sheet,' he explained. 'The Emperor has outlawed opium, but there
are hundreds of thousands of addicts in China, and we
British—and Americans and French—smuggle it in. It
helps to pay for the tea, you see.'

'Is it wise to so deliberately break the Emperor's laws
in his own country? Why does he not like this opium?'

Lieutenant Lewis shrugged carelessly. 'It's highly
addictive. Once a man—or woman—is dependent on it,
they live for nothing else. They don't bother eating,
working... whatever.' He saw her shocked face and
laughed. 'Why worry, Miss Perrault? The problem is the
Chinese Emperor's—and if he weren't so pig-headed
about letting in our English traders, he wouldn't have
the problem in the first place!'

'I see. So all this——' she indicated back towards the European quarter, with all its gracious gardens and opulent houses '—all this is built with money from opium?'

'A lot of it—I wouldn't go so far as to say all of it. There is a fair amount of bona fide trade as well.'

'And the Navy? Why are you here? What do you have to do with this place?'

He tucked her hand into his arm and began to lead her back the way they had come. 'We've nothing here but a convenient place to berth our ships in the Pacific, more's the pity; what this primitive country needs is a decent display of just what His Majesty's Navy can do. They've no navy to speak of themselves, and the entrance to the Pearl River—the main route to Canton—is guarded by the Bogue forts. The cannon in them are so old that when they fire them the balls just pop out and roll down the hill! No, the only way to open this country is to sail two or three ships of the line up the Pearl River and fire a few broadsides. That'd teach them not to call *us* barbarians!'

He mistook her stunned silence for lack of comprehension, and patted her hand in amused consolation. 'You must forgive me for boring you, Miss Perrault! We men tend to take these matters seriously, and I know you ladies don't like to hear about such tedious details! Let me show you the harbour now.'

She would have dearly loved to have learned a great deal more, but had to be content with what she had, rather than risk being thought unladylike by Lieutenant Lewis. She walked alongside him obediently, listening now with only half an ear to his inconsequential chatter, as she thought about what he had said. The arrogance of these English and their Navy seemed limitless! For there was no doubt in her mind but that Kit would concur with every single word the Lieutenant had uttered.

The harbour was crowded with many different vessels—from the small Chinese flat-boats the Lieutenant called 'junks' to the larger sloops and schooners of many trading companies. And among them all in the harbour, tall and graceful, rode the two ships of the line, the *Eagle* and the *Courageous*. The *Courageous* was being cleaned and there seemed to be men swarming all over her, up in the rigging and on scaffolding over the side. Had that ship ever been home to her? It seemed much bigger than she remembered, and now had the same vaguely ominous look of her sister ship. Jara suddenly realised why when she saw that the cannons had been refitted; the ship was no longer a home but a fighting machine once more.

She looked away from the sight and pointed out to Lieutenant Lewis three junks that were anchored a little way out from where they stood. They were covered with brightly coloured Chinese banners, and gaudily painted in red and gold. Even from where they stood, they could hear the sound of laughter and raised voices across the water.

'Flower boats,' Lieutenant Lewis explained. 'They're...ah...not quite legal in Macao, so they anchor just offshore.' Jara still didn't understand until a small window on the side of one of the boats opened and a Chinese girl called out something to them. One glance at the Lieutenant's amused face explained everything.

'I had better go back, I think,' she said quickly, and they turned and went back into the town. Jara thought to herself, not for the first time that day, that this place was not dissimilar to Kororareka after all. Better-dressed, of course, and more sophisticated, but no better under the surface. Perhaps, in a way, it was even worse for its dishonesty. It was not a comforting thought that the rest of the world—which she had so idealised from her little haven in Kororareka in the days of her childhood—would all be just like this. To her dismay, Lieutenant Lewis would not leave the subject of the flower boats alone.

'Dangerous places, of course—a man runs a high risk of ending the night in the water, with empty pockets and a knife in his back. Most sensible men go to the private houses on the shore, where there is less risk of contracting the pox...'

On and on he prattled, while she could only be grateful that the gathering dusk hid her scarlet face. She could not believe that this was the sort of topic on which a gentleman should converse with a lady. Kit would not have spoken to her of such things, but perhaps the Lieutenant was not a gentleman. Or—worse—the Lieutenant did not see her as being a lady. Embarrassment and fear of committing another social *faux pas* sealed her lips, and she listened to the Lieutenant's recital in stony silence.

Encouraged by her apparent acquiescence, and convinced that he had a captivated audience, the Lieutenant went on to describe in further details the more sordid side of life in Macao. None of what he told her would shock her, he knew—he had many times heard Kororareka called 'The hell of the Pacific'. Jara slid her hand from his arm on the pretext of adjusting her glove, and did not replace it, but he scarcely noticed, waxing large as he was on the perils and delights of Chinese mistresses.

On the doorstep of the Hatfields' house he took her hand again and put before her what he regarded as a quite irresistible offer. Then, in anticipation of a favourable response, he kissed her hand and quickly departed, very well pleased with his afternoon's work.

Eustacia had risen during her absence, and now she followed Jara anxiously into her bedroom. 'But you should have woken me, my dear! We have been so con-

cerned about you! Who have you been with? Where did
you go? Anything could have happened to you!'

'I assure you, Eustacia, I am very well, and nothing
has happened to me.' Jara drew off her gloves and threw
them on to the floor. She would wash them later, to
remove whatever taint Lieutenant Lewis had left on
them. 'Has the Captain bothered to come back yet?'

As if in answer to her question the front door crashed
open and she heard Kit demanding of Wei whether she
had returned. Then he strode into her bedroom, his face
so tight with rage that she instinctively took a step back.

'Where the hell have you been?'

'Out.'

'Out where? With whom? Answer me, you
little——'

'Captain!' Eustacia put her frail body between them.
'You can't come in here. This is Jara's *bedroom*! Now
will you please lower your voice and leave?'

'I will not!' he roared indignantly. 'Not until I find
out what this little tramp has been doing and with whom!
Now will you damned well tell me—*where have you
been?*'

He and Jara both side-stepped Eustacia at the same
time—he to grab Jara's arm, and she to swing a punch
at his jaw. Both missed as Eustacia fearlessly threw
herself between them again.

'Stop it! Both of you!' Eustacia cried, and as they
both ignored her she added helplessly, 'Not in Jara's
bedroom! It's not...decent!'

'Murder's not decent anywhere,' Kit said grimly. 'But
if it'll make you feel happier, Eustacia, we'll go into the
drawing-room. Come with me, Jara.' He seized her arm
and proceeded unsteadily down the hallway, with Jara's
teeth firmly embedded in his wrist. He slammed the
drawing room door closed behind them and wrung his
arm free. Her back hit the door and, momentarily

winded, she struggled for her breath, glaring at him as he glared back nursing his mangled wrist.

'Now,' he said at last. 'We'll start again. Where have you been, and with whom?'

'As you said to me this morning in this very room, Captain, it should mean nothing to you!' she spat back.

'And I also said to you that you are my responsibility. If you've been out whoring with God knows who——'

'How dare you? I have not! And it was Lieutenant Lewis, if you must know,' she said haughtily.

'Lewis! That popinjay?' Kit began, when there was a timid knock on the door and it began to open. 'Get out, blast you!' he bellowed and the door quickly shut again.

'I think that was Eustacia,' she said, horrified.

'I don't give a damn who it was!'

'But she is my chaperon!'

'You don't need a chaperon, you need a ball and chain! The moment I turn my back you seduce the first man fool enough to put his foot in the door.'

'He offered to show me Macao,' she spluttered.

'I'll bet he did. And just what else did he offer to show you?'

She bit back the angry words that sprang to her lips and instead drew herself up to stare at him with all the dignity at her command. 'If you insist on knowing, Captain, he has asked me to marry him.'

He stared at her in silence for a second and then threw his head back and roared with laughter. Perplexed, she could only stand and stare at him. This was not the reaction she had expected, nor hoped for. When he recovered his sobriety he went over to the dark, lacquered sideboard and poured two glasses of brandy. She shook her head when he offered one to her, and watched him warily as he sat down in the same chair he had occupied this morning. He was in control of that wild temper of his again, and she knew now he would be

sarcastic, hurtful. She would *not* give him the satisfaction of wounding her again!

He sipped his brandy and then held it up to the light,
admiring the golden liquid glimmering in the cut crystal.
'What makes you think Lewis proposed to you this
afternoon?' he said mildly. 'You know that your English
is a little...inadequate at times. Perhaps you
misunderstood.'

'I misunderstood nothing!' she said hotly. 'I know
what he asked me. Why should you find it so hard to
believe that a man would ask me to marry him?'

'I don't,' Kit said quietly. 'But his wife back in
England might.'

'Oh,' Jara said at last in a small voice. She sank down
into a chair. 'Are you sure? He said nothing about a
wife...'

'Or his two children, apparently.' Kit was still exam-
ining his brandy. 'What exactly did he say?'

She shook her head. 'Exactly? I cannot remember,
but his meaning was clear—I thought. He said he wanted
to provide for me...to protect me...' Her voice trailed
into silence as the realisation of what she was saying sank
in.

'Hmm.' Kit sat in silent contemplation of his drink,
while Jara began to feel very foolish indeed. Lieutenant
Lewis had seemed sincere enough in his murmured
endearments and ambiguous promises on the doorstep.
She had not contemplated what she had taken to be his
offer of marriage for an instant, of course—the man
made her very flesh crawl. But she had hoped to use it
as a weapon against Kit some time, to make him realise
that at least one other man found her desirable. His
amusement made her humiliation even more acute.

But he was not smiling when he spoke again. 'Now
that you know the true value of Lieutenant Lewis's offer,
are you prepared to take it?' He ignored her outraged

denial to continue, 'Because if you are, you can do a great deal better than Lewis.'

'Can I, indeed?' she demanded. 'And just who did you have in mind? Yourself, perhaps? Or do you prefer the flower boats?'

'The flower boats?' he repeated incredulously. 'How the hell did you hear about those? Or did the gallant Lieutenant's tour of Macao extend to more than the purely cultural attractions?'

'He took the time to show me Macao—which is more than you have done! We simply happened to see the flower boats, and I was most interested to hear how you stiff and oh, so proper English officers spend your time when you are not ordering floggings and terrorising your men.'

He raised one eyebrow in surprise. 'Good Lord—how the venom drips from its little fangs! So that's what you think of us, is it?'

'That is what I know to be the truth, Captain Montgomery.' She stared at him directly, refusing to be cowed by the nasty glint in his eyes, and after a moment he shrugged carelessly.

'Think what you like of us, damn you—we're the best Navy in the world. I don't feel the slightest need to prove that to a common whaler's woman.'

She swallowed hard, her hands clenched into tight fists as she struggled to keep her temper in the face of such provocation. 'I will not stay here and listen to this abuse, Captain. But I will forgive you—you are simply ignorant. Ignorant and...arrogant! You think that nothing in the world exists beside your precious Navy...'

'Unlike your Lieutenant, I suppose?'

'Yes, unlike Lieutenant Lewis. At least he can talk about something other than his profession! And besides—what is it to you if he should want to protect me? Are you jealous?' she shot at him.

'Me? Jealous? Hell, no! Lewis is welcome to you—
you're too damned expensive for me!'

'Aah!' She sat bolt upright with delight at this evidence
of his miserliness. 'So you have received the bill for my
dresses?'

'I had a visit from Madame Fouchard, worried about
whether I'd pay for all the clothes you ordered this
morning. I must say a thousand guineas is a little on the
extravagant side, Jara.'

'Good! So you are ruined? Or have you cancelled my
order?'

He smiled blandly. 'No, I'm not exactly ruined, and
I haven't cancelled your order. I'm just curious to know
what you're going to do with all those dinner-gowns in
a nunnery. Are you going to tear them up for bandages?
Silk isn't the most absorbent of materials—you should
have ordered more cotton.'

'Indeed? Then I shall do so tomorrow, Captain
Montgomery,' she said sweetly. 'But now I am not so
sure that I will be leaving for France, after all. There is
so much to see here that I will stay for a while, I think.'

He shrugged. 'Then at least you'll be the best-dressed
whore in Macao. You've certainly come a long way from
the rags you wore when you were touting for business
in Kororareka.'

With a hiss of rage she flew at him, her fingers curved
into claws to rake his hated face open. Caught by surprise, he threw his arm up to protect himself, and the
crystal glass smashed on the wooden floor. He fought
off her efforts to rip his face in silence, the only sound
that of Jara's gasped curses, until Kit twisted her arm
hard up behind her back and she gave a small scream
of pain. He released her at once and stood looking down
on to the top of her bowed head, an expression of shame
that she could not see on his face.

'I've never laid a violent hand on a woman in my life,' she heard him mutter, 'but you . . . oh, Christ, Jara, why do you do this to me?'

She looked up, blinking back the tears stinging in her eyes. 'Why do you hate me so much?' she countered.

'Hate you? Jara . . .' He broke off helplessly. His hand came up to trace the outline of her lips. Suspiciously, she flinched away at first, and then stood still under his caress. Then he bent his head and gently kissed her, his arms slowly encircling her waist to pull her against him. She made no effort to resist, indeed after a moment she slid her hands up over his arms and around his neck. How tender he could be, how gentle! He had never kissed her quite like this before, had never held her quite like this . . . All the anger and hatred in her had evaporated at that first sweet touch of his hands. This was the way it should be! This was the way it should always be!

When he raised his head she smiled up at him, but his face was grave. He released her in one motion and stepped back. 'It's getting late. I've got to go out again. I'm sure Eustacia has had dinner kept for you.'

She watched him walk towards the door, trying to make sense of his words. What had just happened? Dinner was the very last thing on her mind at that moment, but she was too unsure as to her own emotions to say so. He paused in the doorway, and when he spoke again, his voice was tight and controlled. 'There's a French ship in port, Jara. I've made arrangements with the Captain for you to be on it when it leaves in two days' time.'

She had still not thought of anything to say when the door clicked shut behind him.

She spent a long and wakeful night, and when she arose late the next morning she knew exactly what she had to do. Kit had already left for Sir Walter's house, and a reproachful Eustacia was the only one that she had to face across the breakfast table. She sat docilely, appearing to listen to her poor chaperon's outpourings and advice, but with her mind on other things completely. The last piece of her plot fell neatly into place when she spied a letter sitting on the table near Eustacia's elbow.

'What is that?' she asked when Eustacia had paused for breath.

'Oh, this?' Eustacia sighed and picked it up. 'I believe it is an invitation for Kit to attend a dinner party tonight at the Meads'. They are with the Honourable Company, and I understand that Mrs Mead knows the Captain's family well. Have you been listening to *anything* I've been saying, Jara?'

'Yes, everything,' Jara assured her. 'May I see the invitation please?' She studied it carefully. 'It says "and partner".'

'That is just a matter of form. I don't expect the Captain will go, at any rate.' Convinced now that she had been wasting her breath, Eustacia began to irritably butter her bread.

'But he has not declined the invitation?'

'No, I don't think so. Not yet...' Light dawned suddenly and Eustacia looked at her charge sternly. 'You couldn't go, Jara—you couldn't possibly! What are you thinking of?'

'But why not? You have said yourself that my table manners are as good as anyone else's, and I have the clothes to wear. I don't think the Captain would be so ashamed to take me now.'

'With a little more instruction, I do think you would pass unremarked, yes,' Eustacia admitted. 'But Jara, people can be so very unkind sometimes—your background is known to everyone here now, and ... I cannot think you would enjoy yourself.'

Jara stared at her unflinchingly. 'I am not ashamed of my background, and the circumstances under which I came here are not of my making. Why should everyone think that I am not a good woman? I have you to chaperon me, and Kit is not ashamed of me.'

'My dear, Kit is different from many others. He has always been...well, he has always done what he thought to be the right thing, irrespective of what others thought. It is what made him such a successful commander during the recent wars and—from what I can gather—that is why he is in such difficulties with the Admiralty now. But he comes from an excellent family...'

Jara shrugged. 'And what is "an excellent family"? What exactly does that mean? That they have money?'

'Well, yes, but they have more than that.' Eustacia tried to think of how to explain the intricacies of the English caste system to such an innocent and finally had to admit defeat. 'He is the only son and as such has considerable responsibilities,' she ended by saying. 'When he marries, he will have to marry a woman who...understands those responsibilities.'

'And not a penniless savage?'

Eustacia could not bring herself to answer and they sat in silence for a time, Jara still intently studying the engraved invitation in her hand. At last she sighed and put it down.

'I am going to go to this dinner party, Eustacia. Will you accept this invitation for us? And then I would like you to tell me again how one acts at these affairs. How we will be served, what we will eat, how to eat it...everything.'

'Jara——' Eustacia began, but Jara shook her head stubbornly.

'No. I have decided. Kit tells me that I will leave here in two days' time, and before I go I would like to do this. Please, Eustacia—it is very important to me.'

Eustacia sat twisting her hands together distractedly, her poor face a picture of indecision, and Jara allowed herself to relax. That was Eustacia's objections taken care of. Now all that remained was to convince Kit. And then . . . she pressed her hand over her stomach to quell the sudden quiverings of nervousness at what she had to do. But she had made her decision, and she would not turn back now; even Kit Montgomery had no power to change what was inevitable.

Which was precisely what Kit was thinking at that very moment, although for entirely different reasons.

He was in his godfather's sitting-room again, but this time the secretary's presence had been replaced by that of Admiral Lord Buckler, the second most highly ranking member of the Admiralty, and the formerly benevolent atmosphere had been replaced with one that was distinctly censorious. This was the day of reckoning that Kit had dreaded for many months.

Christ, he hadn't felt like this since he was a schoolboy being caned for not learning his Latin declensions, Kit thought uneasily. Although he'd have settled for the canings any day—this protracted procedure was infinitely more painful. And infinitely more serious.

Admiral Buckler laid down the copy of Kit's report on the desk before him and looked thoughtfully at it in silence. The old fox has read that at least once before I walked into the room, Kit thought, curbing his irritation. These theatrics weren't his usual style—so what the hell did he have up his devious sleeve this time?

The Admiral cleared his throat. 'Well. A sorry tale, isn't it, Captain? Have you anything further to add?'

'No, sir.'

Admiral Buckler leaned back in his chair, and made a steeple with his fingers. There was another long silence. 'I must say how very disappointed I am to read this report. Very disappointed indeed. You've broken all the rules in the book, young man. And made some serious errors of judgement, as well.'

'Yes, sir.' Now tell me something I *don't* know, Kit thought.

'I remember hearing last year that you were planning to resign your commission soon—due to your father's failing health, I believe? So it would seem that the only question remaining for us to answer is whether you leave the Naval service in disgrace or with your reputation intact. And I think there can be no argument but that yours has been a particularly fine career up until this unfortunate incident, hasn't it?'

He did not seem to expect an answer, and Kit did not volunteer one. He found himself wishing heartily that the old man would stop playing games and get to the ultimatum he was obviously going to put before him. The Admiral cleared his throat again. 'I have also read the papers you were ordered to deliver to me on Norfolk Island. Are you familiar with their contents?'

'Yes, sir.'

'Then would you kindly acquaint Admiral Ashley with the information?' When Kit hesitated he added impatiently, 'Yes, I know what your orders were. But it is important that the Admiral knows—he can be of invaluable assistance in this matter.'

'Very well, sir.' Kit took a deep breath. 'There's been considerable concern in London about the activities of a certain group of smugglers operating from Canton. One of the reasons the Emperor is so adamantly against the import of opium is that it has been known to destroy the morale of entire armies, and that is something the Emperor can't afford—not with the outbreaks of rebellion against the mandarin rulers which he has frequently to deal with. We—the Admiralty—have evidence that a group, funded by at least one of the largest opium traders here in Macao, is smuggling European armaments up the waterways of the Pearl River, under the guise of opium, in order to encourage open armed revolt against the mandarins.'

'Good heavens!' Sir Walter exclaimed. 'But who would be so irresponsible? If the Chinese authorities ever found out, we'd have an instant war on our hands!'

'A war which many traders would welcome, sir, because an English victory would be inevitable and effortless. Fortunately, the Admiralty and the more responsible traders, like the Honourable Company, believe that China should be opened by diplomacy, not guns, and they want to avoid a war at all costs. My orders were to meet Admiral Buckler on Norfolk Island with this information, and then accompany him to Macao to intercept a shipment of these arms which we knew would be leaving Amsterdam for Macao this year.'

'Yes, on the *Dolores*,' Admiral Buckler added. 'She's in port right now. And she hasn't unloaded her cargo on to the *lorcha* to go upriver yet.'

Despite everything, Kit could not stop the smile of relief that crossed his face. 'Thank heavens! Then we have time to stop them!'

'We have the time, Captain Montgomery. But we're not going to stop them.'

The smile faded from Kit's face as he had a sudden sinking feeling in his stomach. Here we go, he thought. 'Sir?'

The Admiral looked at him consideringly. 'You speak Chinese, I hear? And are familiar with the navigation of the Pearl River?'

'I speak a very little Cantonese, and I once helped to escort an ambassadorial party to the city of Canton,' Kit said carefully. 'But I believe very few Europeans engaged in legal trade have gone any further upriver than that.'

'And would *you* be prepared to go further than that? To go as far upriver as it takes in order to find out just who it is at the heart of this smuggling ring?' The Admiral looked at Kit's tense face. 'Do you understand what I am asking you to do?'

Kit nodded slowly. 'I think so. The helmsman on the *Dolores* was the one who gave us the information in the first place. What you are proposing is that the crew be arrested and a new crew installed on the *lorcha* and that the helmsman—and I—take it up the Pearl River to meet whoever it is who is expecting the cargo.'

'Exactly,' the Admiral confirmed. 'A sound enough plan, I think. But I see you disagree.'

Kit shook his head. 'Sir, I'm a six-foot-tall, fair-haired Englishman! Even the best disguise in the world isn't going to make me look Chinese! And if I were captured, or even seen...'

'You would have to be very careful that you weren't. This would not be an official mission, Captain—you must understand that you cannot allow yourself to be taken, under any circumstances. But we must have a trustworthy Englishman making this journey, because the worst thing in the world that we could anticipate is that there is another European somewhere up the Pearl River waiting for the delivery of these arms. That would mean war between China and the European states and— although that is what many people want—it would also be most inadvisable. At this time at least.' He leaned back and watched Kit carefully.

Kit closed his eyes and waited for the cold current of fear running through him to pass and for reason to take over again. He understood this ultimatum very well indeed. To turn it down, and be dishonourably discharged was unthinkable. And if he took it—well, at least he would die a Naval officer. 'I'm damned if I do and damned if I don't,' he thought aloud.

'Kit, my boy, you don't have to do this.' His god-father, who had remained quiet through most of the proceedings, spoke now, his kindly face furrowed with concern.

'I rather think he does,' Admiral Buckler said quietly. 'Don't you, Captain?'

Kit took a deep breath. 'Yes, sir.' Taking such an absurdly suicidal mission was a once-in-a-lifetime act—an act which would at least go part way to erase the memory of what had happened in New Zealand. And in a strange way, he would not rest easy until he had achieved that. 'Yes, sir,' he repeated. 'I do.'

They spent an hour in thoroughly discussing the plan after that—the *Dolores* would unload unimpeded and be allowed to return to Amsterdam, where the owners would be easily traced. The *lorcha*—a small boat with a Western-style hull and Chinese rigging—would be intercepted shortly after, and the crew replaced with Chinese hand-picked and well-paid by the Admiralty. The unloading was expected to take place the following day, and so Kit was advised to go home to rest and prepare himself.

After he had left, Sir Walter turned to the Admiral.

'With respect, sir, I really can't agree with your hand-ling of this matter! He is a fine young man, and his war record was unsurpassed.'

'Yes, yes, we know all that—but young officers like Captain Montgomery need a challenge, even in peace-time. This is a crucial situation, and we could think of no one better to entrust with this mission.'

'I see.' Sir Walter's face was flushed with anger. 'So this was a plot hatched in London even before young Kit took possession of those orders? You had always intended using him in just this way? What would have happened if he hadn't lost the crew of the *Courageous*, eh? How would you have persuaded him then?'

'Captain Montgomery is a professional. He will always follow orders,' Admiral Buckler said sharply. 'What happened in New Zealand was unfortunate—but it was probably also unavoidable, and he did a superb job in recovering the ship. But it simply wouldn't do to let *him* know that. Would it?'

CHAPTER NINE

DUSK was falling by the time Kit let himself quietly into the Hatfields' house. In the drawing-room the scent from the flowers in the overgrown garden was so heavy as to be almost intoxicating, and he went to the window and breathed in deeply. The air was so soft here; fragrant and sensuous, but still with the salt tang of the sea underneath. Across the roofs of the houses, down in the darkening harbour, he could just make out the navigation lamp on the top of the *Courageous*'s main mast, and he watched it steadily for a while as it rocked slowly from side to side in the currents of the evening tide.

He heard the door being opened quietly, and then the swish of skirts coming across the polished floor. He had half hoped that Jara would still be angry after his parting words to her—her anger was always easier to resist than her pleading—but her upturned face, pale in the twilight, was unexpectedly serene. How sweet she could be sometimes, he thought. And how very beautiful. Her skin looked invitingly smooth and he had to make an effort to keep his hand by his side, instead studying and trying to commit to memory her delicate features and her wide, vividly blue eyes. But he somehow completely missed the determined set to her smile.

'Can I pour you a drink? It is brandy that you like, is it not?' Even that maddening accent was seductive, he thought, and as she walked past him he was aware of the clean scent of her hair and skin. Now the urge to touch her again, one last time, suddenly became overwhelming.

'No, thank you,' he heard himself say. 'I need to keep a clear head tonight.'

'Oh?' She turned from the sideboard and looked at him curiously. 'Why is that? Are you going somewhere?'

He shook his head, wishing that he could tell her. But he knew that that would be as impossible as trying to explain the way he was feeling tonight. How could he even begin to explain the deep calm, the unreality of what he was feeling? Over the years he had seen it a thousand times on the faces of his gunners as they squatted beside their cannons waiting for him to give the order to fire; each of them knowing they could have a few seconds, a few hours, or a lifetime still to live. A man might squander his time on earth away, but when death faced him suddenly each moment of life became so infinitely precious that every breath became a benediction. One's heartbeat slowed, and time itself seemed to tremble and pause. At such times the air was sweeter, the English oak of the deck beneath one's feet a solid reminder of home and loved ones... Another fighting man would understand all this, but not Jara. And at such times Kit was aware that—as much as any other man—he was emotionally vulnerable. He must give Jara no reason to suspect that anything tonight was different.

She went and sat on the chaise-longue, arranging the skirts of her yellow, flounced silk gown carefully around her. The effect was not lost on Kit.

'I see Madame Fouchard has been busy. You look...most attractive.'

She glanced up at him in surprise; it was unlike him to offer unsolicited compliments, even such stilted ones, but she could sense that he was in a strange mood this evening. She had not expected him to be still angry with her; he was a man whose rage would flare up explosively, but who could not nurture and brood over that anger. Indeed, she had been counting on the fact that he would have calmed down after their most recent fight, but this courteous detachment he was displaying tonight was something new to her. Presumably it was because he was looking forward to farewelling her from Macao soon. Well, she could only hope that her carefully laid plans for tonight did not go astray.

'Thank you.' She lowered her head and her eyelashes in order to impart an impression of demure femininity while at the same time making it impossible for him to read her expression. That alone should have alerted him, but tonight the soft enchantment of the evening and Jara's beguiling nearness had made him drop his guard. He waited with an indulgent smile for her to speak again. She took a deep breath.

'Kit, we have been invited to a dinner party tonight, at the Meads' house. I hope you don't mind that I...I have accepted the invitation.' She heard his intake of breath and pressed on hurriedly to forestall his inevitable protest. 'I have only another day in Macao, after all, and I would so very much like to go. I have been practising table manners all day long, and I have the most beautiful dress to wear, and...oh, Kit——' she looked up at him with her most appealing expression '—*please* take me with you!'

The last thing he had wanted to do that night was to mix with other people, but for once the imploring look on her face made him hesitate. It would cost him very little effort to take her out tonight, and the Meads were a very pleasant couple, who would certainly try to make her feel welcome. On the other hand, he had no idea who else might be there, and he did not want Jara to be subjected to any more humiliation.

Jara, watching his face carefully and so seeing the conflict within him, went on, 'And poor Eustacia has gone to bed again, with the megrim. But she thought that it was an excellent idea that I go tonight,' she added quickly.

His raised eyebrows indicated that he thought that that was highly unlikely, but all he said was, 'Poor Eustacia, indeed. I hope there is no serious underlying cause of all these megrims she is prone to.'

'I . . . I think that it is us.' She gave him a small, rueful smile. 'Every time we argue—or even when she thinks we will argue—she is stricken. I feel . . . very guilty about that. And that is why I would like her to know that we are friends once more. I will be leaving here in a day or two. I may never again have an opportunity to wear my beautiful dress and see how your people live. Please, Kit, please take me! After all, after tonight . . . we may never see each other again.'

An odd expression flitted over his face and then, much to her surprise, he lifted her fingers to his lips.

'Very well, then, if you are sure that you really want to go.'

'Thank you!' She jumped up and put her arms around his neck, pressing her face lightly against his. 'I will be only a minute, I promise you!' And with a swirl of her skirts she was bounding out of the room in a manner of which Eustacia Ashley would most certainly not have approved.

Kit raised his hand to his face and touched the place where her cheek had rested. For once she had been right—this was his last night with her and after to-morrow he would never see her again. How many times over these past three months had he wanted to touch her, had started to reach out to her, only to remember who he was and why he could not have her? This after-noon his godfather had made some passing but mean-ingful reference to one of Macao's houses of entertainment, a clean and discreet place where Kit knew many of the other officers went for a game of cards or

a sociable drink. There were other amenities available
too, if one requested them, and for a second he was
tempted—perhaps after the dinner... But he had rarely
had to resort to such places before, and the thought of
taking an anonymous woman repelled him. There was
only one woman he wanted, and at this moment she was
busily putting on her best dress, as excited as a little girl
preparing for a birthday party. She was so very young
and innocent of the world... and he would be leaving
her completely unprotected, save for the generous
endowment he had arranged to be left for her on his
departure. And, with her seemingly limitless enthusiasm
for spending money, he had no idea how long that would
last her. The philosophical calm which had held him
earlier had by now vanished, and it was with a heavy
heart that he retired to dress himself.

Jara stared at her reflection in the great carved mirror
over the dressing table and frowned. Her evening dress
was little short of a work of art, in the peacock-blue silk
she had had to fight so hard for and which suited her
colouring so well. It fell and clung in all the right places,
and emphasised all the curves she wanted to bring to
Kit's attention. But why did she not look any older? She
twisted her plait into a bun on the top of her head and
frowned again at the mirror. No, it was no good—she
still looked like a schoolgirl.

She released her plait with a sigh. Tonight it was essential that she looked sophisticated and beautiful and
completely irresistible. If she failed to seduce Kit by the
morning, then she could say goodbye to any chance of
him changing his mind, and no amount of begging or
screaming from her would stop him from putting her on
that ship to France. But if she succeeded, she knew that
all would be well. For all his harshness she knew very
well that Kit possessed a strong streak of chivalry—and
had she not once before successfully appealed to that

very trait in him? She was convinced that he would not abandon her once he felt guilty about seducing her. And she most certainly *would* make him feel guilty!

She took one last, long look at herself. The only flaw in her plan was her own attitude to it. Could she go through with it? She knew the mechanics of the act—had seen it in all its brutal ugliness time and again in Kororareka—and knew that it would not be a comfortable thing to endure. But Kit was not a brutal man, and she trusted him. For a moment she remembered that other time when she had briefly lain with him, and then she shook her head at her reflection. She had to forget that night. Then it had been he who had done the seducing, and she who allowed herself, helpless and senseless with desire, to be used for his pleasure. This time she knew more than to allow herself to be made a fool of again. This time *she* would be in control. Like the women of Kororareka she had to use a man, use his lust for her own purposes, because her very future depended on it. She took a deep breath. Yes, she could do it. She *had* to do it.

She was ready before Kit, waiting for him in the sitting-room, and she could not stifle the audible gasp that escaped her as he walked in. He was in full dress uniform: an epauletted dark blue jacket, gold-laced shirt, white breeches and highly polished boots. He was scowling when he came in, concentrating on buckling on a small ceremonial sword at his side. Thus attired he looked far more the stern, unbending commander than the libidinous victim of her plans, and for one dreadful moment she despaired of ever managing to seduce such a paragon of propriety. Then he looked up and smiled at her, and she promptly regained all of her lost confidence at the open admiration on his face.

'Lovely, Jara. Absolutely lovely.'

She swirled around to show off her dress and then tugged on her plait anxiously. 'I was not sure about my hair. Eustacia said I could put it up, but I am not sure how to do it...'

'Mmm.' Kit finished buckling his sword. 'Go and get a brush and some hairpins, and I'll see what I can do.'

She did as he said, and then stood still as he undid her plait and brushed her hair. Then with a few deft twists he piled it on top of her head and secured the roll with the pins. She peeped out from under her hair at her reflection.

'Kit—that is wonderful! How did you learn to do that?'

He took the last pin out of his mouth and pushed it into her hair. 'A combination of knowing my sailor's knots and being forced to watch my sisters forever at each other's hair. And if you ever tell a living soul about this, I'll wring your neck! Now, shake your head.' She obliged, and her hair stayed intact in a heavy, surprisingly elegant roll on the top of her head. 'Good. I think we're ready at last.'

His hands were on the nape of her neck, tucking away a few stray wisps of hair, and she turned around to face him.

'Thank you, Kit,' she said softly. He did not at once remove his hands, and she moved a fraction closer, throwing her head back and lowering her lashes, in the same look that had driven Moody to such a frenzy. Her lips were only inches from his, tempting him. There was a moment's silence.

'That's quite effective, Jara. Keep practising and you'll soon be able to stun a man at forty paces.'

She opened her eyes and bit down hard on the retort that sprang to her lips. Instead she managed to smile sweetly. 'Thank you, Kit. I always value your opinion. Now—shall we go?'

The sardonic smile was back on his lips, but she was well used to that. She kept the conversation light and inconsequential as they set off to walk the short distance to the Meads' house through the warm, scented night. After a while she slipped her hand from his arm down to his fingers, and held them lightly. He did not, she noted with satisfaction, try to withdraw his hand.

The Meads' home was as large as the Ashleys' house, but with the added attraction of a staircase. Jara had to resist the temptation to run up and down the stairs, and instead stood meekly as Mr and Mrs Mead welcomed them to their home. If the couple were surprised to see her there, they did not show it in any way, and indeed Mrs Mead took her by the arm to lead her to the sitting-room in a gesture of friendliness that touched Jara. There were two other couples dining with them that night and, well schooled by Eustacia, Jara greeted them correctly, speaking only in response to their questions. They all seemed to know about her background—Eustacia had been quite correct about the Macao gossips!—but in no way gave any hint of censure. She was aware of Kit at her side, ready to deflect any difficult or unpleasant comments, but to her pleased surprise there were none. Instead she was kept busy answering their questions about New Zealand, and no reference at all was made as to the manner in which she had left that country.

Perhaps not all the English were as unfriendly as she had at first assumed, she thought as she took her seat at the dinner table later. Dear Eustacia was very sweet, after all, and Mrs Mead seemed kind, and the Holbrooks and the Frasers were most civil... She caught Kit looking at her enquiringly across the table and smiled reassuringly.

Her confidence was not even shaken by the varied array of strange and exotic courses put before her. Eustacia had taken the precaution of sending one of the

Chinese servants—who turned out to be a distant re-
lation of the Meads' cook—to discreetly find out what
the menu for that night was, and she and Jara had prac-
tised for hours at an imaginary dinner table. Soup,
asparagus, an entrée of poached fish, meat with vegetables she was unfamiliar with...

The only difficult part of the evening came when she
was trying to surreptitiously deduce what sort of meat
was on her plate. It smelt delectable, and looked as pale
as chicken meat, but the texture was different.

Seeing her interest, Mrs Mead leaned forward. 'It is
pork, Miss Perrault—suckling pig, to be exact. Our
Chinese cook prepares it in the most delicious way imag-
inable. Have you ever tasted pork before?'

'Oh, yes,' Jara nodded. 'Twice, I think, and I do like
it. The Maoris say that it is just like human flesh, and
almost as good.'

She felt a slight pressure against her foot and looked
across at Kit in surprise. But he appeared to be concentrating on the conversation of Mrs Fraser, and she wondered if it had been accidental.

'Is that right?' Mrs Mead was saying faintly. 'The
Maoris, you say? They are a very fierce people, I believe.'

'Yes, they are.' Jara speared the pork with her fork
and began to cut it. 'There are no native animals in New
Zealand to eat for meat, and so they eat each other.
They killed my parents, you know, but they did not eat
them. At least, I don't think so.'

The pressure on her foot turned into a definite kick,
and this time Kit's brows were drawn into a disap-
proving frown. Too late she remembered Eustacia's
admonition to keep the conversation on subjects that
could not possibly cause offence or distress. One look
at her hostess's face showed her that she had unwittingly
given both, and she subsided into a miserable silence,
her face scarlet. Kit broke the silence which had fallen

over the table with an anecdote about someone and somewhere she had never heard of, and conversation either side of her was quickly resumed. Within a few seconds it was as if she had never made a gaffe, but she decided to play it safe at any rate, and said nothing more than a few carefully agreeable words for the rest of the meal.

She ate very little of the food before her—partly on Eustacia's instructions and partly because her appetite had rapidly diminished with her embarrassment. But with each course a different wine was served, and Eustacia had neglected to say anything about this. A dry white wine with the entrées, a rich red wine with the meats... Jara loved looking at the ornate crystal glasses lined up beside her plate and, although she usually felt most uncomfortable having servants waiting on her, she was intrigued by the silent, unobtrusive manner in which her glass was filled at soon as she emptied it. By her fourth glass of wine she did not feel quite so bad about her comments to Mrs Mead any more, and everyone else at the table seemed to have forgotten it. Besides, the previously rather tedious conversation of Captain Fraser beside her was becoming most amusing. She found herself giggling helplessly at his account of Macao's last typhoon and—while he did not seem in the least put out—she decided against having any more to drink. Like Kit, she needed a clear head tonight.

She kept to her resolution until the pies, custards and syllabubs were served, together with a sparkling wine served in an exquisite flute-shaped glass. Champagne! She had heard of it before, but had never had the opportunity to try it. She took just a little sip, and the mouthful of delicious bubbles slipped down her throat so quickly that she simply had to finish the glass. Surely, she reasoned, something that tasted so light and heavenly could not be intoxicating? Then her glass always seemed to be full, and she became so absorbed in the engaging conversation around her that she forgot all about not drinking any more wine.

Her eyes kept coming to rest on Kit's face across the table, wavering slightly in the heat from the candles set in the ornate centrepiece of fruit, flowers and silver candelabra. She liked the way Kit's new short hairstyle emphasised the clean square lines of his jaw. She even thought she could become used to his uniform after all— the very dark blue suited his fairness, and it had to be admitted that the cut of the jacket showed his broad shoulders very well... She rested her chin on her hand and gave a little sigh. She had never seen a man she thought half so handsome as Kit Montgomery, and she rather doubted that she ever would. Greatly daring, she put out a foot and touched his boot under the table, and was a little disappointed that he did not respond.

At last Mrs Mead stood up. 'Ladies?' she said, looking around the table. Jara remembered what she was supposed to do now and went to stand up to join the rest of the women.

Nothing happened. She pushed against the arms of the chair, leaned forward... but still she could not make her legs obey her! Horrified, she stared across the table at Kit.

She saw his mouth tighten as he comprehended her dilemma in an instant, and he was at once on his feet, apologising for having to hurry away, and pleading an onerous day on the morrow. His hand under her arm propelled her up from the table and out into the hallway, while she mumbled her scattered farewells to the startled faces of her hosts and their guests, and before she realised it they were out on the street again.

'For God's sake, Jara!' Kit muttered as the door closed behind them. 'I hardly expected you to get blind drunk at your first dinner party! What the hell did you think you were doing putting away all that wine? You must have had at least four glasses of the champagne alone.'

Far from terrifying her, his glowering face sent her instead into a fit of giggles and she had to clutch his jacket for support as she almost fell over.

'I am sorry,' she managed to gasp out at last. 'Was I so very bad? Did the Meads mind so much?'

'You were atrocious, and I doubt that anyone there was able to enjoy their pork after your little speech,' he said severely, but there was a tremor in his voice which gave him away.

'Ah! You are not so angry!' she cried in delight. 'You do forgive me!'

'I do no such thing,' he protested. 'What you did was quite unforgivable. And you've provided Macao with enough gossip to keep them occupied for a month!'

'Kit, you are so sweet when you are being pompous!' She gave him an affectionate push on the shoulder, rather too hard, and came close to falling over again. With a martyred look to the heavens, Kit grasped her firmly around the waist and began to march her back home. There were few people around, and it was so dark in any case that no one passing them would have thought anything amiss unless they heard Jara's muffled laughter every time she missed her footing and fell against Kit's arm. Their progress was slow, and when it began to rain lightly, Kit impatiently bent to swing her over his shoulder.

'Kit! Put me down!' she gasped, halfway between horror and hilarity.

'Stay still or I damned well will, and you'll spend the night sleeping it off in a ditch! And if you tear my epaulette...' She was no featherweight, and while regaining his balance he crashed into a neighbouring fence and swore. Jara pounded weakly on his back with her fists.

'Language, Captain! You must not say those bad words in front of a lady!'

'Lady? What lady? Now, will you stop screaming like that and let me concentrate on getting home.'

She was quite damp by the time they got to the front door, and her head felt heavy from her upside-down position, but she hardly noticed. She put her hands over her mouth to smother her giggles as Kit tried to man-oeuvre her skirts through the entrance.

'Sssh!' he hissed as he closed the door. 'Or you'll wake Eustacia, and she'll want to know why you're entering the house backwards. Can you stand now?'

'No—you will have to put me in my bedroom!' she replied in a stage whisper.

Trying to tiptoe in his heavy boots, Kit made it to her room without alerting any of the servants, and shut the door behind them. 'Now . . .'

'Put me on the bed.'

He sighed heavily and strode over to her bed and threw her down on it without any formalities. He would have left then, but she reached up and grasped his lapels. 'I have torn your epaulette. I am sorry—I will sew it up in the morning.'

'Don't worry about it. Just have a good night's rest and sleep it off.' He stayed leaning over her for a moment. A single lantern had been lit and placed on the camphor chest at the foot of the bed, and it threw out long pale gold fingers of light across the room. Kit's face was in shadow, but she could see that he was no longer smiling. 'Goodnight,' he said at last, abruptly, and began to move away.

'Kit?' She took a firmer grip of his jacket and pulled him down towards the bed. It was strange how quickly her head had become clear, but she had to feign intoxi-cation if she were to be able to later blame him for what would happen now. 'Please don't leave me tonight,' she whispered.

He did not answer. Outside she could hear the rain, heavier now, drumming on the roof and splashing softly on the leaves, and the room was filled with the sweet scent of damp vegetation. Scarcely daring to breathe, she raised her eyes from where her hands lay on his jacket up to his face.

Just as she had anticipated, she saw desire burning in his narrowed eyes—the same fierce need that had both frightened and enslaved her that night on the ship—and she felt a chill of apprehension run through her. What had she started? But as she put out a tentative hand to touch his face he turned his head so that his lips brushed her palm with the lightest of caresses, and she was aware with a great rush of relief that he was driven by more than purely physical hunger this time. He cared for her now, and that would make him all the more pliable. This time would be different.

'What are you playing at now, Jara?' he demanded suddenly, softly. 'What new game is this?'

She shook her head, not trusting herself to speak, but she held his eyes as she dropped her hand down to the stiff gold-laced cravat at his neck. Underneath that she undid one of his buttons and slid her fingers through the thick, curling hair of his chest. He made no effort to pull away, but she heard him catch his breath.

'You've had too much to drink——'

'No.' She shook her head again. 'Not so much. I know what I am doing, Kit. What I want...' She reached up and pulled his face down to hers, kissing him with delicate, exploratory kisses. His mouth was tense under hers at first, the muscles of his face hard and resisting. But then he suddenly groaned her name and pulled her roughly to him, his hands feverishly pulling aside the silk and lace of her clothing, and she knew that she had won. After her first shock she made herself respond to his demanding, hungry kisses with a fervour that was almost savage—he must not for a moment know that she did not really want this. She must lie there and receive his passion, satisfy his hunger, tolerate his hands and his body invading hers with such passion. She was aware that he was trying to hold back, to check himself, but she gave him no opportunity to do so and fiercely urged him on. She couldn't allow him the time to think, or to feel the resistance she was disguising with her compliant limbs and whispered words of passion. And besides, the more quickly it was over and done with...

And it was over quickly. She lay staring at the dark shadows on the ceiling with wide dry eyes, with Kit's weight on her and a dull pain where he had been. So this was it. Well, it had been no better than she had expected—and certainly no worse. She had succeeded in what she had so carefully planned—so why did she feel so angry and cheated? She listened to Kit's breathing as it slowed, and felt his fingers as they gently stroked her arm. She wanted to push him away, but it was too early. But after a moment she became aware of something digging uncomfortably in her side, and she wriggled away.

'You are hurting me,' she said petulantly.

Kit at once rolled away from her and looked down. He began to laugh shakily. 'It's my sword. Oh, hell...'

Furious that he should laugh at her at such a time, she quickly slid off the bed, pulling down the hopelessly crushed silk dress as she did so. She made her way unsteadily to the window and raised the blind; it was a pointless thing to do, but it gave her time to think, and she hoped that with her back turned he might decently leave. She could carry out the second part of her plan and reproach him in the morning, when she had gathered her thoughts. Hot tears stung her eyes as she stared unseeingly at the dark rain, and she could hear him moving around the room. He seemed to be taking a long time to leave, and when at last she turned around to say so it was to see him removing his very last article of clothing. She hurriedly turned back to the window.

'You can leave now! I...want you to leave.'

Instead she felt him move behind her and begin to unbutton her dress. She tried to shrug him away, but he persisted.

'I'm not leaving, Jara. Not now.'

'But you have what you wanted...'

'But you haven't, and that's my fault. I thought you were as ready as I was, but...' He paused for a moment before continuing gently, 'Jara, I don't know what all this was in aid of tonight—although I suppose I can guess—but I'm not leaving you like this.' His hands were on her bare shoulders, and his every touch seemed to irritate her skin intolerably. She shook herself free, and he began to unlace the bodice of her chemise.

'Please go away! I don't like you to...laugh at me!'

His hands stopped their wrestling with her laces and he turned her around to face him. 'I wasn't laughing at you! It's just that after waiting all these months—months of sharing a cabin with you, and even a bed on one occasion—I end up making love to you in a house full of servants and a chaperon, and in my full dress uniform! It's not...well, it's not how I had imagined our first time together to be.'

'You...had thought about this?' she demanded incredulously. 'About making love to me?'

'Of course I have. Many times, and far too often to be good for my health.' He grinned unexpectedly. 'Didn't you?'

She looked at him warily. She had expected him to be remorseful and guilty—he *had* to feel guilty!—but he seemed quite the opposite, and indeed even determined to repeat the whole distasteful procedure. His hands were sliding down over her shoulders to pull down her bodice and she grabbed his wrists.

'Stop it! I want you to go. This is finished.'

'No, this isn't finished. In fact, it hasn't even begun yet.' He easily ignored her restraining hand to trace a delicate pattern on her shoulder with the tip of one finger. 'How very beautiful you are, Jara. Like a white rose.' His fingers began to meander lower. 'And how soft your skin is here. And here...and here...' She caught her breath as his hands slipped beneath the material of her bodice to her breasts. She was aware of him watching her intently, but she could not hide the expression of dazed pleasure on her face any more than she could pull away from those wonderful, tantalising fingers. And when his fingers were replaced with his lips she did not pull away, but instead put out a wondering, exploratory hand of her own. His skin was warm and golden in the lamplight, with the hard muscle underneath. He felt so good to touch, and somehow it felt absolutely right that she should. The last of her resistance went as he pulled her against him, and she felt the power of her body's involuntary response to his surging through her. When he drew her back to the bed she found she could offer no protest at all.

And this time it was quite different.

The smallest movement of the bed disturbed her in the early hours of the morning, and she lay still for a moment, halfway between sleep and consciousness. She had fallen asleep in Kit's arms, with her back curled against his chest and their legs intertwined, and now she became aware that there was nothing but a warm depression in the bed behind her. When she opened her eyes it was to see him silently padding around the still-darkened room to where he had put his clothes the previous night.

Her short time with the whalers at Kororareka had left her with the opinion that a man in a state of partial or complete undress always looked a little ridiculous—without the trappings of uniform or weaponry, and with knock-knees or a pot-belly, even the most fearsome of men tended to look comically vulnerable. But such was not true of Kit. Even naked his lean, muscled, perfectly proportioned body looked authoritative. She had a sudden vision of him standing thus at the helm of his ship and had to bite hard on her pillow to choke off her laughter; she was sure that he would not find it funny.

Oh, but how wonderful she felt this morning! Her body told her that what had happened during the night had been real enough, but in the half-light of early dawn it seemed like some wonderful, strange dream, as if it had happened to another woman in another time. But it had been *her* name Kit had whispered again and again against her skin, and it had been she who had once cried out in ecstasy so loudly that Kit had had to put his hand over her mouth in case she woke the house up. They had laughed about that later, as she lay cradled against him. All night it seemed they had laughed, and loved...

She watched him picking up his breeches from the pile of clothes on the chair, and she was intrigued that even in the midst of last night's passion he could still be so neat. Usually his tidiness irritated her profoundly, but this morning she found it almost endearing. In fact, now she came to think about it, everything about him was endearing this morning. He glanced up and saw her peering at him over the coverlet.

'Er...good morning. I'm sorry if I woke you.' She was a little puzzled to see that he looked embarrassed. Surely he wasn't going to be prudish about her seeing him dress after what had taken place the previous night? She smiled and held back the coverlet invitingly.

'It isn't dawn yet—why don't you come back to bed for a little while longer?' He paused in his movements, his eyes dropping to her revealed breasts. She remembered the pleasure he had taken in them just hours before and her smile widened. 'Please come back to bed,' she whispered, confident now in her power to tempt him.

He looked away, and began to button his breeches. 'I've got to leave, I'm sorry,' he said abruptly.

'But why? No one will be awake for an hour or two yet. You can go back to your room then...'

He reached for his shirt. 'No. You don't understand. I've got to *leave*. This morning.'

Suddenly cold, she pulled the coverlet back over her and sat upright. 'What do you mean?'

'I've been given new orders, and I'm leaving this morning. I should have told you last night...'

'Yes, you should have,' she retorted, stung more by his cold tone and averted face than by the unbelievable things he was saying. 'It would have been rather more courteous to have told me last night before you seduced me!'

'*I* seduced *you*?' he said incredulously. 'That's not how I remember it! You literally dragged me into your bed——'

'I did not!' She pointed an accusing finger at his clothes on the chair. 'Look at those! You took those off yourself! How can you accuse me of raping you? You, who are always in command, and control, and who tells me what I should do and say and——'

'I'm not saying that you raped me, woman, for God's sake!' Kit said in exasperation. 'And I'd be the first one to admit that I've very little self-control over some things—and that includes you flaunting yourself the way you did last night!'

'So I am to blame because you wanted me!'

'Of course I wanted you!' he said between his teeth. 'After almost a year at sea I wanted a woman. Any woman. That it happened to be you is a complication I regret, but last night was entirely of your own doing! Presumably you thought you'd seduce me so that I wouldn't make you leave Macao, but it doesn't alter the fact that I have to leave now, and that I want you out of Macao on that ship tomorrow morning.'

'But...last night you said that...you loved me,' she said in a small voice, still unable to believe that he was saying these things to her. He *couldn't* have used her so—not Kit!

'Did I?' He pretended to try to remember before shrugging carelessly. 'I may well have done so in the heat of the moment—it is the polite thing to say in such situations, after all.'

She felt herself flushing with rage and humiliation, and dashed away a hot tear with the corner of the sheet. How could last night have meant such very different things to each of them? At some wonderful, magical moment during their lovemaking she had abandoned forever her carefully laid plans to make him feel responsible for her, so sure had she been that his passion for her was real and lasting. And now here he was, making her feel as stupid and as used as ever! Her head was swimming and she found it hard to collect her thoughts. 'I am not going to France,' was all she could think of to mutter truculantly. 'You cannot make me go.'

'Then go where you damned well want, as long as you leave Macao.' He looked at her in the rumpled bed, his face impassive. 'Obviously the nunnery is out of the question but now that you know a little more about life—and men—I'm sure you'll have no trouble finding an agreeable husband. In fact, after seeing how much you enjoyed last night, I'd suggest you find yourself a husband as quickly as possible. Perhaps Lieutenant Lewis wasn't as far off the mark about you as I'd thought.'

She struggled to keep her voice steady and her hands off his throat. 'How can I leave Macao? I have no money...'

'I've taken care of that. You'll be well enough provided for. And before I leave, I'll make further provision, in case there should be...complications from tonight.' He spoke tersely over his shoulder as he picked up his boots and the clothing still lying on the chair. He had almost reached the door when she leapt out of bed, dragging the coverlet around her.

'I want none of your filthy money! I would not touch a penny of it! And you can have all of the dresses back!'

'No, thanks—I doubt that any of them would fit me.' His hand was on the door-handle when he turned to face her. 'Look—I'm sorry that this is how we have to say goodbye, Jara. I wish...it had been different.'

'I am sure you do!' she screamed. 'How much easier for you had you been able to slink away like a dog in the night! I trusted you—I thought that you were different. But you're as bad as any of them! Just...get out! Get out of my sight!' She seized the nearest thing to hand, which was the heavy metal lamp at the foot of the bed, and Kit only just managed to get out before it hit the door. Small splinters of wood flew into the air, and a pool of oil began to form in a dark circle on the floor amid the smashed glass. On the other side of the door she could hear the muffled sounds of the servants moving about, and Eustacia's high voice raised in enquiry.

She didn't care any more; it didn't matter if everyone in Macao knew what had happened during the night. Suddenly weak and sick with the strength of her emotions she crawled back into the bed that still held the warmth of Kit's body, and pulled the covers over her head. The entire world could go to hell, and Kit Montgomery with it!

By mid-morning, she had cried herself out and then given herself a stern talking-to. She had made a severe mistake in misjudging the extent of Kit's affection for her. She had been foolish to think for even one moment that he was a man of honour—the memory of how he had been prepared to hand her over to the crew of the *Courageous* in the name of expediency was one she had conveniently forgotten. He had beguiled her into trusting him and then—the moment that he had taken what he wanted— he was off again.

It was fruitless to berate him in his absence, she decided. All that had happened had been but a lesson to be learned from, and now she must carefully reconsider her future. Retiring to the nunnery was—as Kit had said—now completely out of the question, as was staying here on Macao. Kit would return eventually, and she was most certainly not going to be here to be further demeaned and ridiculed.

At last she felt composed enough to pull on her clothes and leave her room. More than anything, she was dreading having to face Eustacia's disappointment in her. Jara found her in the garden, cutting flowers to bring inside, and she took a deep breath to steady herself before cautiously calling out.

'Eustacia...?'

The older woman looked up, and to Jara's relief she gave her a half-smile. 'Good morning, my dear. Are you feeling better? I thought it best that we leave you alone for a while.'

She handed Jara the flat basket filled with flowers, and the two women walked slowly down the garden path, dozens of large butterflies fluttering heavily out of their way as they stopped frequently to allow Eustacia to snip off the head of some particularly fetching bloom. The small garden was lushly overgrown with bouganvillaea, hibiscus and scarlet flame-of-the-forest, and above their heads birds twittered quietly in the rising, scented heat. By now Jara was able to identify some of them—there were a number of greenfinches, and one of the small fire-breasted flowerpeckers, and she could hear a mynah chattering to itself somewhere in the trees in the hills behind them. She remembered the *tuis* at Kororareka and suddenly felt a wave of nostalgia for her home. She was used to the muted greens and subtle scents of the New Zealand forest, and found herself mistrusting all this riotous lushness and vivid colour. It seemed that she belonged nowhere now.

She looked across at Eustacia's steady grey eyes and smiled ruefully. 'I had expected a lecture from you. Thank you for...not telling me how foolish I have been.'

Eustacia shook her head kindly. 'I hold myself at least partly to blame—I've been a shabby sort of chaperon, always ill in bed when I should have been giving you more guidance! And I don't intend giving you a lecture—it's far too late for that, I fear. I've never been in love myself, but I was young once too, and I can under-stand——'

'But I am not in love!' Jara said quickly. 'And most certainly not with Captain Montgomery! And after what he said to me this morning...the way he left...'

'That does surprise me,' Eustacia admitted. 'It is hard to believe that he has acted as he has, but... I know that he will have had his reasons. He told me that he had to leave on Navy business—but he didn't take his uniform with him. I find that rather strange.'

'Yes, it is strange,' Jara said slowly. 'But what he does is no longer any of my concern. Now I must decide what to do. I will have to look for work as I have no money...'

'Oh, money is not to be a problem.' Eustacia placed the knife neatly on top of the cut flowers and then took the basket from Jara's arm. 'The Captain was most specific about that, and has given me a letter to his bankers for you. He was insistent only that you leave Macao as soon as possible.'

'So I am being...what is the English expression? Paid off? Is that what one does to discarded mistresses?' Jara demanded. Despite all her resolutions to the contrary the hot, sick, churning anger was beginning to build up inside her all over again. When Eustacia took her by the hand she was surprised to find herself literally trembling with rage.

Eustacia looked at her sadly. 'My dear, I must admit that his actions do seem unfeeling—even callous. It is not what I would have expected of him, but I think that you do have to accept his explanation that he is under orders. I am sure that everything will turn out for the best——' She broke off at the sound of soft-slippered footsteps behind them on the gravelled path. 'Yes, Wei. What is it?'

Wei bowed slightly, his gaze flitting over Jara's pale and strained face and for a second she thought she saw something a great deal like compassion in his keen, hooded eyes. But when she looked harder his face was as impassive as ever.

'Visitor come, young missy. Say Cap'n say come.'

'A visitor for me?' Jara's heart sank. Not Lieutenant Lewis again! She was about to ask Wei to make some excuse for her when her eye was caught by the huge, shambling figure of the man who had grown impatient of waiting and who had ambled out after Wei into the garden. 'Capitaine Ferrier?'

'Mademoiselle Perrault?' With a look of disbelief on his weatherbeaten nut-brown face, the elderly captain opened his arms and Jara flew into their friendly warmth. *'Mais, c'est impossible! A Kororareka, on dit...'* He broke off politely as he caught sight of Eustacia's startled expression, and continued in English for her benefit. 'They told me in Kororareka that your family had died in a Maori raid. I understood that you and your poor parents had all perished. But this is a miracle! Your parents...?'

'They're dead, *Capitaine*. I alone survived. Did...did no one tell you that I went to live with the whalers?'

The captain shook his head in consternation. 'They said nothing of you, but you know what they are like. That wily fox Bjorn Jorgenson... No doubt he had something to hide! But... you lived with them, you say? I can only thank the Lord that you managed an early escape! But how...?'

Briefly, still with her arms around his ample waist as if to reassure herself that he was really there, Jara told him the story of how she had come to Macao. Captain Ferrier looked down at her as she spoke, carefully watching her face, trying to match her story with what he had heard from the coolly courteous young English captain who had come to see him about a passage for an unaccompanied woman. The English captain had told him only that the woman was a lady who was travelling to France for personal reasons, and who was to have every consideration on the voyage. But from the dock-talk he later heard that the woman was the English captain's courtisan, and he had been inclined to refuse passage to such a woman. However, he was a fair man and—unlike others of his kind—the young English captain had not seemed the kind of officer who would so flagrantly dispatch a mistress. And so Captain Ferrier had come to see for himself. That the woman in question should turn out to be the daughter of his old friends the Perraults both gladdened and shocked him.

Realising the connection between them, Eustacia tactfully went into the house to arrange for some vases, and the Captain was able to revert to French again.

'And now, *ma petite*—you are going on to France at last, as your mother always wished. To Rouen?'

She dropped her eyes. 'No, *Capitaine*. I no longer wish to enter the nunnery. That was always what my mother wanted for me and while I loved her dearly and will always cherish her memory...'

The captain read a great deal more from her averted face than she realised. He was still for a moment as his conscience did battle with his heart, and then he patted her gently on the shoulder. It was a tacit signal to her to release him and she did so at once, standing back flushed and anxious to face him.

'I cannot tell you what you should and should not do, Jara. You are not the child I saw last in Kororareka.' She coloured as she took his underlying meaning and he continued more gently, 'If there is something... someone... that you wish to choose instead of a cloistered life, I will not stand in your way. Well?' he prompted as she remained silent.

'There is...no one. Nothing,' she stammered. 'At least—I have not decided...'

She fell silent and after a minute the Captain cleared his throat and said delicately, 'And one must take into consideration, too, the matter of your dowry...'

'My dowry?' She smiled mirthlessly. 'I have no dowry, of course. I have...nothing.'

The Captain's thick eyebrows met in surprise. 'But you do! I refer of course to the dowry for the nunnery; perhaps you did not know that your sainted parents entrusted me with a sum of money to return to France each time I came to Kororareka, and while it was always intended for your dowry at Rouen, I can see no reason why you should not now do with it as you wish.'

She stared at him in amazement, hardly believing what she was hearing. 'Are... you sure?'

'As the executor of your poor parents' will, yes—I am sure. It is... a not inconsiderable sum, Jara—you must take care to use it wisely.'

'But we were not rich...'

Captain Ferrier gave an eloquent shrug. 'You lived simply—and who did not in Kororareka? But my friend Jacques was clever with his money, and he had always intended to return to France when he grew too old to stay in New Zealand. There were many investments made, and wisely—there was money to be made even during the years of the war. As the sole heir of your parents, you are a very wealthy young woman now, Jara.' He looked at her closely. 'Wealthy and alone. The English Captain——'

'Has left Macao. I shall not be seeing him again. I... think perhaps it would be best to go to France after all, Capitaine Ferrier. If you would be so kind as to give me the benefit of your advice...'

'Willingly, *ma petite* In fact, I should consider it an honour if you would allow me to look after you and protect your interests.' Genuinely touched, the old man took her hand and, in a sudden gesture of affection, Jara leant her head against his arm. Since her early childhood she had always regarded this man as an uncle. Now she felt nothing but a great wave of relief sweep over her as the realisation fully dawned on her that she was no longer alone, but truly safe, for the first time since the death of her beloved parents. She thought of Kit, and felt nothing but a slow, gathering heat of anger rise up inside her. What had he done for her but use her from the first moment they had met? It had been a cook for his crew that he had needed first, and then a companion for his bed... How foolish she had been! In her innocence she had believed him, and had even facilitated his seduction of her when all the time he was planning to leave her alone and abandoned...!

She glanced at her hand where it rested on Captain Ferrier's sleeve and saw that it was shaking. Enough of that! This was not the time to give in to her emotions. Indeed, she must forget the events of last night and even those of the preceding three months and instead look forward to a new life. A life without Kit.

Newly resolute, she farewelled Captain Ferrier, arranging to be ready when he came for her that evening, and then went into her bedroom intending to wash and change into a cooler dress. Eustacia came in to be apprised of all that had taken place, and expressed her very real satisfaction at the new turn of events. Before she left she shyly pressed her cheek against Jara's.

'I shall miss you, Jara, but you deserve to be happy. I hope you will write to me wherever you go to?'

'Of course I shall.' Jara embraced her warmly. 'You are a dear and good friend, and I shall never forget you.'

Eustacia stepped back and composed her prim little features, although her eyes were suspiciously moist. 'Why don't you change, then, my dear, and we shall take a last little stroll to the racecourse and see if we can see Captain Ferrier's vessel from there? Good. I shall be waiting for you in the drawing room.'

As the door closed behind her, Jara sighed. It seemed as if she no sooner found one friend than she lost another. She undressed and washed, and then put her blue silk dressing-gown over her underclothes while she sorted out the dress she wanted to wear that afternoon. Absorbed in her search, and with her head bent over the camphorwood chest, she did not hear anything until a hand from behind her clamped a doused cloth over her face. And the hands that caught her as she fell unconscious to the floor ensured that she made no sound either.

CHAPTER TEN

An errant gust of wind caught the sails of the *lorcha*, and the sudden slight shudder that ran through the small craft brought Kit's head up from his chest with a snap. How long had he been asleep? Not for more than a few minutes, he judged from the position of the Chinese crew on the deck. They had barely moved. In fact, the blasted *ship* had barely moved in this still air...

It was warm, and under his jacket his light shirt was clinging to him uncomfortably. He would have liked to have taken it off, but the two loaded pistols lying against his ribs would have been in clear evidence then, and he didn't want to risk it.

On the surface everything seemed calm enough. As far as the eye could see the flat green fields of the estuary spread under a cloudless sky, with only an occasional peasant working in the fields to break the smooth monotony of the scene. The silt-filled brown waters of the Pearl River were similarly smooth and silken, with barely a ripple to mark the slow passage of the *lorcha*. After three days of travelling upriver the familiar salt tang of the sea had long since disappeared, and Kit was feeling like a fish out of water.

His feeling of unease was intensifying by the hour, as he realised that the crew so carefully hand-picked by the Admiralty was as untrustworthy a bunch of thugs as he had ever encountered. Lin Feng, the helmsman of the opium ship *Dolores* who was so trusted by Admiral Buckler, was all smiles and affability, but Kit felt the skin on the back of his neck prickle whenever he came near. It was not a matter of if there would be a mutiny, but when. He touched the two pistols under his jacket as if they were a talisman. His hours might be numbered, but he'd make damned sure that he wouldn't go alone.

He got to his feet and made his way to the covered bow where the barrel of drinking water was kept, aware that the eyes of the crewmen were on his every move. He took a sip of the sour water from the scoop before pouring the rest over his head and then wiping it dry. It helped to cool him but it did nothing to alleviate the feeling of weariness that had plagued him ever since he had left Macao. He'd had precious little sleep these past few nights—he couldn't afford to shut his eyes on this crew for a minute—and every time he did doze off his mind took him back to Macao, and the woman he had left there...

He slammed down the second scoop of water before he brought it to his lips and strode down to where Lin Feng was sitting with one arm over the tiller, like some large, grinning spider.

'Why are we stopping here?'

The man looked at him quizzically, his head on one side, his bright eyes shrewd. 'We no stop, Cap'n. *Maskee, maskee*, no stop.'

Maskee, maskee—don't worry. He had heard that all the way upriver from Canton, and he had come to hate the taunting ring he sensed in the words. And they *were* slowing, and pulling in towards the bank of the river, despite the fact that Lin Feng had insisted that the men awaiting the armaments were a good five days' journey from Canton...

There was nothing on the bank but a small skiff pulled up high into the grass and a bamboo hut some fifty feet away, but every nerve in Kit's body was screaming danger. Slowly, so as not to arouse Lin Feng's suspicions, he slid his hand inside his jacket.

'Cap'n?' Lin Feng smiled up at him and then pointed past his shoulder. 'Lookee, Cap'n.'

Reluctant to take his eyes off the helmsman, Kit glanced towards the covered bow. Then he did a double-take and looked again, scarcely unable to believe his eyes. One of the crew stood there, supporting the sagging body of a woman. She appeared to be wearing very little except for a wildly incongruous blue silk dressing-gown, her hair was long and unkempt over her shoulders, and she looked filthy.

'My God! Jara!' Grasping the handle of one of his pistols, he would have started forward, but Lin Feng was at his side in an instant.

'Cap'n. Gun plees. Two gun.'

'What?'

'Gun plees,' the little man repeated patiently, still with the unwavering smile which had never reached his eyes. When Kit looked back at Jara the crewman holding her had drawn her hair back to reveal a long knife pressed to her throat, and even as he watched a thin trickle of blood ran down her neck and across her collarbone to disappear under her wrap. He hesitated for only another second before allowing the pistols to be taken from his hands.

'Damn you!' he muttered. Lin Feng smiled again.

'Below now, Cap'n. Chop chop.'

As he approached Jara the crewman released her and Kit caught her in his arms and helped her below to the hold. The long boxes of rifles and broken-down cannon were neatly stacked here, and there was a space between them where Jara had obviously been kept. The reason why he had not suspected she was on board all that time was apparent enough when he looked at her closely. The pupils in her dark blue eyes were dilated to pin-points, and her breath had a sweetish smell. She was having trouble keeping her head upright.

How long had it been? Three days! Three days of this opium-induced stupor... At least she had been kept reasonably clean, although he could feel her ribs through the robe and guessed that she had not been fed. But that was the advantage with drugging prisoners like this— they needed very little care and food, and would obediently do anything they were told to. How much of the damned drug had they given her? he wondered. He had lain her down on the rough floor beside a box of ammunition and was bending over her in concern when the hard muzzle of one of his own pistols dug him in the ribs. With a sigh of resignation he allowed Lin Feng's men to tie his hands together in front, and then when they had gone he knelt again beside Jara to shake her gently.

'Jara? Can you hear me? Can you speak?'

After a moment she nodded with what was apparently considerable effort. 'K...Kit...'

'It's all right, Jara. I won't let them give you any more.'

She looked at him blankly before closing her eyes and slumping sideways on to his shoulder. He eased himself into a more comfortable position to support her. Drugged as she was, she could at least have no idea of where she was, and why, and the danger they were in. On the other hand, if she had been coherent and physically able, he might have been able to make some sort of plan of escape.

As he looked up absently at the canvas over their heads one of the crewmen on watch on the deck above caught his movement and spat at him, the sputum landing only inches from Kit's boot. Then he withdrew his knife from the sheath at his side and slowly and explicitly drew it across his neck with a wide smile. Kit looked away quickly. So much for the Admiralty's hand-picked and highly paid men! The chances of an escape suddenly looked so remote as to be ludicrous. It was far more realistic to plan what to do with Jara when the end came. If she was still drugged, she would accept it quietly, but if she were conscious, and their deaths were protracted... He could only hope that—if he had to—he would be strong enough to end it for her.

Hours passed while they lay moored at the riverside, rocking almost imperceptibly on the smooth water. From the snatches of Cantonese Kit heard, it was apparent that they were waiting for someone to come, but that was all he could learn.

They were brought water eventually, and after cautiously tasting it himself Kit managed to fit Jara's head between his two bound arms so that he could get some of the water down her throat. She retched, and he held her head while she brought it back up, together with what he hoped was the residue of the opium-water they had given her. Then she fell asleep again.

It was night when Jara at last regained consciousness. Her head was aching, and every limb felt like lead. She became aware that the firm warmth under her head belonged to someone else's thighs, and she lay quietly for a time, trying to work out where she was. When she tried to move her head, the effort it took was so great that she felt herself break out into a sweat, and she groaned. At once there was a gentle hand on her hair.

'Kit?'

'So you're awake at last.' His voice came deep and comfortingly familiar. 'Can you sit up? I'm getting cramp in my legs.'

With his help she managed to right herself. Her tongue felt swollen in a mouth filled with dust. 'Wa...wa...' she croaked.

She heard him fumble, and then a cup of water was brought up to her lips. At first she thought he was being sadistic, allowing her only the smallest of sips when she

would have thirstily gulped, but as her stomach contracted and threatened to expel even that tiny amount
she understood. After a few measured sips, with a pause
between each to allow her stomach to adjust, she felt
much better and her tongue regained some of its mobility.

'Kit, I cannot see you. It is so dark down here...'

He caught her groping hand and she felt it pressed to
his lips. 'I know. We're still in the hold of the *lorcha*.
You must have been drugged for the last three days at
least—can you remember how they brought you
aboard?'

She shook her head, although he could not have seen
the movement in the profound darkness. 'I remember
only... being in my bedroom. I was dressing, I think.
Then... I was in darkness, and something foul and
stinking was over my head all the time. Someone would
get me up occasionally, and I was given some water to
drink, which tasted horrible and sweet, and sometimes
I could not drink it. But they would hold me until I did,
and then... I seemed to sleep all the time.' She paused
for breath, her tongue still heavy and clumsy in her
mouth. 'For three days, Kit? Is that how long I have
been asleep?'

'Drugged. They've given you opium to keep you
silent.'

'But... why?'

She felt him shrug. 'For insurance. To make sure that
I'd surrender at the appropriate time.'

She rested her head on his shoulder, taking comfort
from his body heat and the faint male scent of his skin.
His shirt did not have the crisp, freshly washed smell
she had come to associate with him, and she wondered
what state of dishevellment he was in.

'What are we doing here?' she asked calmly, surprised
that she did not really care whether he told her or not—
there was a strange feeling of unreality about everything

that had happened, and she was still not convinced that she was not having some unpleasantly vivid dream. Still, dream or not, she found comfort in Kit's shoulder under her head and she snuggled closer into him.

'I suppose that's a reasonable enough question to ask,' Kit said dubiously—he did not want to waste precious energy on an explanation if she was going to fall asleep in the middle of it. 'Do you remember my telling you that I had new orders?'

'Oh, yes,' she said slowly. 'I remember. Such important orders that you would not stay with me...'

'Yes, well... I'd been ordered by the Admiralty to take this *lorcha* upriver to meet whoever it was who is expecting it. On board is a load of weaponry and ammunition such as the Chinese have never seen before, shipped from Holland for the express purpose of starting a revolution here in China. My orders were to find out who is behind it all.'

'All by yourself?'

He laughed shortly. 'So I thought, until you made such a dramatic appearance! The last person I'd expected to see a hundred miles up the Pearl River in her dressing-gown...'

She frowned with concentration. 'Why am I here?'

'As I said—for insurance. The crew that the Admiralty sent with this *lorcha* have other loyalties. You were kidnapped and brought along so that they could be sure that I would do as I was told. I'm fairly sure that they plan to hand me over to the Chinese authorities when the time is right—perhaps when their revolution is well under way. You can imagine the furore that the discovery of an English Naval officer is going to cause then—the foreign barbarians will receive all the blame for the revolt and whoever is behind all this will get just what they want. War. And there is no way the Chinese could ever win that; not against the English. Jara, are you taking in any of this?'

'Yes, of course,' she muttered. Her head was aching from simply listening to him, and nothing he said made any sense, but his voice was comforting all the same. She wished he would put his arms around her, but did not have the energy to say so. Now he was talking again, more to himself than to her.

'I still don't believe that it is the Chinese who are behind this—there are a fair number who will join a revolution against the Emperor, but I'm convinced that the driving force behind all this is a European. It *has* to be.'

His words now were but a soothing background noise. Vaguely she understood that he was worried—even apprehensive—but could not recall exactly why. It was enough that he was here, and beside her. She closed her eyes and, with a small sigh of contentment that Kit heartily envied, she fell asleep again.

Kit's shout of protest and the sharp pain in her arm came suddenly and simultaneously, both serving to jerk her sharply out of unconsciousness and into a world of confusion. She raised her head and saw the face of one of the Chinese crewmen inches away, his teeth showing in a malignant mask. He said something rapidly that she did not understand, and his fingers bit hard into her arm in a gesture that she *did* understand. Obediently she rocked her upper body forward in an attempt to stand, but her cramped muscles refused to obey her, and she fell forward.

'I told you to leave her!' she heard Kit say angrily. 'She can't stand, damn you! Leave her alone!'

She raised her head to see him standing a few feet away in the shadow of the hold while a crewman re-tied the length of rope that bound his hands. This was presumably what they wanted to do to her as well. Vague memories of what Kit had told her last night of their situation began to surface, and she looked apprehensively at the man gripping her arm. He gave her another vicious tug and she whimpered more from fear than pain.

The next sound in the hold was a loud crack as Kit swung his bound hands up and under the chin of the man in front of him, and the sailor's feet left the ground as he was thrown sideways. The sailor who had been holding Jara released her to stand up and was flung backwards, propelled by Kit's boot in his stomach. It was all over in a few seconds, as Jara sat staring in dazed wonder at all this activity. Kit was frantically pulling at the rope restricting his wrists when a voice directly above them made him freeze.

'You stupid, Englis'man. Where you tink you go? Lookee, lookee.'

Kit looked up at the pistol in Lin Feng's hands that was pointing directly at Jara and his shoulders slumped as he expelled his breath in a groan of frustration. Once again, his face tight and his stance rigid, he stood tamely as his hands were re-tied behind him this time, the ropes being pulled so hard that Jara saw him wince. Her wrists were bound in much the same fashion, but either the rope was not as tight or the feeling had not yet fully returned to her limbs. As she staggered drunkenly to her feet with the aid of the crewman, she tended to think it was the latter.

Her head was pulled roughly back and she obediently gulped the cloudy liquid from the bowl that was held to her lips. Once, a long time ago it seemed now, she had tried to resist, but she had soon learned that any resistance was futile. Now she drank quickly, having also learned that to do otherwise would only mean retching up the foul mixture and then having to undergo the ordeal once more.

Then they were led blinking up on to the deck into the bright light of day, and taken directly to the side of the *lorcha*. Jara was helped over the side and into the small skiff alongside with few problems, but Kit's larger frame was more difficult to manoeuvre. Because he was unable to help himself with his hands tied so restrictively, it took four men to lower him into the skiff. The crewman who had woken Jara took the opportunity of slamming Kit's head hard against the side of the *lorcha* during the procedure, but if Kit made any sound of pain or protest Jara did not hear it.

On the riverbank they were walked the short distance down a well-worn path to a low bamboo hut with a thatched roof. It stood alone in the cultivated fields, with no sign of any other habitation nearby. She had only a brief moment to look up at the fluffy white clouds scudding across an azure sky, to hear the monotonous chirruping of the crickets, to take a few deep breaths of the grass-scented breeze. Then it was back into confinement—this time that of the small windowless hut. It contained nothing but a heavy wooden peg buried deep into the centre of the dirt floor, and it was to this that the ends of the ropes that bound their wrists were tied.

'What happens now?' Kit asked conversationally as Lin Feng oversaw their tethering.

'Now you wait.' They were sitting on the floor with their backs to each other, and Lin Feng stepped forward to try their ropes. He grunted in satisfaction. 'You wait number one man. No long time.'

The door creaked shut behind him and they were alone. Jara turned to speak but Kit abruptly silenced her with a jerk of his head. She felt the dirt floor beneath them tremble slightly with the thud of feet moving away, and then slowly the chorus of crickets rose again.

'Right,' Kit said decisively after a moment. 'Now to get these blasted ropes off.' Even in her somnolent state this statement sounded ridiculous, but he was twisting himself around so that his right side was against her back. She felt the high side of his boot press against her hands. 'Can you reach?'

'What?'

'The knife in my boot. Can you reach it?'

She managed to push her fingers down inside his boot where they at once touched the cool, hard hilt of the small knife Kit always carried. Her fingers felt heavy and unresponsive, and it was with considerable difficulty that she finally withdrew the knife.

'Watch that point, dammit, Jara! Now hold it steady— yes, like that—and I'll move my hands.'

It seemed to take a long time for Kit to saw through his bonds, and it was hard to maintain her grip. More than once the knife slipped from her numbed hands and they were both cut and bleeding by the time Kit fumbled on the ground for it and put it back into her fists. Her heart wrung every time she heard Kit's agonised intake of breath, but she herself felt no pain.

It dimly concerned her that she was not panicking, because her common sense told her that she should be. In addition to that, she should be both starving and very uncomfortable, but she was neither. The only reason she could think of was that she was still affected by the opium. How long had it been since they had last given her some of that sickeningly sweet drink? Yesterday? No, she seemed to remember it being more recent than that. She screwed up her face as she tried to make sense of the jumbled memories in her head. Time seemed just now to be expanding and contracting in the most alarming way. She could remember only flashes of her childhood and of her voyage to Macao. Oddly enough, her clearest memories were of a night spent in rapturous happiness in Kit's arms. Something had happened after that…but she could not remember exactly what. It didn't matter now. Nothing very much mattered now, except Kit's pain. That, at least, still affected her.

With a gasp of relief Kit broke free, and turned at once to untie Jara. That done, he went to kneel down by the door. Like the hut, the door was made of lengths of bamboo woven together to form a strong fabric yet one which still allowed the sunlight to seep through. She clambered over to join him as he eased the side of the door open to look out.

'That's interesting,' he muttered. 'They've taken the *lorcha* away.'

She peered out over his shoulder, squinting in the bright light. There was nothing to see except for the dark shapes of two of the *lorcha*'s crew squatting under the shade of a tree beside the river.

'Do we leave now?' she asked, not needing him to remind her to keep her voice down.

He shook his head, still not looking at her. 'No. Not now. Not until the man—or men—we're waiting for arrive. Besides—you're in no condition to go anywhere.'

She sat down heavily on the earth floor, relieved that he did not expect any physical feats from her. The needle-thin strips of light that lay across the dirt floor shone softly like a carpet of sunshine. How pretty, she thought. How she would like to curl up on that softness and light and go to sleep now... She wondered aloud if Kit would mind.

'Jara...!' he began in exasperation, but then he turned to look at her and she saw his eyes soften. He reached over and drew her against him so that she sat with her back to him, and his arms around her. It was, she realised dimly, a position which still enabled him to keep an ever-watchful eye on the two figures by the river. He lifted one of her hands up before her face. 'Have you seen your wrists?'

She looked at her wrist in surprise, and at his beside it. The ropes had cut deep red marks in their skin, and in parts blood slowly oozed from where the skin had been broken. Both of them had several deep cuts where the knife had slipped while they had been freeing themselves. She grimaced at the sight.

'You can't feel that, can you?'

'No. Well, only a very little.' She turned around to look up at him. 'I don't understand...'

'And how is your throat?' He ran a finger along the underside of her chin, and she felt something raised on the skin. 'They cut you there yesterday. You don't feel any pain? It's quite a nasty gash.' He looked at her stricken face and smiled. 'Maybe it's no bad thing they've kept you drugged. We can't think of leaving here until after this "number one" man comes, anyway. Why don't you go back to sleep and I'll wake you when our friends decide to come back?'

His voice was so soothingly quiet and even that she did not think to question what he was saying. Dreamily, she leaned back against the support of his arms and took her first proper look at him since Macao. There was dust in his hair and over his clothes, and a large bruise was turning purple on his right cheek where the crewman must have pushed him against the side of the *lorcha*. He looked very tired and pale under his tan, and he had not shaved for some days. She had never seen him look less than immaculate before, and the change in him vaguely disturbed her, although she could not have said why. Absently she put out a finger and ran it over his stubble.

'You do not look like a captain any more.' She frowned, trying to concentrate her thoughts. 'Do I look as dreadful as you?'

'I've seen you look worse,' Kit replied in absolute truthfulness, and his arms tightened around her. Damn it, he should have left her in Kororareka! As debased as

that place had been, she would still have been afforded
some kind of casual protection by her own people. He
bent and kissed her on the top of her head, remembering
with a pang how she had looked the first time he had
seen her. Filthy, smelling abominably...a little savage
on a savage shore. Could he honestly say he had im-
proved her life by taking her away?

'Kit?' she said sleepily.

'Mmmm?'

'I love you.'

He rested his cheek against her hair. 'I love you too,
Jara.'

There was a moment of silence before she spoke again.
'Kit, will you marry me?'

He laughed softly. 'Yes, of course I will. If that's what
you want.'

'Yes, please,' she muttered happily, and closed her
eyes. 'I want to marry you very much. And we will have
many children. But where will we live?'

'Where will we live? Now let me see...' One of the
men squatting under the willow by the river had got to
his feet, and Kit carefully kept his voice steady, even
while his body tensed with anticipation. 'How about
England? You'd like it there, and my family will soon
come to love you as much as I do. There are all my
sisters—and the twins are about your age—and you'll
get on famously with them. And we'll live in the house
where I was born, in Kent. It's very old—parts of it were
built over five hundred years ago—and very big, especially with most of the girls gone now. My mother has
had the gardens done in the Italian style, and there are
orchards all around. The apples from the trees on our
estate are held to be the best in all Kent.'

'It sounds lovely, Kit. What is your room like in this
house?'

The man by the river was sitting down again. Jara, lost in her happy thoughts, did not feel Kit's body relax slightly.

'My room is in the old wing, and it has a big mullioned window that looks out over the orchards, and a fireplace.'

'A fireplace in a bedroom?' She frowned, and a note of disbelief crept into her voice. 'Why do you have to cook in your bedroom?'

'No, the fireplace is there only to provide warmth; it gets so cold in England that it generally snows in winter. I don't suppose you've ever seen snow, have you? At night we'll lie in our bed when the snow is falling outside and listen to the fire, and watch the shadows...' His voice faltered and Jara opened her eyes.

'Kit...?' she began, and for the first time she looked worried.

To reassure her he bent his head and kissed her on the lips. It was an instinctive action, and he was quite unprepared for Jara's response. Lulled by the gentleness of his voice, contentedly half-asleep in his arms, her mouth opened under his and she pressed herself against him in a gesture of unmistakable invitation. As his hand involuntarily dropped to slide under the thin robe she wore, Jara moaned deep in her throat with longing and the memories that his hands on her bare skin revived in her.

For just one moment Kit was lost. The scent of her skin, the soft, acquiescent feel of her... For a moment he felt all the tenderness and passion of that last night in Macao start to gather inside him, and almost overwhelm him.

But it was only for a moment. Slowly, and with an immense effort of will, he took his lips from hers, loosened his arms about her, and gently extracted his hand from inside her robe. Jara grumbled something and pushed his hand back.

'Please, Jara...' He was finding it difficult to steady his breathing. She was lying back against his arm, her eyes half-closed in invitation and her lips reddened from his kisses. Under any other circumstances...

He looked past her head and saw with a cold jolt of apprehension that the *lorcha* was back.

'Jara! Sit up! Come on, now!' He pushed her away and then bodily half carried and half dragged her the few feet to the centre of the tiny hut. 'Now—are you able to sit upright? With your hands behind your back like this? Good. Now please, Jara, on your life...don't move or speak, no matter what happens. *On your life!* Do you understand what I am saying?'

She nodded, wide-eyed. For the first time his urgency had somehow penetrated the fog of unreality that had thus far surrounded her and as she took in Kit's tense face she felt a small shiver of fear run down her spine. He sat with his back to hers, just as they had first been left, and when he took her hands and gave them a warm reassuring squeeze, it was all she could do to respond. Where they were...how they had got here...slowly she was starting to make some horrible sense of it all.

Through the ground she felt the vibrations of approaching footsteps. Who were they to wait for? She delved through her muddled mind for the answer. The number one man? That was it. The European who should not be here, any more than they should... She tried to imagine what he would look like, but could only come up with the image of Bjorn: big, red-haired and threatening.

She was taken aback, therefore, when the door of the hut opened to reveal not a red-haired giant but the small form of the helmsman, Lin Feng. But what Feng lacked in stature he made up for in the look of sheer ferocity on his face. Without a word he stood over Kit and struck him—a single, resounding blow with his closed fist. Kit's fingers closed over hers in a reflexive movement of pain but he even then did not move to defend himself.

'How clever you must think you are,' Feng hissed, his English suddenly and chillingly perfect. 'And how foolish you must think *we* are! I was ashore at Macao for only a few hours...'

'That was all the time we needed.'

'Obviously. Yes.' Feng gave a hard, mirthless snort of laughter. 'All the time you needed to take ashore all the cargo I had brought from Holland and to replace it with bags of sand and a few pieces of old rifles on the top in case anyone was curious enough to look.'

The last word was punctuated with yet another blow and this time Kit gave a small grunt of pain. She twisted around to see if he was all right but he still did not relax his grip on her wrists and she stayed silent only because she knew that he desperately wanted her to be.

'Are you...the number one man? The one behind...all this?'

Feng stood back and stared at him with eyes like cold stone. 'You would like it to be a European, *neh*? A European opium-smuggler, so that you and your kind would have good reason to finish the opium-trade. Yes, that would have been convenient, Captain Montgomery. But life is never...*convenient*.'

'Are you the number one man?'

'Am I the number one man?' Feng suddenly swooped down and grasped a handful of Kit's hair and pulled it back painfully. His face was a mask of rage. 'Am I the number one man? Who else do you think I would entrust with a fortune in armaments brought thousands of miles across the seas? Yes, I am. And you, Captain, *you*——' another resounding blow '—you are a dead

man. You have yourself destroyed the only reason you—
and this female—have been kept alive. Now...'

He had raised his arm for yet another blow when Kit
sprang. Before Jara could realise quite how it was
achieved, Feng was lying flat on his back and Kit was
over him, his hands on his throat and one knee over his
groin. Feng tried to bring his hands up to Kit's eyes but
his arms fell back as Kit pressed his knee down hard.

Jara got unsteadily to her feet, staring at the two men
in horror and disgust. The diminutive Feng suddenly
looked pathetic and defenceless, sobbing in silent agony
under Kit's ministrations. She had seen seamen in vicious brawling at Kororareka, and had seen for herself
Kit's style of fighting on the *Courageous*, but after
having adjusted to the civilised Captain Montgomery in
Macao she found herself shocked by his use of such low
tactics. Besides, her mind seemed to be getting clearer
by the minute, and now she was remembering much more
about Macao, and their last night together, and what he
had said and done... Oh, yes, she was remembering now
with dreadful clarity exactly what he had said!

'Look out of the door—no, don't open it wide! Now.
What is there?'

'Nothing.' She opened the door a little more to enable
her to look up and down the river for a distance of several
hundred yards. The river slipped by tranquilly, glinting
in the hazy sun, and only a slight breeze trembled the
long reeds growing down by the banks. 'I see no
boats...no people.'

'Then go down to the riverbank. Keep off the track,
and I want you to crawl, so that you keep below the level
of the grass. When you get there, just stay still and wait
for me.'

'But...'

'Don't argue with me, Jara. Just get the hell out of
here!'

He hadn't once looked at her, and she could only stare helplessly at his back, as if that would provide some clues as to just what was going on. Why did he want her to leave without him? What was he going to do with Feng? When she failed to move, he turned his head to glare at her in exasperation. His face was pale with dust, but the purpling bruises on his cheek and jaw were already evident. Blood trickled steadily from the cut in his lip and made him look even more ferocious. She fled.

She half crawled, half slithered down to the river, although she was fast approaching a state in which she no longer cared if she was found or not. She slithered down to the river edge, and lay still in the rushes for a moment. Her heart seemed to be pounding uncommonly quickly and even the slight exertion of movement had made her breathing difficult. It must be the last effects of the days of opium-induced sleep, she thought and pressed her hand firmly over her stomach to quell the churning there. And when had she last eaten...?

The waters of the Pearl River looked clean enough to safely drink, but to reach them she would have to cross several yards of mud, with no rushes to hide her from view. A little further down river, however, the rushes grew over the water, and it would be safe enough to reach down from there. She got up on all fours to go there, but was suddenly propelled forward again as a hand reached over and covered her mouth. With a whoosh of air the breath was knocked out of her and she lay in impotent rage with her chin in the mud. Damn Kit! She might be past caring now what happened to her, but this really was completely unnecessary!

She wrenched the hand away from her mouth to say so, but the face she turned to look at was not Kit's. It was not until he whispered urgently that she realised who it was.

'Missy all right? Where is Captain?'

'Wei! But . . .' She could only stare at his anxious, furrowed face in consternation. This man served her breakfast and answered the door to visitors, and saw to the smooth running of the little house in Macao. He should still be there. He should not be *here*, in the mud and rushes, God knew how many miles from sanity and civilisation. With a groan she hid her eyes in her hands.

'You are not here,' she muttered into her palms. 'When I open my eyes none of this is going to be here. I am going to wake up in my bedroom in Macao, and——'

A very real hand prised away her fists. 'Where is Captain, missy? You are not alone here?'

'No, she's not.' Kit slithered down beside them and at once reached out to clasp Wei's shoulder in a gesture of gratitude and friendship. 'Wei. Thank God.'

'Thank Admiralty, Captain. I just follow orders, like always.' As the two men grinned at each other Jara laid her head on her knees and closed her eyes. She didn't understand any of this. Nothing made sense any more. Vaguely she heard Wei's voice in tight enquiry, and Kit's in response, but the words meant nothing. She offered no resistance when Kit scooped her up and carried her a short distance down the riverbank. She opened her eyes, however, when he laid her down on a quilt in the dark bow of a low, narrow, extraordinarily long boat. There must have been forty men sitting in it, one behind the other, all with short, spoon-like paddles in their hands. She sat bolt upright.

'What is this?'

'It's what they call a centipede boat. Usually used by the opium smugglers for speed down the waterways of the Pearl River to evade the Chinese custom men. We'll be back in Macao in no time at all in this.' He passed a hand wearily across his face. 'Have something to eat—there's some fruit down there by your hand—and then

I think you'd better sleep. You need it . . . we both need it.'

Even as he spoke the centipede boat was pulling out from the shore and the rowers were starting to build up speed, with oars dipping into the still water with rhythmic grace. Kit crouched down as their pace suddenly increased and the bow beneath her seemed to lift out of the water. The riverbanks either side of them were going by so quickly in a blur of green and dusty gold that her head began to spin. But she stopped Kit when he would have drawn the canvas cover over her.

'No. I want to know—what did you do to Feng?'

'Look, we're not getting into this right now. When we get back to Macao——'

'You killed him. I know you did. You need not deny it.'

He looked at her tense, accusing face and then looked away again. 'I had to, Jara, there was no other way. When we get back to Macao I'll tell you why.'

'Why when we get to Macao? Will the reasons have changed by the time we get there?'

'No, but——'

'Then tell me now. Why could he not have lived?'

'Because if he'd lived he would have caused infinite destruction. The man was a fanatic, Jara—one way or another he would have been responsible for many more deaths than just his own.'

'You don't know that.'

'Yes, I do.' His flat, final tone infuriated her.

'Then . . . why could you not have brought him back to Macao? If you knew that Wei was here . . .'

'But I didn't. That is, I couldn't be sure that he was. Don't you see—I needed to be absolutely sure that Feng was the last man in the chain of revolutionaries and then I had to kill him. To have brought him out with us was impossible; it would have been tantamount to kidnapping a Chinese subject, because we have no charges to bring against him—to let the Chinese government know what has been going on puts the Europeans on very shaky ground . . .'

'You make no sense to me.' She turned her back on him and began to pull the canvas cover over her, no longer able to fight the desperate need for sleep, for oblivion. 'Please leave me alone now.'

'Jara . . .' His voice was suddenly gentle now, almost pleading. She felt his hand smooth back her lank locks of hair and caress the back of her neck. 'When we get back to Macao, and you're rested properly, we need to talk . . .'

'Please leave me,' she repeated stonily, and after a moment she felt his hand leave her neck. She pulled the cover over her head and curled up on the quilt in the darkness, ignoring even the bag of fruit beside her.

By now she had almost total recall of all the events of that last night in Macao, and she most definitely did not want to talk to him when they returned there. As ever, it would be him who did all the talking. More lies, more manipulations . . . How could she know when to believe him any more? She had made such a fool of herself already, giving herself to him so completely, and he had spurned her, laughed at her and the love she had offered him so unreservedly . . .

But now she had no love to offer, even if he should care to dally further with her. He had murdered her love no less than he had murdered Lin Feng and God knew how many others in his ruthless pursuit of his *duty*. Or perhaps she had never loved him at all, but had simply felt physical desire for him. After all, it was all that men felt for women and they called it love . . .

She dashed away the huge hot tears that were scalding her eyes and agreed with herself that that was all it had been. Desire. Lust. A hunger now satisfied and thus able to be dismissed forever. There was no need for her to wait until Kit deemed it time to spell that out to her in his condescending way—there would be his report to the Admiralty to make, people to see... She could be well on the way to France by the time he thought of talking to her. And if Captain Ferrier had already left Macao, then she would take the first boat she could to any-where. Anywhere as long as it was somewhere where Kit Montgomery was not.

The sound of the water rushing past the bow through mere inches of wood was loud but not unpleasant, and the lulling rocking motion of the boat was irresistible. It felt good to be back on the water again, even under these conditions, and it was not long before she closed her eyes and either slept or fell into unconsciousness.

CHAPTER ELEVEN

WHEN Jara next opened her eyes it was to the familiar comforting walls of her little bedroom in Macao. Cautiously she raised her aching body up on her elbows and looked around her in disbelief. It was just as if nothing at all had changed since she had last been in this room. The bamboo shades were down, but through them she could see the strong light of the midday sun, and from outside she could hear the muted sound of the gardener humming to himself and the rasping of the rake over the paving stones. She could smell freshly cut grass and . . . food.

Her mouth filled with saliva and she threw back the bedclothes and went to stand up. After only one step forward the room began to swim around her and she sat down hurriedly again. She was dressed in her nightgown, and her skin felt fresh and clean and scented with soap. Even her hair had been washed and re-tied in a neat plait down her back. But that was impossible—she would surely have remembered someone doing *that* to her?

Unless . . . unless it really had all been a dream—a long, horribly realistic dream from which she had been unable to wake up. The long, stifling hours under a filthy sack on a rocking boat, and Kit and that awful man Feng and that little hut . . . had it all been nothing but a product of an over-active imagination? A night's sleep disturbed by indigestion? Something she had eaten at the dinner party, perhaps? Unlikely as that seemed, it was at least an explanation, and the only one she had. She was filled with a sudden, wonderful surge of relief.

Then her eyes fell on her wrists, bared as the sleeves of her nightgown were drawn up, and she saw the neat strips of bandage bound around them. Her hand flew to her throat. That had not been bandaged, but some kind of salve had been applied to the long, shallow cut there.

It had been no dream, then. No nightmare.

As if in response to her moan of despair the door opened at that moment and Eustacia edged into the room, laden with a tray.

'It's all right, my dear, I'm here. I heard you stirring, although I had hoped you would sleep for many more hours yet...'

She looked so sweet and familiar and so reassuringly *Eustacia* that Jara could not help but burst into tears at the sight of her. Then it was hugs and kisses and a few tears from Eustacia herself, followed by stern admonitions that Jara was not to stir from her bed.

'We've had the doctor in to look at you, and he said complete bed-rest for at least a week. And just a little soup and toast to start with, and then lots of little nourishing meals until you have built your strength up again...'

'Soup and toast?' Jara wailed as her stomach audibly growled. 'But I am starving, Eustacia! I could eat an entire ox!'

But even the light soup was hard to get down, with her stomach knotting in protest at every sip, and her first meal in days was far from the pleasurable event she had anticipated. While she ate Eustacia chattered away companionably, every now and then reaching out to smooth back Jara's hair, or squeeze her hand affectionately. There was no doubt at all but that she was genuinely delighted to have Jara back, and safe.

'...And even dear Constance has been asking every day after you! And Mrs Mead came to visit twice, but

of course we couldn't tell her that you were missing—
Sir Walter wouldn't permit it. We had not the slightest
idea of where you had gone, but could only surmise that
you had been kidnapped. And—when we heard nothing
further, Sir Walter said that he was sure it had something to do with the Captain's leaving. Oh, we were all
so worried about you! And then Wei left shortly after—
we know why now, of course, but it was all so very
distressing... Mrs Mead brought you some flowers
yesterday—those ones over by the window there. We had
had to tell her that you were too indisposed to have
visitors, and so she sent her very best wishes for your
recovery...'

'Really?' Jara swallowed a mouthful of toast with difficulty and looked at her in surprise. 'I would have
thought that after the dreadful exhibition I made of
myself at her dinner party she wouldn't have wanted
anything further to do with me!'

Now it was Eustacia's turn to blink in surprise.
'Exhibition? I don't think so, my dear—I gather you
made a most favourable impression. Not that I am surprised, of course, after all the hard work we put into
making you presentable! And people would make al-
lowances, too, for your...ah...unusual upbringing.
Indeed, Mrs Mead mentioned to me how very refreshing
she found you after all the silly young females one is
used to meeting in Macao. No, you appear to have done
very well, and I think you can be very pleased with your
debut into polite society.'

'I doubt that Kit would agree with you,' Jara said re-
flectively, taking another bite of toast. 'I seemed to do
everything wrong. Hasn't he told you what happened
that night?'

'We have exchanged only a few words since he came
back—the poor man was so utterly exhausted by all that
he had been through these past few days. After he

brought you home to us last night he had to go straight out again to see some members of the Admiralty, and he only came back an hour or two ago. He fell asleep at once, and I don't expect him to stir for a very long time.' She stood up to take away Jara's empty tray. 'And you must follow his example, my dear. Back to sleep, and I don't want you to move from that bed until your strength is completely recovered.'

'And Captain Ferrier?' Jara asked slowly. 'I suppose that he has left Macao by now?'

'Bless you, no! He has been another constant visitor, asking at least once every day if you were all right. He was here just a little time ago, and I took the liberty of telling him something about what had happened, seeing that you were safely back with us, and that he was such a close friend of your parents. He was most distraught, and said to tell you that he will stay in Macao harbour until you are quite well enough to sail. Such a kind man.'

'Yes he is.' Suddenly determined, Jara threw back the sheets and swung her legs out of bed. 'I am not going to keep him waiting, Eustacia. Would you mind helping me dress and packing a few of my clothes for me?'

'Jara! Are you mad? You can't possibly——'

She made her way shakily across the room to the wardrobe. 'I can, and I will. With or without your help. I am not going to remain in Macao an hour longer than I have to.' She opened the wardrobe door and began to select some of her favourite clothes. She had once told Kit that she would not take any of the things he had brought her, but she had nothing else to wear. Three day dresses, some underclothes, a nightgown...that should suffice. She was bundling them together on the bed when Eustacia at last moved.

'Oh, very well then, if you are as determined as that to go! Don't fold them up so, Jara, or they will crush most dreadfully. I shall get you a trunk to put them in, and then I shall help you dress. But please, my dear...*please*. Won't you reconsider? I really don't want to wake up the Captain...'

'No, of course not,' Jara said quickly. 'But he is expecting me to go at the first opportunity and...I shall write him a letter of farewell. I promise.'

But when she was ready to leave and she sat down at the escritoire in the drawing-room to compose a note she found that there was nothing to say. For five full minutes she stared at the reproachfully blank sheet of paper before she threw down the pen and stood up. No words were adequate—her departure would be eloquent enough.

Eustacia accompanied her to Captain Ferrier's ship, the *Juliette*, and saw her on board, her poor face blotched and anxious and tearful. The Captain was delighted to see her, and waved away her stammered explanations of her tardy arrival.

'Later, *ma petite*. Later. We have time to catch the afternoon tide if we hurry, and then you will have three months—maybe more—to tell me all that has happened. Come, I will show you to your cabin, and then we will talk tonight.'

As she rose to follow him he turned and took her hand in his own great paw, raising it gallantly to his lips. 'I am glad to see that you are well again, Jara. And glad that you have decided at last to have done with the English Captain.'

'Thank you.' She didn't know what else to say, and she lowered her eyes modestly. She wished he would let go of her hand. He kissed it once more, thoughtfully, and then released it.

'Yes. I am glad. Now that you are a young woman of fortune, the question of who you marry is of even greater importance. There will be fortune-hunters, rakes...you need a husband who will protect and cherish and guide you, Jara.'

'I...I had not thought of marriage...'

'But of course you hadn't! But you shouldn't feel that such a prospect is out of the question now, even if you *have* been ruined by the Englishman. A mature man, one such as myself, can often find it in himself to overlook a single indiscretion. The Englishman took advantage of your youth and vulnerability...' He smiled at her stricken face and patted it consolingly. 'No, I don't hold you to blame. Most men would, I know, but I am far too fond of you for that. But I see that I have taken you by surprise, speaking of marriage to you so soon. We have a whole voyage to talk of such things, and I even have a priest travelling back with us who will be more than willing to perform the ceremony when...I mean if...you agree to do me the honour of becoming my wife.' He bent down and gently kissed her forehead, his greying beard brushing across her nose. 'I shall speak no more of it, but shall take you to your cabin at once. Come, *ma petite*.'

She had forgotten how quickly it became dark here in Macao. For hours it seemed the huge ball of the sun hovered over the opaque sea, sending lengthening silver shimmers of light across the water and turning everything else a glowing orange. Then, abruptly, it was gone. The sky was black, the sea was black, the grass she sat on was black. A few uncertain stars began to appear in the sky, as if in pale response to the lamps being lit in the town below, and a cool night wind swept in to claim the land.

She shuddered and slowly got to her feet, her body aching from the stillness she had imposed on it for many hours now. She had to go back to the house sooner or later, and she could hardly spend another eight hours crouched in the grass up here in the hills above the town, pretending to herself that she still had any choices left. She had firmly closed the last open door when she had fled from the *Juliette*. That had been a decision born of panic and the certain knowledge that she did not want to become Madame Ferrier; the grateful bride of a kindly, and condescending older man.

Ah, but it seemed that she had always known what she did *not* want, and never what she *did* want! She had not wanted to stay in Kororareka or to go to the nunnery or to marry Captain Ferrier... So—what did she want?

It had been quiet up here in the hills, with the only sounds those of the crickets whirring busily by her feet, and the rustling of the grass, and the birds in the trees above her. It occurred to her that it was the first time she had been alone—really alone—since her childhood in the New Zealand forest. And she *had* been a child then. Until her parents died, and she met the fair-haired stranger with the kind brown eyes...

She remembered all his tiny acts of kindness now; how he had watched over her, protected her and taught her how to survive. It was true that there had been many times when he had been off-hand, even cruel to both her and others... but he had always had his reasons, and it was only because she had somehow always known what he was really like under the steel exterior that those times had hurt so deeply. He had tried to explain to her once what it meant to be a professional sailor, and it had taken her a very long time to realise that his arrogance and his brutality were not in his nature but were qualities demanded of him by his rank. Only now did she feel that she could accept that part of his life.

And she also believed that he loved her, after his own fashion. Marriage to him, however, was another matter. They had spoken before of love, and once of marriage, but that of course was impossible; women like her were the mistresses of men like him, but never their wives. She remembered the little hut on the Pearl River, and the laughter in his voice as he had pretended to accept her proposal; anything to humour her. She remembered Lady Ashley's cold hostility, and Eustacia's flustered explanations of Kit's position, and Kit's family, and Kit's responsibilities...

No wonder he had laughed at her. He would never belong to her, but he was all she had, and all she would ever want.

With a heart as heavy as the portmanteau in her hand she made her way down the hillside, stumbling occasionally over an unseen stone in her path, down past the tiny shanties of the Chinese labourers, down through the streets of the Chinese quarter and along the beautiful wide streets where the Portuguese merchants made their homes. It was easier to see here, with the light pooling out across the streets from the lamps hanging from each front door, but she did not increase her speed. Indeed, by the time she got to the Hatfields' front door she slowed to a stop altogether. The lamp outside had not been lit, and to her surprise the front door was open.

She put out a hand to open it further when it was pulled out of her hand and Kit narrowly missed crashing into her on his way out.

'Jara! Oh, thank God...' He flung his arms around her and hugged her so tightly to him that her feet left the ground for a second. She dropped her portmanteau but resisted the impulse to return his embrace. She squeezed back the tears pricking her eyes—she must not embarrass him, or herself...

He released her at last and led her inside but not, as she had expected, to the drawing-room. It was not until they reached the door to her bedroom that it dawned on her what he intended.

'Kit, what are you doing? You cannot be serious! Where is everyone?'

'Out looking for you! Come on, Jara, we haven't much time...' Suddenly uneasy, she tried to wrest her arm away but he easily pulled her into the bedroom and shut the door firmly behind them. He was back in uniform once more and that fact—as well as the confident smile on his face—brought back a sudden rush of memories she had wanted to forget. 'No, Kit!' she said as firmly as she could. 'I came back only because I wanted to talk to you.'

'We'll talk. Afterwards.' He was advancing on her now, pulling off his Naval jacket as he came. The back of her legs made contact with the bed at the same moment as his jacket landed on the floor. Her eyes widened at such uncharacteristic untidiness and his smile widened. 'And that's the last time I'm ever wearing the goddamned thing. You will never, ever see me in uniform again, Jara. I swear it.'

His sword was the next item of apparel to clatter to the floor, and his shirt would have followed shortly after had Jara not attempted a sudden dash to the door. She had not covered more than a couple of steps when Kit's leg swept her feet out from under her and she landed heavily on her back on the bed with Kit on top of her. Any protest she might have made when she got her breath back was drowned by the kisses he began to rain on her lips and face. It was not until he began to pay some attention to her lower regions that either of them spoke.

'Damnation,' he muttered, as he felt around under her bodice. 'This does up differently from the other one.'

'Are you adding rape to your list of sins, Captain?' she managed to gasp, now that her mouth was free.

'I've committed so many transgressions this afternoon that I might as well,' he said cheerfully as he solved the last intricacy of her underwear. He buried his face in the hollow between her breasts and sighed blissfully. 'Wonderful. Although not as much as there used to be.'

'I should hope not. Lady Ashley said I was too big and——'

Kit raised his head and looked at her sternly. 'Lady Ashley can go to hell. I'm the one who makes love to you and I can't abide a scrawny female. You're a lovely, generous, unique woman, and I don't want you ever to change a single hair on your head. Do you understand?'

'That sounds like an order,' she grumbled, half delighted and half piqued. She felt him smile against her skin as he continued his explorations.

'It wasn't meant to. I'm not in the Navy now. I've resigned. And now——' he began to run his hand down the length of her skirts '—I can spend all my time with you. Well, the next hour, anyway.'

'What does that mean?' She tried to sit up to look at him. 'And what did you mean by your "transgressions this afternoon"? What have you done? Kit, stop it! I can't think while you're doing that to me!'

'I can't, either. Marvellous, isn't it?'

She crossed her legs firmly and pushed his hand away. 'Tell me! What have you done?'

'I'll tell you later. Later, Jara. Oh, Lord...'

'No! Tell me now!'

Slowly he leaned away and lay on one elbow, his eyes dancing with laughter. He looked very young, suddenly, and very happy. For the first time she realised that the lines around his eyes had smoothed out, and that the watchful, slightly tense look he had always worn—even in their most relaxed moments—had left his face completely. The cuts on his lip were still there, and there was a darkened bruise still on his temple, and she ached to touch them. But she kept her hands by her sides.

'Tell me now,' she repeated. 'What have you done?'

'Well, first of all, when Eustacia woke me to tell me that you'd left, I commandeered the *Courageous* and took her out to sea this afternoon, without Admiralty approval.'

'Did you? But . . . is that so bad? She was your ship, after all, and——'

'But I had resigned my commission twelve hours earlier.'

'Oh.'

'But I didn't tell the men on board that. Which is why I was still in uniform when you came back.'

'I see.'

'And then I caught up with the *Juliette*, and when that foul-tempered Frenchman wouldn't stop I put a shot across his bows.'

'Kit!'

'Well, I didn't like the idea of having to cross the Pacific alongside him while I pleaded with him to stop and let me take you off his blasted little merchant tug! But of course, when I boarded him—under arms—it was to find you'd never left Macao. So I came straight back here to find you. And so did Captain Ferrier—to lay a complaint against me with the Admiralty for piracy.'

She lay in stunned silence, staring up at him. She could not even begin to grasp just how much trouble he was in, and here he was—relaxed and happy, acting as if he had not a care in the world.

'Will . . . they arrest you?'

'In all probability. So let's not waste any more time——'

'No!' She slapped his hand away. 'How could you do such things? How could you resign your commission?'

Now it was his turn to stare at her in surprise. 'Don't you know?'

'No I don't! You loved the Navy . . .'

'But I love you a great deal more. And I know how you disliked the fact that I was an officer, and you hated the things that I had to do. I didn't think you'd marry me unless I resigned, and so...I resigned. As soon as we got back.'

'You...you want to marry me?' she stammered. 'You are proposing?'

He pretended to look affronted. 'I'm accepting! Don't you remember proposing marriage not two days ago? We were in a little bamboo hut at the time, I believe, and... What's the matter, Jara? Oh, for God's sake, don't cry...'

'It's just that...oh Kit!' She threw herself into his arms and he held her tightly for a long time, rocking her gently and smoothing away the tears as they fell with one tender finger. And in time the tender touch became a passionate one, and Jara's sobs turned to gasps, and it was only the sound of Sir Walter's booming voice in the hallway, demanding to know the whereabouts of his godson, that made them reluctantly and slowly separate.

'Don't worry,' Kit said as he pulled on his jacket and snatched one last kiss from her at the same time. 'I can always rely on my godfather to put in a good word for me. And I think the Admiralty owes me at least one indiscretion.'

'And I will talk to Captain Ferrier about him charging you with piracy,' Jara promised as she straightened his jacket collar. 'And if that does not work...remember that it was a convict captain that I first fell in love with, after all!'

'Very true.' He put an arm about her waist and placed yet another last kiss on her nose. 'And I understand Australia is not at all a bad place to live. Do you mind if...?'

'Not at all.' She put her arm around his waist and together they opened the door to face the world.

Look out for the two intriguing

MASQUERADE *Historical*

Romances coming next month

DEAR REBEL

Mary Nichols

Like many men in his position, Lord Carthorne was more concerned to protect his property, the lovely manor of Waterlea in the Fens of East Anglia, than to take sides in the escalating war between Charles I and his Parliament.
So he had no hesitation about using the childhood betrothal between his daughter Alys and Cromwell's captain, Sir Garret Hartswood, to get out of trouble. This was an enormous shock to Alys, who had forgotten the betrothal, and was a fervent Cavalier to boot! There seemed to be no escape from Garret's relentless intention to honour the agreement . . .

NOBLE BUCCANEER

Yvonne Purves

Debtor's prison — or marriage to a stranger!

Elena Worth agreed to marry Anthony Drew, an East India trader living in Malaysia. But on arrival, after a long and arduous journey, she discovered Anthony was dead — and that he had willed her to Dutchman Lord Stephan Van Coen!

Trapped on Lord Stephan's island, Elena was horrified to learn that everyone there was involved with piracy — but even with every course of action seemingly blocked, Elena refused to admit defeat . . .

Available in September